FOR LOVE OF
COUNTRY

A Story of Land and Sea in the Days of the Revolution

CYRUS TOWNSEND BRADY

1st WORLD
LIBRARY
Literary Society

For Love of Country

Cyrus Townsend Brady

© 1st World Library, 2007
PO Box 2211
Fairfield, IA 52556
www.1stworldlibrary.com
First Edition

LCCN: 2007927808

Softcover ISBN: 978-1-4218-4518-0
Hardcover ISBN: 978-1-4218-4434-3
eBook ISBN: 978-1-4218-4602-6

Purchase *"For Love of Country"*
as a traditional bound book at:
www.1stWorldLibrary.com/purchase.asp?ISBN=978-1-4218-4518-0

1st World Library is a literary, educational organization
dedicated to:

- Creating a free internet library of downloadable ebooks

- Hosting writing competitions and offering book publishing
scholarships.

Interested in more 1st World Library books? contact:
literacy@1stworldlibrary.com
Check us out at: www.1stworldlibrary.com

1ˢᵗ World Library Literary Society

Giving Back to the World

"If you want to work on the core problem, it's early school literacy."

- James Barksdale, former CEO of Netscape

"No skill is more crucial to the future of a child, or to a democratic and prosperous society, than literacy."

- Los Angeles Times

"Literacy... means far more than learning how to read and write... The aim is to transmit... knowledge and promote social participation."

- UNESCO

"Literacy is not a luxury, it is a right and a responsibility. If our world is to meet the challenges of the twenty-first century we must harness the energy and creativity of all our citizens."

- President Bill Clinton

"Parents should be encouraged to read to their children, and teachers should be equipped with all available techniques for teaching literacy, so the varying needs and capacities of individual kids can be taken into account."

- Hugh Mackay

TO THE

Society of the Sons of the Revolution,

And those kindred organizations whose chief function is to cultivate a spirit of patriotism and love of country in the present by recalling the struggles and sacrifices of the past.

PREFACE

Since the action of this story falls during the periods, and the book deals with personages and incidents, which are usually treated of in the more serious pages of history, it is proper that some brief word of explanation should be written by which I might confirm some of the romantic happenings hereafter related, which to the casual reader may appear to draw too heavily upon his credulity for acceptance.

The action between the Randolph and the Yarmouth really happened, the smaller ship did engage the greater for the indicated purpose, much as I have told it; and if I have ventured to substitute another name for that of the gallant sailor and daring hero, Captain Nicholas Biddle, who commanded the little Randolph, and lost his life, on that occasion, I trust this paragraph may be considered as making ample amends. The remarkable fight between those two ships is worthy of more extended notice than has hitherto been given it, in any but the larger tones (and not even in some of those) of the time. As far as my information permits me to say, there never was a more heroic battle on the seas.

Again, it is evident to students of history that the character of Washington has not been properly understood hitherto, by the very people who revere his name, though the excellent books of Messrs. Ford, Wilson, Lodge, Fiske, and others are doing much to destroy the popular canonization which made of the man a saint; in defence of my characterization of him I am able to say that the incidents and anecdotes and most of the conversations in which he appears are absolutely historical.

If I have dwelt too long and too circumstantially upon the Trenton and Princeton campaigns for a book so light in character as is this one, it may be set down to an ardent admiration for Washington as man and soldier, and a design again to exhibit him as he was at one of the most critical and brilliant points of his career. Furthermore, I find that the school and other histories commonly accessible to ordinary people are not sufficiently awake to the importance and brilliancy of the campaign, and I cherish the hope that this book may serve, in some measure, to establish its value.

I have freely used all the histories and narratives to which I had access, without hesitation; and if I have anticipated a distinguished arrival, or hastened the departure of a ship, or altered the date of a naval battle, or changed its scene, I plead the example of the distinguished masters of fiction, to warrant me.

In closing I cannot refrain from thanking those who have so kindly assisted me with advice and correction during the writing of this story and the reading of the proof, especially the Rev. A. J. P. McClure.

C. T. B.

PHILADELPHIA, PENNA.,
November, 1897.

CONTENTS

BOOK III - THE LION AT BAY

BOOK IV - A DEATH GRAPPLE ON THE DEEP

BOOK V - THE DEAD ALIVE AGAIN

BOOK I

THE EVENTS OF A NIGHT

CHAPTER I

KATHARINE YIELDS HER INDEPENDENCE

If Seymour could have voiced his thought, he would have said that the earth itself did not afford a fairer picture than that which lay within the level radius of his vision, and which had imprinted itself so powerfully upon his impressionable and youthful heart. It was not the scenery of Virginia either, the landscape on the Potomac, of which he would have spoken so enthusiastically, though even that were a thing not to be disdained by such a lover of the beautiful as Seymour had shown himself to be,—the dry brown hills rising in swelling slopes from the edge of the wide quiet river; the bare and leafless trees upon their crests, now scarce veiling the comfortable old white house, which in the summer they quite concealed beneath their masses of foliage; and all the world lying dreamy and calm and still, in the motionless haze of one of those rare seasons in November which so suggests departed days that men name it summer again. For all that he then saw in nature was but a setting for a woman; even the sun itself, low in the west, robbed of its glory, and faded into a dull red ball seeking to hide its head, but served to throw into high relief the noble and beautiful face of the girl upon whom he gazed,—the girl who was sun and life and light and world for him.

The most confirmed misogynist would have found it difficult to challenge her claim to beauty; and yet it would require a more severe critic or a sterner analyst than a lover would be likely to prove, to say in just what point could be found that which would justify the claim. Was it in the mass of light wavy brown hair, springing from a low point on her forehead and gently rippling back, which she wore plaited and tied with a ribbon and destitute of powder? How sweetly simple it looked to him after the bepowdered and betowered misses of the town with whom he was most acquainted! Was it in the broad low brow, or the brown, almost black eyes which laughed beneath it; or the very fair complexion, which seemed to him a strangely delightful and unusual combination? Or was it in the perfection of a faultless, if somewhat slender and still undeveloped figure, half concealed by the vivid "Cardinal" cloak she wore, which one little hand held loosely together about her, while the other dabbled in the water by her side?

Be this as it may, the whole impression she produced was one which charmed and fascinated to the last degree, and Mistress Katharine Wilton's sway among the young men of the colony was-well-nigh undisputed. A toast and a belle in half Virginia, Seymour was not the first, nor was he destined to be the last, of her adorers.

The strong, steady, practised stroke, denoting the accomplished oarsman, with which he had urged the little boat through the water, had given way to an idle and purposeless drift. He longed to cast himself down before the little feet, in their smart high-heeled buckled shoes and clocked stockings, which peeped out at him from under her embroidered camlet petticoat in such a maliciously coquettish manner; he longed to kneel down there in the skiff, at the imminent risk of spoiling his own gay attire, and declare the passion which consumed him; but something—he did not know what it was, and she did not tell him—constrained him, and he sat still, and felt himself as far away as if she had been in the stars.

In his way he was quite as good to look at as the young maiden; tall, blond, stalwart, blue-eyed, pleasant-featured, with the frank engaging air which seems to belong to those who go down to the sea in ships, Lieutenant John Seymour Seymour was an excellent specimen of that hardy, daring, gallant class of men who in this war and in the next were to shed such imperishable lustre upon American arms by their exploits in the naval service. Born of an old and distinguished Philadelphia family, so proud of its name that in his instance they had doubled it, the usual bluntness and roughness of the sea were tempered by this gentle birth and breeding, and by frequent attrition with men and women of the politest society of the largest and most important city of the colonies. Offering his services as soon as the news of Lexington precipitated the conflict with the mother country, he had already made his name known among that gallant band of seamen among whom Jones, Biddle, Dale, and Conyngham were pre-eminent.

The delicious silence which he had been unwilling to break, since it permitted him to gaze undisturbed upon his fair shipmate, was terminated at last by that lady herself.

She looked up from the water with which she had been playing, and then appearing to notice for the first time his steady ardent gaze, she laughed lightly and said,—

"Well, sir, it grows late. When you have finished contemplating the scenery, perhaps you will turn the boat, and take me home; then you can feast your eyes upon something more attractive."

"And what is that, pray?" he asked.

"Your supper, sir. You must be very anxious for it by this time, and really you know you look quite hungry. We have been out so long; but I will have pity on you, and detain you no longer here. Turn the boat around, Lieutenant Seymour, and put me on shore at once. I will stand between no man and his dinner."

"Hungry? Yes, I am, but not for dinner,—for you, Mistress Katharine," he replied.

"Oh, what a horrid appetite! I don't feel safe in the boat with you. Are you very hungry?"

"Really, Miss Wilton, I am not jesting at all," he said with immense dignity.

"Oh! oh! He is in earnest. Shall I scream? No use; we are a mile from the house, at least."

"Oh, Miss Wilton—Katharine," he replied desperately, "I am devoured by my—"

"Lieutenant Seymour!" She drew herself up with great hauteur, letting the cloak drop about her waist.

"Madam!"

"Only my friends call me Katharine."

"And am I not, may I not be, one of your friends?"

"Well, yes—I suppose so; but you are so young."

"I am just twenty-seven, madam, and you, I suppose, are—"

Cyrus Townsend Brady

"Never be ungallant enough to suppose a young lady's age. You may do those things in Philadelphia, if you like, but 't is not the custom here. Besides, I mean too young a friend; you have not known me long enough, that is."

"Long enough! I have known you ever since Tuesday of last week."

"And this is Friday,—just ten days, ten long days!" she replied triumphantly.

"Long days!" he cried. "Very short ones, for me."

"Long or short, sir, do you think you can know me in that period? Is it possible I am so easily fathomed?" she went on, smiling.

Now it is ill making love in a rowboat at best, and when one is in earnest and the other jests it is well-nigh impossible; so to these remarks Lieutenant Seymour made no further answer, save viciously to ply the oars and drive the boat rapidly toward the landing.

Miss Katharine gazed vacantly about the familiar river upon whose banks she had been born and bred, and, finally noticing the sun had gone down, closing the short day, she once more drew her cloak closely about her and resumed the neglected conversation.

"Won't you please stop looking at me in that manner, and won't you please row harder, or is your strength all centred in your gaze?"

"I am rowing as fast as I can, Miss Wilton, especially with this—"

"Oh, I forgot your wounded shoulder! Does it hurt? Does it pain you? I am so sorry. Let me row."

"Thank you, no. I think I can manage it myself. The only pain I have is when you are unkind to me."

At that moment, to his great annoyance, his oar stuck fast in the oar-lock, and he straightway did that very unsailorly thing known as catching a crab.

Katharine Wilton laughed. There was music in her voice, but this time it did not awaken a responsive chord in the young man. Extricating his oar violently, he silently resumed his work.

"Do you like crabs, Mr. Seymour?" she said with apparent irrelevance.

"I don't like catching them, Miss Wilton," he admitted ruefully.

"Oh, I mean eating them! We were talking about your appetite, were we not? Well, Dinah devils them deliciously. I'll have some done for you," she continued with suspicious innocence.

Seymour groaned in spirit at her perversity, and for the first time in his life felt an intense sympathy with devilled crabs; but he continued his labor in silence and with great dignity.

"What am I to infer from your silence on this important subject, sir? The subject of edibles, which everybody says is of the first importance—to men—does not appear to interest you at all!"

He made no further reply.

The young girl gazed at his pale face at first in much amusement; but the laughter gradually died away, and finally her glance fell to the water by her side. A few strong strokes, strong enough, in spite of a wounded shoulder, to indicate wrathful purpose and sudden determination to the astute maiden, and the little boat swung in beside the wharf. Throwing the oars inboard with easy skill, Seymour sat motionless while the boat glided swiftly down toward the landing-steps, and the silence was broken only by the soft, delicious lip, lip, lip of the water, which seemed to cling to and caress the bow of the skiff until it finally came to rest. The man waited until the girl looked up at him. She saw in his resolute mien the outward and visible sign of his inward determination, and she realized that the game so bravely and piquantly played since she met him was lost. They had nearly arrived at the foregone conclusion.

"Well, Mr. Seymour," she said finally, "we are here at last; for what are you waiting?"

"Waiting for you."

"For me?"

"Ay, only for you."

"I—I—do not understand you."

"You understand nothing apparently, but I will explain." He stepped out on the landing-stage, and after taking a turn or two with the painter to secure the boat, he turned toward his captive with a ceremonious bow.

"Permit me to help you ashore."

"Oh, thank you, Lieutenant Seymour; if I only could, in this little boat, I would courtesy in return for that effort," she answered with tremulous and transparent bravery. But when the little palm met his own brown one, it seemed to steal away some of the bitterness of the moment. After he had assisted her upon the shore and up the steps into the boathouse, he held her hand tight within his own, and with that promptitude which characterized him he made the plunge.

"Oh, Miss Wilton—Katharine—it is true I have known you only a little while, but all that time—ever since I saw you, in fact, and even before, when your father showed me your picture—I have loved you. Nay, hear me out." There was an unusual sternness in his voice. My lord appeared to be in the imperative mood,—something to which she had not been accustomed. He meant to be heard, and with beating heart perforce she listened. "Quiet that spirit of mockery but a moment, and attend my words, I pray you. No, I will not release you until I have spoken. These are troublous times. I may leave at any moment—must leave when my orders come, and I expect them every day, and before I go I must tell you this."

Her downcast eyes could still see him blush and then pale a little under the sunburn and windburn of his face, as he went on speaking.

"I have no one; never had I a sister, I can remember no mother; believe me, I entreat you, when I tell you that to no woman have I ever said what I have just said to you. We sailors think and speak and act quickly, it is a part of our profession; but if I should wait for years I should think no differently and act in no other way. I love you! Oh, Katharine, I love you as my soul."

There was a note of passion in his voice which thrilled her

Cyrus Townsend Brady

heart with ecstasy; the others had not made love this way.

"You seem to me like that star I have often watched in the long hours of the night, which has shown me the way on many a trackless sea. I know I am as far beneath you as I am beneath that star. But though the distance is great, my love can bridge it, if you will let me try. Katharine—won't you answer me, Katharine? Is there nothing you can say to me? 'Dost thou love me, Kate?'" he quoted softly, taking her other hand. How very fair, but how very far away she looked! The color came and went in her cheek. He could see her breast rise and fall under the mad beating of a heart which had escaped her control, though hitherto she had found no difficulty in keeping it well in hand. There was a novelty, a difference, in the situation this time, a new and unexpected element in the event. She hesitated. Why was it no merry quip came to the lips usually so ready with repartee? Alas, she must answer.

"I—I—oh, Mr. Seymour," she said softly and slowly, with a downcast face she fain would hide, he fain would see. "I—yes," she murmured with great reluctance; "that is—I think so. You see, when you defended father, in the fight with the brig, you know, and got that bullet in your shoulder you earned a title to my gratitude, my—"

"I don't want a title to your gratitude," he interrupted. "I want your love, I want you to love me for myself alone."

"And do you think you are worthy that I should?" she replied with a shadow of her former archness.

He gravely bent his head and kissed her hand. "No, Katharine, I do not. I can lay no claim to your hand, if it is to be a reward of merit, but I love you so—that is the substance of my hope."

"Oh, Mr. Seymour, Mr. Seymour, you overvalue me. If you do that with all your possessions, you will be—Oh, what have I said?" she cried in sudden alarm, as he took her in his arms.

"My possessions! Katharine, may I then count you so? Oh, Kate, my lovely Kate—" It was over, and over as she would have it; why struggle any longer? The landing was a lonely little spot under the summer-house, at the end of the wharf; no one could see what happened. This time it was not her hand he kissed. The day died away in twilight, but for those two a new day began.

The army might starve and die, battles be lost or won, dynasties rise and fall, kingdoms wax and wane, causes tremble in the balances,—what of that? They looked at each other and forgot the world.

CHAPTER II

THE COUNTRY FIRST OF ALL

"Oh, what is the hour, Mr.—John? Shall I call you Seymour? That is your second name, is it not? But what would people say? I—No, no, not again; we really must go in. See! I am not dressed for the evening yet. Supper will be ready. Now, Lieutenant Seymour, you must let me go. What will my father think of us? Come, then. Your hand, sir."

The hill from the boat-landing was steep, but Mistress Kate had often run like a young deer to the top of it without appreciating its difficulties as she did that evening. On every stepping-stone, each steep ascent, she lingered, in spite of her expressed desire for haste, and each time his strong and steady arm was at her service. She tasted to the full and for the first time the sweets of loving dependence.

As for him, an admiral of the fleet after a victory could not have been prouder and happier. As any other man would have done, he embraced or improved the opportunity afforded him by their journey up the hill, to urge the old commonplace that he would so assist her up the hill of life! And so on. The iterations of love never grow stale to a lover, and the saying was not so trite to her that it failed to give her the little thrill of loving joy which seemed, for the moment at least, to tame her restless spirit, that spirit of subtle yet merry mockery which charmed yet drove him mad. She was so unwontedly quiet and subdued that he stopped at the brow of the hill, and said, half in alarm, "Katharine, why so silent?"

She looked at him gravely; a new light, not of laughter, in her brown eyes, saying in answer to his unspoken thought: "I was thinking of what you said about your orders. Oh, if they should come to-day, and you should go away on your ship and be shot at again and perhaps wounded, what should I do?"

"Nonsense, Katharine dear, I am not going to be wounded any more. I've something to live for now, you see," he replied, smiling, taking both of her hands in his own.

"You always had something to live for, even before—you had me."

"And what was that, pray?"

"Your country."

"Yes," he replied proudly, taking off his laced hat, "and liberty; but you go together in my heart now, Kate,—you and country."

"Don't say that, John—well, Seymour, then—say 'country and you.' I would give you up for that, but only for that."

"You would do well, Katharine; our country first. Since we have engaged in this war, we must succeed. I fancy that more depends, and I only agree with your father there, upon the issue of this war than men dream of, and that the battle of liberty for the future man is being fought right here and now. Unless our people are willing to sacrifice everything, we

Cyrus Townsend Brady

cannot maintain that glorious independence which has been so brilliantly declared." He said this with all the boldness of the Declaration itself; but she, being yet a woman, asked him wistfully,—

"Would you give me up, sacrifice me for country, then?"

"Not for the whole wide—" She laid a finger upon his lips.

"Hush, hush! Do not even speak treason to the creed. I am a daughter of Virginia. My father, my brother, my friends, my people, and, yes, I will say it, my lover are perilling their lives and have engaged their honor in this contest for the independence of these colonies, for the cause of this people, and the safeguarding of their liberties; and if I stood in the pathway of liberty for a single instant, I should despise the man who would not sweep me aside without a moment's hesitation." She spoke with a pride and spirit which equalled his own, her head high in the air, and her eyes flashing.

She had released her hands and had suited the gesture to the word, throwing out her hand and arm with a movement of splendid freedom and defiance. She was a woman of many moods and "infinite variety." Each moment showed him something new to love. He caught the outstretched hand,— the loose sleeve had fallen back from the wrist,—he pressed his lips to the white arm, and said with all his soul in his voice,—

"May God prevent me from ever facing the necessity of a choice like that, Katharine! But indeed it is spirit like yours which makes men believe the cause is not wholly desperate. When our women can so speak and feel, we may confidently expect the blessing of God upon our efforts."

"Father says that it is because General Washington knows

the spirit of the people, because he feels that even the youths and maidens, the little children, cherish this feeling, he takes heart, and is confident of ultimate success. I heard him say that no king could stand against a united people."

"Would that you could have been in Paris with your father when he pleaded with King Louis and his ministers for aid and recognition! We might have returned with a better answer than paltry money and a few thousand stand of arms, which are only promised, after all."

"Would that I were a man instead of being a weak, feeble woman!" she exclaimed vehemently.

"Ah, but I very much prefer you as you are, Katharine, and 't is not little that you can do. You can inspire men with your own patriotism, if you will. There, for instance, is your friend Talbot. If you could persuade him, with his wealth and position and influence in this country, to join the army in New Jersey—" As she shook her head, he continued:

"I am sure if he thought as I do of you, you could persuade him to anything but treachery or dishonor." His calm smile of superiority vanished in an expression of dismay at her reply,—

"Talbot! Hilary Talbot! Why, John, do you know that he is— well, they say that he is in love with me. Everybody expects that we shall marry some day. Do you see? These old estates join, and—"

"Kate, it is n't true, is it? You don't care for him, do you?" he interrupted in sudden alarm.

"Care for him? Why, of course I care for him. I have known him ever since I was a child; but I don't love him. Besides, he stays at home while others are in the field. Silly boy, would I have let you kiss me in the summer-house if it were so? No, sir! We are not such fine ladies as your friends in the city of Philadelphia, perhaps, we Virginia country girls upon whom your misses look with scorn, but no man kisses us, and no man kisses me, upon the lips except the one I—that I must— let me see—is the word 'obey'? Shall you make me obey you all the time, John?"

"Pshaw, Katharine, you never obey anybody,—so your father says, at least,—and if you will only love me, that will be sufficient."

"Love you!"—the night had fallen and no one was near— "love you, John!" She kissed him bravely upon the lips. "Once, that's for me, my own; twice, that's for my country; there is all my heart. Come, sir, we must go in. There are lights in the house."

"Ah, Katharine, and there is light in my heart too."

As they came up the steps of the high pillared porch which completely covered the face of the building, they were met, at the great door which gave entrance to the spacious hallway extending through the house, by a stately and gracious, if somewhat elderly gentleman.

There was a striking similarity, if not in facial appearance, at least in the erect carriage and free air, between him and the young girl who, disregarding his outstretched hand and totally disorganizing his ceremonious bow, threw her arms about his neck and kissed him with unwonted warmth, much to his dismay and yet not altogether to his displeasure. Perhaps he suspected something from the bright and happy faces of the two young people; but if so, he made no comment, merely telling them that supper had been waiting this long time, and bidding them hasten their preparation for the meal.

Katharine, followed by Chloe, her black maid, who had been waiting for her, hastily ran up the stairs to her own apartments, upon this signal, but turned upon the topmost stair and waved a kiss to the two gentlemen who were watching her,—one with the dim eyes of an old father, the other with the bright eyes of a young lover.

"Colonel Wilton," exclaimed Seymour, impulsively, "I have something to say to you,—something I must say."

"Not now, my young friend," replied the colonel, genially. "Supper will be served, nay, is served already, and only awaits you and Katharine; afterward we shall have the whole evening, and you may say what you will."

"Oh, but, colonel—"

"Nay, sir, do not lay upon me the unpleasant duty of commanding a guest, when it is my privilege as host to entreat. Go, Mr. Seymour, and make you ready. Katharine will return in a moment, and it does not beseem gentlemen, much less officers, to keep a lady waiting, you know. Philip and Bentley have gone fishing, and I am informed they will not return until late. We will not wait for them."

"As you wish, sir, but I must have some private conversation with you as soon as possible."

"After supper, my boy, after supper."

CHAPTER III

COLONEL WILTON

Left to himself for a moment, the colonel heaved a deep sigh; he had a premonition of what was coming, and then paced slowly up and down the long hall.

He was attired, with all the splendor of an age in which the subject of dress engrossed the attention of the wisest and best, in the height of the prevailing mode, which his recent arrival from Paris, then as now the mould of fashion, permitted him to determine. The soft light from the wax candles in their sconces in the hall fell upon his thickly powdered wig, ran in little ripples up and down the length of his polished dress-sword, and sparkled in the brilliants in the buckles of his shoes. His face was the grave face of a man accustomed from of old not only to command, but to assume the responsibility of his orders; when they were carried out, his manner was a happy mixture of the haughty sternness of a soldier and the complacent suavity of the courtier, tempered both by the spirit of frankness and geniality born of the free life of a Virginia planter in colonial times.

In his early youth he had been a soldier under Admiral Vernon, with his old and long-deceased friend Lawrence Washington at Cartagena; later on, he had served under

Wolfe at Quebec. A visitor, and a welcome one too, at half the courts of Europe, he looked the man of affairs he was; in spite of his advanced age, he held himself as erect, and carried himself as proudly as he had done on the Heights of Abraham or in the court of St. Germain.

Too old to incur the hardships of the field, Colonel Wilton had yet offered his services, with the ardor of the youngest patriot, to his country, and pledged his fortune, by no means inconsiderable, in its support. The Congress, glad to avail themselves of the services of so distinguished a man, had sent him, in company with Silas Deane and Benjamin Franklin, as an embassy to the court of King Louis, bearing proposals for an alliance and with a request for assistance during the deadly struggle of the colonies with the hereditary foe of France. They had been reasonably successful in a portion of their attempt, at least; as the French government had agreed, though secretly, to furnish arms and other munitions of war through a pseudo-mercantile firm which was represented by M. de Beaumarchais, the gifted author of the comedy "Le Mariage de Figaro." The French had also agreed to furnish a limited amount of money; but, more important than all these, there were hints and indications that if the American army could win any decisive battle or maintain the unequal conflict for any length of time, an open and closer alliance would be made. The envoys had despatched Colonel Wilton, from their number, back to America to make a report of the progress of their negotiations to Congress. This had been done, and General Washington had been informed of the situation.

The little ship, one of the gallant vessels of the nascent American navy, in which Colonel Wilton had returned from France, had attacked and captured a British brig of war during the return passage, and young Seymour, who was the first lieutenant of the ship, was severely wounded. The wound had been received through his efforts to protect Colonel Wilton, who had incautiously joined the boarding-party which had captured the brig. After the interview with Congress, Colonel Wilton was requested to await further instructions before returning to France, and, pending the result of the deliberations of Congress, after a brief visit to the headquarters of his old friend and neighbor General Washington, he had retired to his estate. As a special favor, he was permitted to bring with him the wounded lieutenant, in order that he might recuperate and recover from his wound in the pleasant valleys of Virginia. That Seymour was willing to leave his own friends in Philadelphia, with all their care and attention, was due entirely to his desire to meet Miss Katharine Wilton, of whose beauty he had heard, and whose portrait indeed, in her father's possession, which he had seen before on the voyage, had borne out her reputation. Seymour had been informed since his stay at the Wiltons' that he had been detached from the brig Argus, and notified that he was to receive orders shortly to report to the ship Ranger, commanded by a certain Captain John Paul Jones; and he knew that he might expect his sailing orders at any moment. He had improved, as has been seen, the days of his brief stay to recover from one wound and receive another, and, as might have been expected, he had fallen violently in love with Katharine Wilton.

There were also staying at the house, besides the servants and slaves, young Philip Wilton, Katharine's brother, a lad of sixteen, who had just received a midshipman's warrant, and was to accompany Seymour when he joined the Ranger, then outfitting at Philadelphia; and Bentley, an old and veteran sailor, a boatswain's mate, who had accompanied Seymour from ship to ship ever since the lieutenant was a midship-man,—a man who had but one home, the sea; one hate, the English; one love, his country; and one attachment, Seymour.

Colonel Wilton was a widower. As Katharine came down the stairway, clad in all the finery her father had brought back for her from Paris, her hair rolled high and powdered, the old family diamonds with their quaint setting of silver sparkling upon her snowy neck, her fan languidly waving in her hand, she looked strikingly like a pictured woman smiling down at them from over the mantel; but to the sweetness and archness of her mother's laughing face were added some of the colonel's pride, determination, and courage. He stepped to meet her, and then bent and kissed the hand she extended toward him, with all the grace of the old regime; and Seymour coming upon them was entranced with the picture.

He too had changed his attire, and now was clad in the becoming dress of a naval lieutenant of the period. He wore a sword, of course, and a dark blue uniform coat relieved with red facings, with a single epaulet on his shoulder which denoted his official rank; his blond hair was lightly touched with powder, and tied, after the fashion of active service, in a queue with a black ribbon.

"Now, Seymour, since you two truants have come at last, will you do me the honor to hand Miss Wilton to the dining-room?" remarked the colonel, straightening up.

With a low bow, Seymour approached the object of his adoration, who, after a sweeping courtesy, gave him her hand. With much state and ceremony, preceded by one of the servants, who had been waiting in attention in the hall, and followed by the colonel, and lastly by the colonel's man, a stiff old campaigner who had been with him many years, they entered the dining-room, which opened from the rear of the hall.

The table was a mass of splendid plate, which sparkled under the soft light of the wax candles in candelabra about the room or on the table, and the simple meal was served with all the elegance and precision which were habitual with the gentleman of as fine a school as Colonel Wilton.

At the table, instead of the light and airy talk which might have been expected in the situation, the conversation assumed that grave and serious tone which denoted the imminence of the emergency.

The American troops had been severely defeated at Long Island in the summer, and since that time had suffered a series of reverses, being forced steadily back out of New York, after losing Fort Washington, and down through the Jerseys, relentlessly pursued by Howe and Cornwallis. Washington was now making his way slowly to the west bank of the Delaware. He was losing men at every step, some by desertion, more by the expiration of the terms of their enlistment. The news which Colonel Wilton had brought threw a frail hope over the situation, but ruin stared them in the face, and unless something decisive was soon accomplished, the game would be lost.

"Did you have a pleasant ride up the river, Katharine?" asked her father.

"Very, sir," she answered, blushing violently and looking involuntarily at Seymour, who matched her blush with his own.

There was a painful pause, which Seymour broke, coming to the rescue with a counter question.

"Did you notice that small sloop creeping up under the west bank of the river, colonel, this evening? I should think she must be opposite the house now, if the wind has held."

"Why, when did you see her, Mr. Seymour? I thought you were looking at—at—" She broke off in confusion, under her father's searching gaze. He smiled, and said,—

"Ah, Katharine, trained eyes see all things unusual about them, although they are apparently bent persistently upon one spot. Yes, Seymour, I did notice it; if we were farther down the river, we might suspect it of being an enemy, but up here I fancy even Dunmore's malevolence would scarcely dare to follow."

Katharine looked up in alarm. "Oh, father, do you think it is quite safe? Chloe told me that Phoebus told her that the raiders had visited Major Lithcomb's plantation, and you know that is not more than fifty miles down the river from us. Would it not be well to take some precaution?"

"Tut, tut, child! gossip of the negro servants!" The colonel waved it aside carelessly. "I hardly think we have anything to fear at present; though what his lordship may do in the end, unless he is checked, I hardly like to imagine."

"But, father," persisted Katharine, "they said that Johnson was in command of the party, and you know he hates you. You remember he said he would get even with you if it cost him his life, when you had him turned out of the club at Williamsburg."

"Pshaw, Katharine, the wretch would not dare. It is a cowardly blackguard, Seymour, whom I saw cheating at cards at the Assembly Club at the capital. I had him expelled from the society of gentlemen, where, indeed, he had no right of admittance, and I scarcely know how he got there originally. He made some threats against me, to which I naturally paid no attention. But what did you think of the vessel?"

"I confess I saw nothing suspicious about her, sir," replied Seymour. "She seemed very much like the packets which ply on the river; I only spoke idly of the subject."

"But, father, the packet went up last week, the day before you came back, and is due coming down the river now, while this boat is coming up," said Katharine.

"Oh, well, I think we are safe enough now; but, to relieve your unusual anxiety, I will send Blodgett down to the wharf to examine and report.—Blodgett, do you go down to the boat-landing and keep watch for an hour or two. Take your musket, man; there is no knowing what you might need it for."

The old soldier, who had stationed himself behind the colonel's chair, saluted with military precision, and left the room, saying, "Very good, sir; I shall let nothing escape my notice, sir."

"Now, Katharine, I hope you are satisfied."

"Yes, father; but if it is the raiders, Blodgett won't be able to stop them."

"The raiders," laughed the colonel; and pinching his daughter's ear, he said, "I suspect the only raiders we shall see here will be those who have designs upon your heart, my bonny Kate,—eh, Seymour?"

"They would never dare to wear a British uniform in that case, father," she retorted proudly.

"Well, Seymour, I hear, through an express from Congress to-day, that Captain Jones has been ordered to command the Ranger, and that the new flag—we will drink to it, if you please; yes, you too, Katharine; God bless every star and stripe in it—will soon be seen on the ocean."

"It will be a rare sight there, sir," said Seymour; "but it will not be long before the exploits of the Ranger will make it known on the high seas, if rumor does not belie her captain."

"I trust so; but do you know this Captain Jones?"

"Not at all, sir, save by reputation; but I am told he has one requisite for a successful officer."

"And what is that?"

"He will fight anything, at any time, or at any place, no matter what the odds."

Colonel Wilton smiled. "Ah, well, if it were not for men of that kind, our little navy would never have a chance."

"No, father, nor the army, either; if we waited for equality before fighting, I am afraid we should wait forever."

"True, Katharine. By the way, have you seen Talbot to-day?"

"No, father."

"I wish that we might enlist his services in the cause. I don't think there is much doubt about Talbot himself, is there?"

"No. It is his mother, you know; she is a loyalist to the core. As were her ancestors, so is she."

The colonel nodded gently; he had a soft spot in his heart for the subject of their discussion. "With her teaching and training, I can well understand it, Katharine. Proud, of high birth, descended from the 'loyal Talbots,' and the widow of one of them, she cannot bear the thought of rebellion against the king. I don't think she cares much for the people, or their liberties either."

"Yes, father; with her the creed is, the king can do no wrong."

"Ah, well," said the colonel, reflectively, "I thought so too once, and many is the blow I have struck for this same king. But liberty is above royalty, independence not a dweller in the court; so, in my old age, I find myself on a different side." He sipped his wine thoughtfully a moment, and continued,—

"Madam Talbot has certainly striven to restrain the boy, and successfully so far. He is a splendid fellow; I wish we had him. He would be of great service to the cause, with his name and influence, and the money he would bring; and then the quality of the young man himself would be of value to us. You have met him, Seymour, I believe?"

"Yes, sir, several times; and I agree with you entirely. It is his mother who keeps him back. I have had one or two conversations with her. She is a Tory through and through."

"Not a doubt of it, not a doubt of it," said the colonel. "Katharine, can't you do something with him?"

"Oh, father, you know that I have talked with him, pleaded with him, and begged him to follow his inclination; but he remains by his mother."

"Nonsense, Katharine! Don't speak of him in that way; give him time. It is a hard thing: he is her only son; she is a widow. Let us hope that something will induce him to come over to us." He said this in gentle reproof of his spirited daughter; and then,—

"Permit me to offer you a glass of wine, Seymour,—you are not drinking anything; and to whom shall we drink?"

Seymour, who had been quaffing deep draughts of Katharine's beauty, replied promptly,—

"If I might suggest, sir, I should say Mistress Wilton."

"No, no," said Katharine. "Drink, first of all, to the success of our cause. I will give you a toast, gentlemen: Before our sweethearts, our sisters, our wives, our mothers, let us place—our country," she exclaimed, lifting her own glass.

The colonel laughed as he drank his toast, saying, "Nothing comes before country with Katharine."

And Seymour, while he appreciated the spirit of the maiden, felt a little pang of grief that even to a country he should be second,—an astonishing change from that spirit of humility which a moment since contented itself with metaphorically kissing the ground she walked upon.

"By the way, father, where is Philip?" asked Katharine.

"He went up the branch fishing, with Bentley, I believe."

"But is n't it time they returned? Do you know, I feel nervous about them; suppose those raiders—"

"Pshaw, child! Still harping on the raiders? and nervous too! What ails you, daughter? I thought you never were nervous. We Wiltons are not accustomed to nervousness, you know, and what must our guest think?"

"Nothing but what is altogether agreeable," replied Seymour, a little too promptly; and then, to cover his confusion, he continued: "But I think Miss Wilton need feel under no apprehension. Master Philip is with Bentley, and I would trust the prudence and courage and skill of that man in any situation. You know my father, who was a shipmaster, when he died aboard his ship in the China seas, gave me, a little boy taking a cruise with him, into Bentley's charge, and told him to make a sailor and a man of me, and from that day he has never left me. At my house, in Philadelphia, he is a privileged character. There never was a truer, better, braver man; and as for patriotism, love of country is a passion with him, colonel. He might set an example to many in higher station in that particular."

"Yes, I have noticed that peculiarity about the man. I think Philip is safe enough with him, Katharine, even if those—Ha! what is that?" The colonel sprang to his feet, as the sound of a musket-shot rang out in the night air, followed by one or two pistol-shots and then a muffled cry.

CHAPTER IV

LORD DUNMORE'S MEN PAY AN EVENING CALL

"Oh, father, it must be the raiders! That was Blodgett's voice," cried Katharine, looking very pale and clasping her hands.

"Let me go and investigate, colonel," said Seymour, leaping to his feet and seizing his sword.

"Do so, Seymour," cried the colonel, as the sailor hastily left the room. "Phoebus," to the butler, "go tell Caesar to call the slaves to the house. You, Scipio," to one of the footmen, "go open the arm-chest. Katharine, reach me my sword. See that the doors are closed, Billy," said the colonel to the other servant, rapidly and with perfect coolness. "I think, Katharine, that perhaps you would better retire to your room;" but even as he spoke the sound of hurried footsteps and excited voices outside was heard. After a few moments one of the field-hands, followed by Seymour, burst panting into the room, his mouth working with excitement and his eyes almost starting from his head.

"Well, sir, what is it?" said the colonel.

"Foh de Lawd's sake, suh, dey'se a-comin', suh, dey'se

a-comin'. Dey'se right behin' me; dey'll be heah in a minute, suh."

"Who is coming, you idiot!" exclaimed the colonel.

"De redcoats, de British sojuhs, suh; dey 'se fohty boat-loads ob 'em; dey'se come off fum de lil' sloop out in de ribah, and dey 'se gwine kill we all, and bu'n de house down. Dey done shot Mars' Blodgett, and dey'se coming heah special to get you, suh, Mars' Kunnel, kase I heahd dem say, when I was lyin' down on de wha'f, dat de man dey wanted was dat Kunnel Wilton."

"It is quite true, sir; they seem to be a party of raiders of some sort," said Seymour, coolly. "I fear that Blodgett has been killed, as I heard nothing of him. I saw them from the brow of the hill. Perhaps you may escape by the back way, though there is little time for that. Do you take Miss Wilton and try it, sir; leave me to hold these men in play."

"Yes, yes, father," urged Katharine; "I know it must be Lord Dunmore's men and Johnson. They know that you have come back from France, and now the man wants to take you prisoner. You remember what the governor told you at Williamsburg, that he would make you rue the day you cast your lot in with the colonists and refused to assist him in the prosecution of his measures. And you know we have been warned at least a dozen times about it. Oh, what shall we do? Do fly, and let me stay here and receive these men."

"What! my daughter, do you think a Wilton has ever left his house to be defended by his guest and by a woman! Seymour, I believe, however, as an officer in the service of our country, your best course is to leave while there is yet time."

"I will never leave you, sir; I will stay here with you and Mistress Katharine, and share whatever fate may have in store for you."

But even as he spoke, the crowding footsteps of many men were heard at both entrances to the wide hall-way which ran through the house. At the same moment the door was violently thrown open, and the dining-room was filled with an irregular mass of motley, ragged, red-coated men, whose reckless demeanor and hardened faces indicated that they had been recruited from the lowest and most depraved classes of the inhabitants of the colony. They were led by a middle-aged man of dissipated appearance, whose rough and brutal aspect was not concealed by the captain's uniform he wore, nor was the malicious triumph in his bearing and in his voice veiled by the mock courtesy with which he advanced, pistol in hand.

"What means this intrusion, sir?" shouted Colonel Wilton, in a voice of thunder.

"This is Colonel Wilton, I believe, is it not?" said the leader of the band, taking off his hat.

"Yes, sir, it is; you, Mr. Johnson, should be the last to forget it, and I desire to know at once the meaning of this outrageous descent upon a peaceful dwelling."

The man bowed low with mock courtesy. "I shall have to ask your pardon, my dear sir, for appearing before the great Colonel Wilton so unceremoniously. But my orders, I regret to say, allow me no discretion whatever; they are imperative. You are my prisoner. I have been sent here by my Lord Dunmore, the governor of this colony of Virginia, to secure the persons of some of the principal rebellious subjects of his majesty King George, and your name, unfortunately, is the first and chiefest on the list. I shall have to request you to accompany me at once."

The master of the situation smiled mockingly, and the colonel, white with anger, looked about the room. Resistance was perfectly hopeless; all the windows even were now blocked up by the irregular soldiery.

"He has chosen a fit man to do his work," said the colonel, in haughty scorn; "failing gentlemen, he must needs take blackguards and bullies into his service as housebreakers and raiders."

Johnson flushed visibly, as he said with another bow, "Colonel Wilton would better remember that I am master now."

"Sir, I am not likely to forget it. There is the family plate. I presume, from what I know of your habits, that will not be overlooked by you."

"Quite so," he returned; "it will doubtless be a welcome contribution to the treasury of his majesty's colony. Mistress Wilton's diamonds also," he said meaningly; and then, turning to two of his men, "Williams, you and Jones bundle up the plate in the tablecloth, get what's on the sideboard too;" and laying his pistols down upon the table, he continued:

"But before Colonel Wilton insults me again, it might be well for him to remember that I am master not only of his person, but of the persons of all others who are in this room."

The colonel started, and Johnson laughed, looking with insolence from Katharine to her father.

"What, sir! I reach through your insolent pride now, do I? Curse you!" with sudden heat, throwing off even the mask of politeness he had hardly worn. "I swore I would have revenge for that insult at Williamsburg, and now it's my hour. You are to go with me, and go peaceably and quietly, or, by God, I'll have you kicked and dragged out of the building, or killed like that old fool who tried to stop us coming up on the landing."

"What! Blodgett, my old friend Blodgett! You villain, you haven't dared to kill him, have you? Oh, my faithful—"

"Silence, sir! We dare anything. What consideration has a rebel a right to expect at the hands of his majesty's faithful Rangers? You, Bruce and Denton, seize the old man. If he makes any trouble, knock him down, or kill him, for aught I care. One of you, take the girl there. As for you, sir," to Seymour, who had been quietly watching the scene, "I don't know who you are, but you are in bad company, and you will have to consider yourself a prisoner; I trust you have sense enough to come without force being used. And so," clapping his hat on his head defiantly, "God save the king!"

Two of the soldiers seized the colonel in spite of the vigorous resistance he made; another approached Katharine, who had stood with clasped hands during the whole of the colloquy between Johnson and her father. The soldier rudely chucked her under the chin, saying, "Come on, my pretty one! you'll give us a kiss, won't you, before we start?" As she drew back, paling at the insult, Seymour, who had seen and heard it all, quick as a flash drew his sword, and threw himself upon the soldier; one rapid thrust at the surprised man he made, with all the force and skill begotten of long practice and a strong arm, and the hilt of his blade crushed against the man's throat, and he fell dead upon the floor. At the same instant one of the other soldiers, who had observed the action, struck Seymour over the head with his clubbed musket, and he also fell heavily to the floor, and lay there senseless and still, blood running from a fearful-looking wound in his forehead. The room was filled with tumult in an instant, and with shouts of "Kill him!" "Shove your bayonet through the damn rebel hound!" "Shoot him!" "Kill him!" the men moved towards Seymour. Johnson looked on unconcernedly.

"Good God!" shrieked the colonel, writhing in the grasp of the men who held him, "are you going to allow a senseless, wounded man to be murdered before your eyes? Oh, how could anybody ever mistake you for a gentleman for an instant?" he added, with withering contempt; and then turning his head toward the fierce soldiery, "Stop, stop, you bloody assassins!" he cried.

"Silence, sir! He might as well die this way as on the gallows. Besides, he struck the first blow, and he has killed one of his majesty's loyal soldiers. The soldier only wanted to kiss the girl anyway, and she will find, before she gets to camp, that kisses are cheap."

"Oh, my God," groaned the father, "and they call this war!"

At this moment one of the soldiers lifted his bayonet to plunge it into the prostrate form of the unconscious sailor. There was a blinding flash of light in the room, and a quick, sharp report. The man's arm dropped to his side, and he shrieked and groaned with pain. Katharine, unnoticed in the confusion, had slipped to the side of the table, and had quickly picked up one of the pistols which Johnson had laid upon it after the silver had been taken away. Her ready decision and unerring aim had saved her lover's life. She threw the smoking pistol she had used with such effect down at her feet, and, seizing the other, she stepped over to the side of her unconscious lover.

"I swear," she said, in a shrill, high-pitched voice which just escaped a scream, and which trembled with the agitation of the moment, "by my hope of heaven, if a single man of you lay hands on him, he shall have this bullet also, you cowards!"

After a moment's hesitation, amid shouts of "Kill the girl!" the men surged toward her. Chloe, her black maid, flung herself upon her mistress' breast.

"Oh, honey, I let dem kill me fust."

"Well done, Kate! It's the true Wilton blood. Oh, if I had a free arm, you villains!" cried the still struggling colonel.

"Seize the girl," Johnson commanded promptly, "and let us get out of this."

The men made a rush toward the table where Katharine stood undaunted, her face flushed with excitement, her mouth tense with resolution. She cried,—

"Have a care, men! have a care!"

One life she could still command with her loaded pistol. Her hands did not tremble. She waited to strike once more for love and country, but it would be all over in a moment.

The colonel groaned in agony, "Kate, Kate!" but they were almost upon her, when a new voice rose above the uproar,—

"Hold! Are you men? Do you war with old men and women? Back with you! Get back, you dogs! Back, I say!"

CHAPTER V

A TIMELY INTERFERENCE

A young man in the uniform of a British naval lieutenant leaped in front of the girl with drawn sword, with which he laid about him lustily, striking some of the men with the flat of it, threatening others with the point; and backing his actions by the prompt commands of one not accustomed to be gainsaid, he soon cleared the space in front of her.

"How dare you interfere in this matter, my lord?" shouted Johnson, passionately. "I command this party, and I intend—"

"I know you do," replied the officer, "and that I am only a volunteer who has chosen to accompany you, worse luck! but I am a gentleman and a lieutenant in his Britannic majesty's navy, and by heaven! when I see old men mishandled, and wounded helpless men about to be assassinated, and young women insulted, I don't care who commands the party, I interfere. And I don't propose to bandy words with any runagate American partisan who uses his commission to further private vengeance. And I swear to you, on my honor, if you do not instantly modify your treatment of this gentleman, and call off this ragamuffin crew, you shall be court-martialled, if I have any influence with Dunmore or Parker or Lord Howe, or whoever is in authority, and I will have the rest of you hung as high as Haman. This is outrage and robbery and murder; it is not fighting or making prisoners," continued the young officer. "You are not fit to be an officer; and you, you curs, you disgrace the uniform you wear."

Johnson glanced at his men, who stood irresolute before him fiercely muttering. A rascally mob of the lowest class of people in the colony, to whom war simply meant opportunity for plunder and rapine, they would undoubtedly back up their leader, in their present mood, in any attempt at resistance he might make the young officer. But he hesitated a moment. Desborough was a lord, high in the confidence of Governor Dunmore, and a man of great influence; his own position was too precarious, the game was not worth the candle, and the risk of opposition was too great.

"Well," he said in sulky acquiescence, "the men meant no special harm, but have it your own way. Fall back, men! As to what you say to me personally, you shall answer to me for that at a more fitting time," he continued doggedly.

"When and where you please," answered Desborough, hotly, "though I'd soil a sword by passing it through you. What was Dunmore thinking of when he put you in charge of this party and sent you to do this work, I wonder? Give your orders to your men to unhand this gentleman instantly. You will give your parole, sir? I regret that we are compelled to secure your person, but those were the orders; and you, madam," turning to Katharine, "I believe no order requires you to be taken prisoner, and therefore you shall go free."

But Katharine had knelt down by her prostrate lover as soon as the space in front of her had been cleared, and was entirely oblivious to all that was taking place about her.

"Allow me to introduce myself, colonel," he resumed. "I am Lord Desborough. I have often heard my father, the Earl of Desmond, in Ireland, speak of you. I regret that we meet under such unpleasant circumstances, but the governor's orders must be carried out, though I wish he had sent a more worthy representative to do so. I will see, however, that everything is done for your comfort in the future."

"Sir," said the colonel, bowing, "you have rendered me a service I can never repay. I know your father well. He is one of the finest gentlemen of his time, and his son has this day shown that he is worthy of the honored name he bears. I will go with you cheerfully, and you have my parole of honor. Katharine, you are free; you will be safe in the house, I think, until I can arrange for your departure."

She looked up from the floor, and then rose. "Oh, father, he is dead, he is dead," she moaned. "Yes, I will go with you; take me away."

"Nay, my child, I cannot."

"Enough of this!" broke in the sneering voice of Johnson. "She has been taken in open resistance to the king's forces, and, warrant or no warrant, orders or no orders, or court-martial either," this with a malevolent glance at Desborough, "she goes with us as a prisoner."

"I will pledge my word, Colonel Wilton, that no violence is offered her," exclaimed Desborough, promptly, and then, turning to Katharine,—

"Trust me, madam."

"I do, sir," she said faintly, giving him her hand. "You are very kind."

"It is nothing, mistress," he replied, bowing low over it, as he raised it respectfully to his lips. "I will hold you safe with my life."

"Very pretty," sneered Johnson; "but are you coming?"

"What shall we do with these two, captain?" asked the sergeant, kicking the prostrate form of Seymour, and pointing to the body of the man who had been slain.

"Oh, let them lie there! We can't be bothered with dead and dying men. One of them is gone; the other soon will be. The slaves will bury them, and those other three at the foot of the hill—d' ye hear, ye black niggers? There's hardly room enough on the sloop for the living," he continued with cynical indifference.

"All right, captain! As you say, poor Joe's no good now; and as for the other, that crack of Welsh's was a rare good one; he will probably die before morning anyhow," replied the sergeant, there being little love lost among the members of this philosophic crew; besides, the more dead, the more plunder for the living. And many of the band were even now following the example of their leader, and roaming over the house, securing at will whatever excited their fancy, the wine-cellar especially not being forgotten.

"Oh, my God! John," whispered Katharine, falling on her knees again by his side, "must I leave you now, oh, my love!" she moaned, taking his head in her arms, and with her handkerchief wiping the blood from off his forehead, "and you have died for me—for me."

The colonel saw the action, and knew now what was the subject of the interview after supper which Seymour had so much desired. He knelt down beside his daughter, a great pity for her in his soul, and laid his hand on the prostrate man's heart.

"He is not dead, Katharine," he whispered. "I do not even think he will die; he will be all right in an hour. If we don't go soon, Katharine, Philip and Bentley will return and be taken also," he continued rapidly. "Come, Katharine," he said more loudly, rising. "Dearest child, we must go,—you must bear this, my daughter; it is for our country we suffer." But the talismanic word apparently had lost its charm for her.

"What's all this?" said Johnson, roughly; "she must go." She only moaned and pressed her lover's hands against her heart.

"And go now! Do you hear? Come, mistress," laying his hand roughly upon her shoulder.

"Have a care, sir," said Desborough, warningly. "Keep to yourself, my dear sir; no harm is done. But we must go; and if she won't go willingly, she will have to be carried, that's all. Do you hear me? Come on!"

"Come, Katharine," said the colonel, entreatingly.

"Oh, father, father, I cannot leave him! I love him!"

"I know you do, dear; and worthy he is of your love too. Please God you shall see him once again! But now we must go. Will you not come with me?"

"I cannot, I cannot!" she repeated.

"But you must, Kate," said the colonel, lifting her up, in deadly anxiety to get away before his son returned. "You are a prisoner."

"I can't, father; indeed I can't!" she cried again.

She struggled a moment, then half fainted in his arms.

"Who else is here?" said Johnson.

"Only the slaves," replied the colonel.

"Well, we don't want them. Move on, then! Your daughter can take her maid with her if she wishes," he said with surly courtesy. "Is this the wench? Well, get your mistress a cloak, and be quick about it!"

Assisted by Chloe, the maid, and Lord Desborough, the colonel half carried, half led, his daughter out of the room.

"Seymour, Seymour!" she cried despairingly at the door; but he lay still where he had fallen, seeing and hearing nothing.

CHAPTER VI

FAITHFUL SUBJECT OF HIS MAJESTY

A few miles up the river from Colonel Wilton's plantation, upon a high bluff, from which, as at that point the river made a wide bend, one could see up and down for a long distance in either direction, was the beautiful home of the Talbots, known as Fairview Hall.

On the evening of the raid at the Wilton place, Madam Talbot and her son were having a very important conversation. Madam Talbot was a widow who had remained unwedded again from choice. Rumor had it that many gentlemen cavaliers of the neighborhood had been anxious to take to their own hearthstones the person of the fair young widow, so early bereft, and incidentally were willing to assume the responsibility of the management of the magnificent estate which had been left to her by her most considerate husband. Among the many suitors gossip held that Colonel Wilton was the chief, and it was thought at one time that his chances of success were of the best; but so far, at least, nothing had come of all the agitation, and Madam Talbot lived her life alone, managing her plantation, the object of the friendly admiration of all the old bachelors and widowers of the neighborhood. She had devoted herself to the successful development of her property with all the energy and capacity of a nature eminently calculated for success, and was now one of the richest women in the colony. One son only had blessed her union with Henry Talbot, and Hilary Talbot was a young man just turned twenty-five years of age, and the idol of her soul. Too self-contained and too proud to display the depth of her feelings, except in rare instances, and too sensible to allow them to interfere in the training of the child, she had spared neither her heart nor her purse in his education, with such happy results that he was regarded by all who knew him as one of the finest specimens of young Virginia that it were possible to meet. Of medium height, active, handsome, dark-eyed, dark-haired, fiery and impetuous in temperament, generous and frank in disposition, he was a model among men; trained from his boyhood in every manly sport and art, and educated in the best institutions of learning in the colonies, his natural grace perfected by a tour of two years in England and abroad, from which he had only a year or so since returned, he perfectly represented all that was best in the young manhood of Virginia. For many years there had been hopes in the minds of Colonel Wilton and Madam Talbot, that the affection between the two young people, who had played together from childhood with all the frankness and simplicity permitted by country life, would develop into something nearer and dearer, and that by their marriage at the proper time the two great estates might be united.

The two children, early informed of this desire, had grown up under the influence of the idea; as they reached years of discretion, they had taken it for granted, considering the arrangement as a fact accomplished by tacit understanding and habit rather than by formal promise. Personally attached to each other, nay, even fondly affectionate, the indefinite tie seemed sufficiently substantial to bring about the desired result. Katharine had, especially during Talbot's absence in Europe, resisted all the importunities and rejected all the proposals made to her, and on his account refused all the hearts laid at her feet. Since Talbot's return, however, and especially since he refused, or hesitated rather, to cast his lot in with her own people, his neighbors and friends, in the Revolution, the affair had, on her part at least, assumed a new phase. Still, there had been nothing said or done to prevent this consummation so devoutly to be wished until the advent of Seymour. Then, too, Talbot, calm and confident in the situation, had not noticed Seymour's infatuation, and was entirely ignorant that the coveted prize had slipped from his grasp. The insight of the confident lover was not so keen as that of the watchful father.

It was believed by the principal men of Virginia that Talbot's sympathies were with the revolted colonies; but the influence of his mother, to whom he had been accustomed to defer, had hitherto proved sufficient to prevent him from openly declaring himself. His visit to England, and the delightful reception he had met with there, had weakened somewhat the ties which bound him to his native country, and he found himself in a state of indecision as humiliating as it was painful. Lord Dunmore and Colonel Wilton had each made great efforts to enlist his support, on account of his wealth and position and high personal qualities. It was hinted by one that the ancient barony of the Talbots would be revived by the king; and the gratitude of a free and grateful country, with the consciousness of having materially aided in acquiring that independence which should be the birthright of every Englishman, was eloquently portrayed by the other. When to the last plea was added the personal preference of Katharine Wilton, the balance was overcome, and the hopes of the mother were doomed to disappointment.

For his own hopes, however, the decision had come too late, and it may be safely presumed that his hesitation was one of the main causes through which the woman he loved escaped him; for Katharine's heart was given to young Seymour, after a ten days' courtship, almost before his eyes. In any event, a wiser man would have seen in Seymour a possible, nay, a certain rival by no means to be disregarded. An officer who had devoted himself to the cause of his country in response to the first demand of the Congress, who had been conspicuously mentioned for gallantry in general orders and reports, who had been severely wounded while protecting Katharine's father at the risk of his life; as well bred and as well born as Talbot, of ample fortune, and with a wide knowledge of men and things acquired in his merchant voyagings as captain of one of his own ships in many seas,—Seymour's single-hearted devotion eminently fitted him to woo and win Miss Katharine Wilton, as he had done.

Nevertheless, a friendship had sprung up between Seymour and the unsuspecting Talbot which bade fair to ripen into intimacy; and it may be supposed that the stories of battles in which the older man had participated, his attractive personality, the consideration in which the young sailor was held by men of weight and position in the colonies, as a man from whom much was to be expected, had large influence in determining Talbot in the course he proposed taking, and which he had not yet communicated to his mother.

The evening repast had just been finished, and the mother and son were walking slowly up and down the long porch overlooking the river in front of the house. There was a curious and interesting likeness between the two,—a facial resemblance only, for Madam Talbot was a slender, rather frail little woman, and looked smaller by contrast as she walked by the side of her son, who had his arm affectionately thrown over her shoulder. She was as straight, however, as he was himself, in spite of her years and cares, and bore herself as proudly erect as in the days of her youth. Her black eyes looked out with undiminished lustre from beneath her snowy-white hair, which needed no powder and was covered by the mob cap she wore. She looked every inch the lady of the manor, nor did her actions and words belie her appearance. The subject of the conversation was evidently a serious one. There was a troubled expression upon her face, in spite of her self-control, which was in marked contrast to the hesitating and somewhat irresolute look upon the handsome countenance of her son.

"My son, my son," she said at last, "why will you persist in approaching me upon this subject? You know my opinions. I have not hesitated to speak frankly, and it is not my habit to change them; in this instance they are as fixed and as immutable as the polar star. The traditions and customs of four hundred years are behind me. Our family—you know your father and I were cousins, and are descended from the same stock—have been called the 'loyal Talbots.' I cannot contemplate with equanimity the possibility even of one of us in rebellion against the king."

"Mother—I am sorry—grieved—but I must tell you that that is a possibility I fear you must learn to face. I have—"

"Oh, Hilary, do not tell me you have finally decided to join this unrighteous rebellion. Pause before you answer, my boy—I entreat you, and it is not my habit to entreat, as you very well know. See, you have been the joy of my heart all my life, the idol of my soul,—I will confess it now,—and for you and your future I have lived and toiled and served and loved. I have dreamed you great, high in rank and place, serving your king, winning back the ancient position of our family. I have shrunk from no sacrifice, nor would I shrink from any. 'Tis not that I do not wish you to risk your life in war,—I am a daughter of my race, and for centuries they have been soldiers, and what God sends soldiers upon the field, that I can abide,—but that you should go now, with all your prospects, your ability, the opportunity presented you, and engage yourself in this fatal cause, in this unholy attack upon the king's majesty, connect yourself with this beggarly rabble who have been whipped and beaten every time they have come in contact with the royal troops,—I cannot bear it. You are a man now. You have grown away from your mother, Hilary, and I can no longer command, I must entreat." But she spoke very proudly, for, as she said, entreaty was not so usual to her as command.

"Oh, mother, mother, you make it very hard for me. You know the colonists have been badly treated, and hardly used by king and Parliament. Our liberties have been threatened, nay, have been abrogated, our privileges destroyed, none of our rights respected, and unless we are to sink to the level of mere slaves and dependants upon the mother country, we have no other course but an appeal to arms."

"I know, I know all that," she interrupted impatiently, with a wave of her hand. "I have heard it all a thousand times from ill-balanced agitators and popular orators. There may be some truth in it, of course, I grant you; but in my creed nothing, Hilary, nothing, will justify a subject in turning against his king. The king can do no wrong. All that we have is his; let him take what he will, so he leaves us our honor, and that, indeed, no one can take from us. It is the principle that our ancestors have attested on a hundred fields and in every other way, and will you now be false to it, my boy?"

"I must be true to myself, mother, first of all, in spite of all the kings of earth; and I feel that duty and honor call me to the side of my friends and the people of this commonwealth. I have hesitated long, mother, in deference to you, but now I have decided."

"And you turn against two mothers, Hilary, when you take

this course,—old England, the mother country, and this one, this old mother, who stands before you, who has given you her heart, who has lived for you, who lives in you now, whose devotion to you has never faltered; she now humbly asks with outstretched arms, the arms that carried you when you were a baby boy, that you remain true to your king."

"Nay, but, mamma," he said, calling her by the sweet name of his boyhood, taking her hand and looking down at her tenderly with tear-dimmed eyes full of affection, "one must be true to his idea of right and duty first of all, even at the price of his allegiance to a king; and, after all, what is any king beside you in my heart? But I feel in honor bound to go with my people."

The irresolution was gone from his expression now, and the two determined faces—one full of pity, the other of apprehension—confronted each other.

CHAPTER VII

THE LOYAL TALBOTS

"Your people, son?" she said after a long pause. "Come with me a moment." She drew him into the brilliantly lighted hall. As they entered, he said to the servant in waiting,—

"See that my bay horse is saddled and brought around at once, and do you tell Dick to get another horse ready and accompany me; he would better take the black pony."

"Are you going out, Hilary?"

"Yes, mother, when our conversation is over, if there is time. I thought to ride over to Colonel Wilton's. The night is pleasant, and the moon will rise shortly. What were you about to say to me?"

She led him up to the great open fireplace, on the andirons of which a huge log was blazing and crackling cheerfully. Over the mantel was the picture of a handsome man in the uniform of a soldier of some twenty years back.

"Whose face is pictured there, Hilary?"

"My honored father," he answered reverently, but in

some surprise.

"And how died he?"

"On the Plains of Abraham, mother, as you well know."

"Fighting for his king?"

"Yes, mother."

"And who is this one?" she said, passing to another picture.

"Sir James Talbot; he struck for his king at Worcester," he volunteered.

"Yes, Hilary; and here is his wife, Lady Caroline Talbot, my grandmother. She kept the door against the Roundheads while the prince escaped from her castle, to which he had fled after the battle. And over there is Lord Cecil Talbot, her father; he fell at Naseby. There in that corner is another James, his brother, one of Prince Rupert's men, wounded at Marston Moor. Here is Sir Hilary, slain at the Boyne; and this old man is Lord Philip, your great-uncle. He was out in the '45, and was beheaded. These are your people, Hilary," she said, standing very straight, her head thrown back, her eyes aflame with pride and determination, "and these struck, fought, lived, and died for their king. I could bear to see you dead," she laid her hand upon her heart in sudden fear at the idea, in spite of her brave words, "but I could not bear to see you a rebel. Think again. You will not so decide?" She said it bravely; it was her final appeal, and as she made it she knew that it was useless. The sceptre had departed out of her hand.

He smiled sadly at her, but shook his head ominously. "Mother, do you know these last fought for Stuart pretenders against the house of Hanover? George III., in your creed, has no right to the place he holds. Do I not then follow my ancestors in taking the field against him?"

"Ah, my child, 't is an unworthy subterfuge. They did fight for the house of Stuart, God bless it! It was king against king then, and at least they fought for royalty, for a king; but now the house of Stuart is gone; the new king occupies the throne undisputed, and our allegiance is due to him. These unfortunate people who are fighting here strive to create a republic where all men shall be equal! Said the sainted martyr Charles on the scaffold, "T is no concern of the common people's how they are governed.' A common man equal to a Talbot! Fight, my son, if you must; but oh, fight for the king, even an usurper, before a republic, a mob in which so-called equality stands in very unstable equilibrium,—fight for the rightful ruler of the land, not against him."

"Mother, if I am to believe the opinions of those whom I have been taught to respect, the rightful rulers of this colony, of our country, of any country, are the people who inhabit it."

"And who says that, pray, my boy?"

"Mr. Henry."

"And do you mean to tell me, a Talbot, that you have been taught to look up to men of the social stamp of Patrick Henry, or to respect their opinions?" she said with ineffable disdain.

"Mother, the logic of events has forced all men to do so. Had you heard his speeches before the Burgesses at Williamsburg, you would have thought that he was second to no man in the colony, or in the world beside; but if he be not satisfactory, there is his excellency General Washington."

"Mr. Washington," she replied with an emphasis on the "Mr." "Now there, I grant you, is a man," she said reluctantly. "I cannot understand the perversion of his destiny or the folly of his course."

"And, mother, you know his family was as loyal as our own. One of his forefathers held Worcester for King Charles with the utmost gallantry and resolution. And he had as a companion in arms in that brave attempt Sir George Talbot, one of our ancestors. There is an example for you. I have often heard you speak with the greatest respect of George Washington."

"It is true, my son," she replied honestly, "but I am at a loss to fathom his motive. What can it be?"

"Mother, I am persuaded of the purity of his motives; his actions spring from the very highest sense of his personal obligation to the cause of liberty."

"'Liberty, liberty,' 't is a weak word when matched with loyalty. But be this as it may, my son, it is beside the question. Our family, these men and women who look down upon us, all fought for principles of royalty. It makes no difference whether or no they fought for or against one or another king, so long as it was a king they fought for. Such a thing as a democracy never entered their heads. And if you take this course, you will be false to every tradition of our past. In my opinion, the people are not fit to govern, and you will find it so. In the impious attempt that is being made to reverse what I conceive to be the divinely appointed polity and law of God, disaster must be the only end."

"Mother, I must follow my convictions in the present rather

than any examples in the past. But this is a painful discussion. Should we not best end it? I honor your opinions, I love you, but I must go."

There was a long silence. She broke it. "Well, my child," she said in despair, "you have reached man's estate, and the men of the Talbot race have ever been accustomed to do as their judgment dictates. If you have decided to join Washington's rabble and take part among the rebels in this fratricidal contest, I shall say no more. I cannot further oppose you. I cannot give you my blessing—as I might in happier circumstances—nor can I wish success to your cause. I too am a Talbot, and have my principles, which I must also maintain; but at least I can gird your sword about you, and express the hope and make the prayer, as I do, that you may wear and use it honorably; and that hope, if you are true to the traditions of our house, will never be broken,—I feel sure of that, at least."

The young man bent and kissed his mother, a new light shining in his eyes. "Mother, I thank you. At least, as far as I am concerned, I will endeavor to do my duty honorably in every field. And now I think, with your permission, I will go over and tell Katharine that I have at last made up my mind and cast my lot in with her—I mean with our country," he said, blushing, but with the thoughtless disregard of youth as to the meaning and effect of his words.

"Go, my son, and God be with you!" she said solemnly.

He stepped quickly out on the porch, and, swinging into the saddle of the horse which awaited him, with the ease and grace of an accomplished horseman, galloped off in the moonlight night followed by the groom.

The little old woman stood rigidly in the doorway a moment,

looking after her departed son, and then she walked quickly down to a rustic seat on the brow of the hill and sat down heavily, following with straining eyes and yearning heart his rapidly disappearing figure. The same pang that every mother must feel, those who have a son at least, once in her life if no more, came to her heart; all her prayers had been unavailing, her requests unheeded, her pleas and wishes disregarded. She had an idea, not altogether warranted perhaps, but still she had it, that the influence was not so much the example of General Washington, nor the eloquence of Patrick Henry, nor the force of neighborly example, nor rigid principle, but the influence of a sunny head, and a pair of youthful eyes, and a merry laugh, and a young heart, and a pleading voice. These have always stood in the light of a mother since the world began, and these have taken her son from her side. All her hopes gone, her dreams shattered, her sacrifice vain, her love wasted, she bowed her white head upon her thin hands, and wept quietly in the silent night. The deep waters had gone over her soul, and the rare tears of the old woman bespoke a breaking heart.

CHAPTER VIII

AN UNTOLD STORY

There were two roads which led from Fairview Hall to the home of the Wiltons,—one by the river, and the other over the hills farther inland. Talbot had chosen the river-road, and was riding along with a light heart, forgetful of his mother and those tears which indeed she would not have shown him, and full of pleasant anticipations as to the effect of his decision upon Katharine.

As he rode along in the moonlight, his mind, full of that calm repose which comes to men when they have finally arrived at a decision upon some point which has troubled them, felt free to range where it would, and naturally his thoughts turned toward the girl he loved. He was getting along in life, twenty-four his last birthday, while Katharine was several years his junior. It was time to settle himself; and if he must ride away to the wars, it were well, pleasant at least, to think that he was leaving at home a wife over whom he had thrown the protecting aegis of his name.

Katharine would be much happier,—his thoughts dwelt tenderly upon her,—and the definite arrangement would be better than this tacit understanding, which of course was sufficiently binding; though, now he thought of it, Katharine had seemed a little difficult of late, probably because of the indefinite character of the tie. He laughed boyishly in pleasure at his own thought. It was another proof that she loved him, that she resented any assumption on his part based on hopes indulged in and plans formed by her father and his mother. He must declare himself at once. Poor mother! it was hard for her; but she would soon get over all that, and when he came back distinguished and honored by the people, she would feel very differently. As for the capricious Katharine, he would speak out that very night, never doubting the issue, and get it done with. Of course, that was all that was necessary.

When she knew that he was engaged heart and soul in the cause of the Revolution, she would be ready to yield him anything. Not that he had any doubt of the result of his proposal in any case; as soon doubt that the nature and orderly sequence of events should be suddenly and violently interrupted, as imagine that these cherished plans, in which they had both acquiesced so long ago, should fall through. And so my lord was prepared to drop the handkerchief at the feet of my lady for her to pick up! It was a time, however, he might have remembered, in which the old established order of events in other fields, which men had long since conceived of as fixed as natural laws, was being rudely broken and destroyed. Many things which had heretofore been habitually taken for granted, now were required to be proved, and Talbot was destined to meet the fate of every over-confident lover. Devotion, self-abnegation, persistency,—these during ten days had held the field; and the result of the campaign had been that inevitable one which may always be looked for when the opposing forces, even after years of possession, muster under the banner of habit, assurance, confidence, and neglect.

So musing, the light-hearted gentleman galloped along. The

intervening distance was soon passed over, and Talbot found himself entering the familiar stretch of woodland which marked the beginning of the colonel's estate. Under the trees and beneath the high bank of the river the shadows deepened; scarcely any light from the moon fell on the road. It was well, therefore, that our cavalier drew rein, and somewhat checked the pace of his horse, advancing with some caution over the familiar yet unseen road; for just as he came opposite the land end of the pier which led out to the boat-house, the animal stopped with such suddenness that a less practised rider would have suffered a severe fall. The horse snorted and trembled in terror, and began rearing and backing away from the spot. Looking down in the darkness, Talbot could barely discern a dark, bulky object lying in the road.

"Here, Dick!" he called to the groom, who had stopped and reined in his own horse, apparently as terrified as the other, a few paces back of his master; and tossing his bridle rein toward him, "take my horse, while I see what stopped him."

Lightly leaping to the ground, and stepping up to the object before him, he bent down and laid his hand upon it, and then started back in surprise and horror. "It's a man," he exclaimed; "dead, yet warm still. Who can it be?" The moonlight fell upon the pebbly beach of the river a little farther out; overcoming his reluctance, he half lifted, half carried the body out where the light would fall upon its face. This face, which was unknown to him, was that of a desperate-looking ruffian, who was dressed in a soiled and tattered uniform, the coat of which was red; the man's hand tightly clasped a discharged pistol; he had been shot in the breast, for where his coat had fallen open might be seen a dark red stain about a ragged hole in his soiled gray shirt; the bullet had been fired at short range, too, for there were powder marks all about his breast. Talbot noticed these

Cyrus Townsend Brady

things rapidly, his mind working quickly.

"Oh, Mars' Hil'ry—wha-wha's de mattah? I kyarnt hol' dese hosses; dey'se sumfin wrong, sho'ly," broke in the groom, his teeth chattering with terror.

"Quiet, man! don't make so much noise. This is the dead body of a man, a soldier; he has been shot too. Take the horses back beyond the old tree on the little bend there; tie them securely, and come back here quickly. Make no noise. Bring the pistols from your holsters."

As the man turned to obey him, Talbot glanced about in perplexity, and his eyes fell upon a small sloop rapidly disappearing down the river, under full sail in the fresh breeze which had sprung up. She was too far away now to make out any details in the moonlight, but the sight was somewhat unusual and alarming, he scarcely knew why.

"I got dem tied safe, Mars' Hil'ry," called out the voice of the boy from the road.

"All right, Dick! We will leave this one here, and try to find out what's wrong; you follow me, and keep the pistols ready."

"Yes, Mars', I got dem." The man was brave enough in the presence of open danger; it was only the spiritual he feared.

They had scarcely gone ten paces farther toward the path, when, at the foot of it, they stumbled over another body.

"Here is another one. What does it mean? See who it is, Dick."

The groom, mastering his instinctive aversion, bent down

obediently, and lifting the face peered into it. It was lighter here, and he recognized it at once.

"Hit's Mars' Blodgett, de kunnel's old sojuh man. Him got a bullet-hole in de fohaid, suh; him a dead man sholy, an' heah is his gun by his han'," he said in an awestruck whisper.

"Blodgett! Good God, it can't be."

"Yes, suh, it's him, and dere's anoder one ober dah. See, suh!" He laid his hand upon another body, in the same uniform as the first one. This man groaned slightly.

"Dis one's not daid yit," said Dick, excitedly; "he been hit ober de haid, his face all bloody. Oh, Mars' Hil'ry, dem raidahs you done tell me 'bout been heah. Mars' Blodgett done shot dat one by de riber on de waf, an' den hit dis one wid his musket, an' den dey done shoot Mars' Blodgett. Oh, Mars' Hil'ry, le"s get out ob heah."

Talbot saw it all now,—the slow and stealthy approach of the boat from the little sloop out in the river (it had disappeared round the bend, he noticed), Blodgett's quiet watch at the foot of the path, the approach of the men, Blodgett's challenge, the first one shot dead as he came up, the pistol-shot which missed him, the rush of the men at the indomitable old soldier, the nearest one struck down from the blow of the clubbed musket of the sturdy old man, the second pistol-shot, which hit him in the forehead, his fall across the path. Faithful unto death at the post of duty. The little drama was perfectly plain to him. But who were these raiders? Who could they be? And Katharine?

"Oh, my God," he exclaimed, stung into quick action at the thought of a possible peril to his love. "Come, Dick, to the house; she may be in danger."

"But dis libe one, Mars' Hil'ry?"

"Quick, quick! leave him; we will see about him later."

With no further attempt at caution, they sprang recklessly up the steep path, and, gaining the brow of the hill, ran at full speed toward the house. He noticed that there were no lights in the negro quarters, no sounds of the merry-making usually going on there in the early evening. Through the open windows on the side of the house, he had a hasty glimpse of the disordered dining-room. The great doors of the hall were open. They were on the porch now,—now at the door of the hall. It was empty. He paused a second. "Katharine, Katharine!" he called aloud, a note of fear in his voice, "where are you? Colonel Wilton!" In the silence which his voice had broken he heard a weak and feeble moan, which struck terror into his heart.

He ran hastily down the hall, and stopped at the dining-room door aghast. The smoking candles in the sconces were throwing a somewhat uncertain light over a scene of devastation and ruin; the furniture of the table and the accessories of the meal lay in a broken heap at the foot of it, the chairs were overturned, the curtains torn, the great sideboard had been swept bare of its usual load of glittering silver.

At his feet lay the body of a man, in the now familiar red uniform, blood from a ghastly sword-thrust clotted about his throat, the floor about his head being covered with ominous stains. A little farther away on the floor, near the table, there was the body of another man, in another uniform, a naked sword lying by his side; he had a frightful-looking wound on his forehead, and the blood was slowly oozing out of his coat-sleeve, staining the lace at his left wrist. Even as he looked, the man turned a little on the floor, and the same low moan broke from his lips. Talbot stepped over the first body to the side of the other.

"My God, it's Seymour," he said. He knelt beside him, as Katharine had done. "Seymour," he called, "Seymour!" The man opened his eyes slowly, and looked vacantly at him.

"Katharine," he murmured.

"What of her? is she safe?" asked Talbot, in an agony of fear.

"Raiders—prisoner," continued Seymour, brokenly, in a whisper, and then feebly murmured, "Water, water!"

"Here, Dick, get some water quickly! First hand me that decanter of wine," pointing to one which had fortunately escaped the eyes of the marauders. He lifted Seymour's head gently, and with a napkin which he had picked up from the floor, wiped the bloody face, washing it with the water the groom quickly brought from the well outside.

Then he poured a little of the wine down the wounded man's throat, next slit the sleeve of his coat, and saw that the scarcely healed wound in the arm had broken out again. He bandaged it up with no small skill with some of the other neglected table linen, and the effect upon Seymour of the stimulant and of these ministrations was at once apparent. With a stronger voice he said slowly,—

"Dunmore's men—Captain Johnson—colonel a prisoner—Katharine also—God grant—no harm intended."

"Hush, hush! I understand. But where are the slaves?"

"Terrified, I suppose—in hiding."

"Dick, see if you can find any of them. Hurry up! We must take Mr. Seymour back to Fairview tonight, and report this outrage to the military commander at Alexandria. Oh that I had a boat and a few men!" he murmured. Katharine was gone. He would not tell his story to-night; she was in the hands of a gang of ruffians. He knew the reputation of Johnson, and the motives which might actuate him. There had been a struggle, it was evident; perhaps she had been wounded, killed. Agony! He knew now how he loved her, and it was too late.

Presently the groom returned, followed by a mob of frightened, terror-stricken negroes who had fled at the first advent of the party. Talbot issued his orders rapidly. "Some of you get the carriage ready; we must take Lieutenant Seymour to Fairview Hall. Some of you go down to the landing and bring up the bodies of the three men there. You go with that party, Dick. Phoebus, you get this room cleared up. Hurry, stir yourselves! You are all right now; the raiders have gone and are not likely to return."

"Why, where is Master Philip, I wonder? Was he also taken?" he said suddenly. "Have any of you seen him?" he asked of the servants.

"He done gone away fishin' wid Mars' Bentley," replied the old butler, pausing; "and dey ain't got back yit, tank de Lawd; but I spec 'em ev'y minute, suh."

CHAPTER IX

BENTLEY'S PRAYER

As he spoke, a fresh youthful voice was heard in the hall. "Father, Kate, where are you? Come see our string of—Why, what's all this?" said a young man, standing astonished in the door of the room. It was Philip Wilton, holding a long string of fish, the result of their day's sport; behind him stood the tall stalwart figure of the old sailor. "Talbot—you? Where are father and Kate? What are these men doing in the dining-room? Oh, what is that?" he said, shrinking back in horror from the corpse of the soldier.

"Dunmore's raiders have been here."

"And Katharine?"

"A prisoner, with your father, Philip, but I trust both are uninjured."

"Mr. Seymour, sir, where is he?" said the deep voice of the boatswain, as he advanced farther into the room. The light fell full upon him. He was a splendid specimen of athletic manhood; tall, powerful, long-armed, slightly bent in the shoulders; decision and courage were seen in his bearing, and were written on his face, burned a dull mahogany color

Cyrus Townsend Brady

by years of exposure to the weather. He was clothed in the open shirt and loose trousers of a seafaring man, and he stood with his feet slightly apart, as if balancing himself to the uneasy roll of a ship. Honesty and fidelity and intelligence spoke out from his eyes, and affection and anxiety were heard in his voice.

"Lieutenant Seymour," he repeated, "where is he, sir?"

"There," said Talbot, stepping aside and pointing to the floor.

"Not dead, sir, is he?"

"Not yet, Bentley," Seymour, with regaining strength, replied; "I am not done for this time."

"Oh, Mr. John, Mr. John," said the old man, tenderly, bending over him, "I thank God to see you alive again. But, as I live, they shall pay dear for this—whoever has done it,—the bloody, marauding, ruffians!"

"Yes, Bentley, I join you in that vow," said Talbot.

"And I too," added Philip, bravely.

"And I," whispered the wounded man.

"It's one more score that has got to be paid off by King George's men, one more outrage on this country, one more debt we owe the English," Bentley continued fiercely.

"No; these were Americans, Virginians,—more's the shame, —led by that blackguard Johnson. He has long hated the colonel," replied Talbot.

"Curses on the renegades!" said the old man. "Who is it that loves freedom and sees not that the blow must be struck to-day? How can any man born in this land hesitate to—" He stopped suddenly, as his eyes fell upon Talbot, whose previous irresolution and refusal had been no secret to him.

"Don't stop for me, Bentley," said that young man, gently; "I am with you now. I came over this evening to tell our friends here that I start north tomorrow as a volunteer to offer my services to General Washington."

"Oh, Hilary," exclaimed Philip, joyfully, "I am so glad. Would that Katharine and father could hear you now!"

Seymour lifted his unwounded arm, and beckoned to Talbot. "God bless you, Talbot," he said; "to hear you say that is worth a dozen cracks like this, and I feel stronger every minute. If it were not for the old wound, I would n't mind this thing a bit. But there is something you must do. There is an armed cutter stationed up the river at Alexandria; send some one to notify the commander of the Virginia naval militia there. They will pursue and perhaps recapture the party. But the word must be carried quickly; I fear it will be too late as it is."

"I will go, Hilary, if you think best."

"Very well, Philip; take your best horse and do not delay a moment. Katharine's liberty, your father's life perhaps, depend upon your promptness. Better see Mr. West as you go through the town,—your father's agent, you know,—and ask him to call upon me to-morrow. Stop at the Hall as you come back."

"All right, Hilary, I will be in Alexandria in four hours," said Philip, running out.

"Bentley, I am going to take Lieutenant Seymour over to my plantation. Will you stay here and look after the house until I can notify Colonel Wilton's agent at Alexandria to come and take charge, or until we hear from the colonel what is to be done? You can come over in the morning, you know, and hear about our protege. I am afraid the slaves would never stay here alone; they are so disorganized and terrorized now over these unfortunate occurrences as to be almost useless."

"Ay, ay, sir; if Lieutenant Seymour can spare me, I will stay."

"Yes, Bentley, do; I shall be in good hands at Fairview Hall."

"This is arranged, then," said Talbot. "It is nine o'clock. I think we would better start at once. I will go out and see that the arrangements about the carriage are made properly, myself," he said, stepping through the door.

Seymour's hand had closed tightly over something which had happened to fall near where it lay. "Bentley," he called, "what is this in my hand?"

"It is a handkerchief, Mr. John,—a woman's handkerchief too, sir, and covered with blood."

"Has it any marks on it?" said Seymour, eagerly.

"Yes, sir; here are the letters K. W. embroidered in this corner."

"I thought so," he smiled triumphantly. "Will you put it inside my waistcoat, there, over my heart? Yes," he added, as if in answer to the old man's anxious look, "it is true; I love her, and she has confessed that she loves me. Oh, who will protect her now?"

"God, sir," said Bentley, solemnly, but with a strange pang of almost womanly jealousy in his faithful old heart.

"Ay, old friend, He will watch over her. He knows best. Now help me up."

"No, sir. Beg pardon for disobeying orders, but you are to lie still. We will carry you to the carriage. Nay, sir, you must. You are too weak from loss of blood with two wounds on you to stand it. A few days will bring you about all right, though, I hope, sir."

"All ready, Bentley?" said Talbot, coming into the room. "The negro boys have rigged up a stretcher out of a shutter, and with a mattress and blankets in the carriage, I think we can manage, driving carefully, to take him over without any great discomfort. I have sent Dick on ahead to ride over to Dr. Craik's and bid him come to the Hall at once; so Mr. Seymour will be well looked after. By the way, Blodgett is dead. I had almost forgotten him. He evidently met and fought those fellows at the landing. We found him at the foot of the steps by the boat-landing with two bodies. That reminds me, one of them was alive when we came by. I told the men to bring all three of the bodies up. Here they are now. Are any of them alive yet, Caesar?"

"No, suh, dey'se all ob 'em daid."

"Take the two redcoats into the dining-room with the other one. Lay Blodgett here in the hall. He must have been killed instantly. Well; good-by, I shall be over in the morning," he exclaimed, extending his hand.

"Good-by, sir," said the seaman, taking it in his own huge palm. "Take care of Lieutenant Seymour."

"Oh, never fear; we will."

"And may God give the men who did this into our hands!" added Bentley, raising his arms solemnly.

"Amen," said Talbot, with equal gravity.

Seymour was tenderly lifted into the carriage, and attended by Talbot, who sat by his side. Followed by two servants who had orders to get the horses, which they found tied where they had been left, the carriage drove off to the Hall. With what different thoughts was the mind of the young man busy! Scarcely an hour had elapsed since he galloped over the road, a light-hearted boy, flushed with hope, filled with confidence, delighted in his decision, anticipating a reception, meditating words of love. In that one hour the boy had changed from youth to man. The love which he had hardly dreamed was in his heart had risen like a wave and overwhelmed him; the capture and abduction of his sweetheart, the whole brutal and outrageous proceeding, had filled him with burning wrath. He could not wait to strike a blow for liberty against such tyranny now, and his soul was full of resentment to the mother he had loved and honored, because she had held him back; all of the devoted past was forgotten in one impetuous desire of the present. To-morrow should see him on the way to the army, he swore. He wrung his hands in impotent passion.

"Katharine, Katharine, where are you?" he murmured. Seymour stirred. "Are you in pain, my friend?"

"No," said the sailor quietly, his heart beating against the blood-stained handkerchief, as he echoed in his soul the words he had heard: "Katharine, Katharine, where are you? where are you?"

CHAPTER X

A SOLDIER'S EPITAPH

Left to himself in the deserted hall, the old sailor walked over to the body of the old soldier. Many a quaint dispute these two old men had held in their brief acquaintance, and upon no one thing had they been able to agree, except in hatred of the English and love of their common country. Still their disputes had been friendly, and, if they had not loved, they had at least respected each other.

"I wish I had not been so hard on the man. I really liked him," soliloquized the sailor. "Poor Blodgett, almost forgotten, as Mr. Talbot says. He died the right way, though, doing his duty, fighting for his country and for those he loved. Well, he was a brave man—for a soldier," he murmured thoughtfully.

Out on the river the little sloop was speeding rapidly along. Ride as thou wilt, Philip, she cannot be overtaken. Most of the exhausted men lay about the decks in drunken slumber. Johnson stood moodily by the man at the helm; his triumph had been tempered by Desborough's interference. Two or three of the more decent of his followers were discussing the events of the night.

"Poor Joe!" said one.

"Yes, and Evans and Whitely too," was the reply.

"Ay, three dead, and nobody hurt for it," answered the other.

"You forget the old fellow at the landing, though."

"Yes, he fought like the devil, and came near balking the whole game. That was a lucky shot you got in, Davis, after Evans missed and was hit. That fellow was a brave man—for a rebel," said the raider.

In the cabin of the sloop Colonel Wilton was sitting on one of the lockers, his arm around Katharine, who was leaning against him, weeping, her hands before her face. Desborough was standing respectfully in front of them.

"And you say he made a good fight?" asked the colonel, sadly.

"Splendid, sir. We stole up to the boat-house with muffled oars, wishing to give no warning, and before he knew it half of us were on the wharf. He challenged, we made a rush; he shot the first man in the breast and brained the next with his clubbed musket, shouting words of warning the while. The men fell back and handled their pistols. I heard two or three shots, and then he fell, never making another sound. But for Johnson's forethought in sending a second boat load to the upper landing to get to the back of the house, you might have escaped with the warning and the delay he caused. He was a brave man, and died like a soldier," continued the young man, softly.

"He saved my life at Cartagena, and when I caught the fever there, he nursed me at the risk of his own. He was faithfulness itself. He died as he would have liked to die, with his face to the enemy. I loved him in a way you can hardly understand. Yes, he was a brave man,—my poor old friend."

On the rustic bench beside the driveway overlooking the river sat a little woman, older by ten years in the two hours which had elapsed since she looked after the disappearing figure of her son.

She heard the sound of wheels upon the gravel road, and recognized Colonel Wilton's carriage and horses coming up the hill; there were her own two horses following after, but neither of the riders was her son. What could have happened? She rose in alarm. The carriage stopped near her.

"What, mother, are you still here?" said Hilary, opening the door and stepping out, his voice cold and stern.

"Yes, my son; what has happened?"

"Dunmore's men have raided the Wilton place. Katharine and her father have been carried away by that brute Johnson, who commanded the party. Seymour has been wounded in defending Katharine. I have brought him here. This is the way," he went on fiercely, "his majesty the king wages war on his beloved subjects of Virginia."

"'They that take the sword, shall perish with the sword,'" she quoted with equal resolution.

"And Blodgett is killed too," he added.

"What else have those who rebel against their rightful monarch a right to expect?" she replied. "Is Mr. Seymour seriously wounded?"

"No, madam," answered that young man, from the carriage; "but I fear me my cause makes me an unwelcome visitor."

"Nay, not so, sir. No wounded helpless man craving assistance can ever be unwelcome at my—at the home of the Talbots, whatever his creed. How died Blodgett, did you say, Hilary?"

"Fighting for his master, at the foot of the path, shot by those ruffians."

"So may it be to all enemies of the king," she replied; "but after all he was a brave man. 'T is a pity he fell in so poor a cause."

And that was thy epitaph, old soldier; that thy requiem, honest Blodgett,—from friend and foe alike,—"He was a brave man."

BOOK II

KNIGHTS ERRANT OF THE SEA

CHAPTER XI

CAPTAIN JOHN PAUL JONES

"You would better spread a little more canvas, Mr. Seymour. I think we shall do better under the topgallantsails. We have no time to lose."

"Ay, ay, sir," replied the young executive officer; and then lifting the trumpet to his lips, he called out with a powerful voice, "Lay aloft and loose the topgallantsails! Man the topgallant sheets and halliards!"

The crew, both watches being on deck, were busy with the various duties rendered necessary by the departure of a ship upon a long cruise, and were occupied here and there with the different details of work to be done when a ship gets under way. Some of them, their tasks accomplished for the moment, were standing on the forecastle, or peering through the gun ports, gazing at the city, with the tall spire of Christ Church and the more substantial elevation of the building even then beginning to be known as Independence Hall, rising in the background beyond the shipping and over the other buildings which they were so rapidly leaving. In an instant the quiet deck became a scene of quick activity, as the men left their tasks and sprang to their appointed stations. The long coils of rope were thrown upon the deck and seized by the groups of seamen detailed for the purpose; while the rigging shook under the quick steps of the alert topmen springing up the ratlines, swarming over the tops, and laying out on the yards, without a thought of the giddy elevation, in their intense rivalry each to be first.

"The main royal also, Mr. Seymour," continued the captain. "I think she will bear it; 'tis a new and good stick."

"Ay, ay, sir. Main topgallant yard there."

"Sir?"

"Aloft, one of you, and loose the royal as well."

"Ay, ay, sir."

After a few moments of quick work, the officers of the various masts indicated their readiness for the next order by saying, in rapid succession,—

"All ready the fore, sir."

"All ready the main, sir."

"All ready the mizzen, sir."

"Handsomely now, and all together. I want those Frenchmen there to see how smartly we can do this," said the captain, in reply, addressing Seymour in a tone perfectly audible over the ship.

"Let fall! Lay in! Sheet home! Hoist away! Tend the braces there!" shouted the first lieutenant.

Amid the creaking of blocks, the straining of cordage, and

the lusty heaving of the men, with the shrill pipes of the boatswain and his mates for an accompaniment, the sheets were hauled home on the yards, the yards rose on their respective masts, and the light sails, the braces being hauled taut, bellied out in the strong breeze, adding materially to the speed of the ship.

"Lay down from aloft," cried the lieutenant, when all was over.

"Ay, that will do," remarked the captain. "We go better already. I am most anxious to get clear of the Capes before nightfall. Call the men aft, and request the officers to come up on the quarterdeck. I wish to speak to them."

"Ay, ay, sir.—Mr. Wilton," said the young officer, turning to a young midshipman, standing on the lee-side of the deck, "step below and ask the officers there, and those forward, to come on deck. Bentley," he called to the boatswain, "call all hands aft."

"Ay, ay, sir."

Again the shrill whistling of the pipes was heard, followed by the deep tones of Bentley, which rolled and tumbled along the decks of the ship in the usual long-drawn monotonous cry, which could be heard, above the roar of the wind or the rush of the water or the straining of the timbers, from the truck to the keelson: "All hands lay aft, to the quarter-deck."

The captain, standing upon the poop-deck, was not, at first glance, a particularly imposing figure. He was small in stature, scarcely five and a half feet high at best, with his natural height diminished, as is often the case with sailors, by a slight bending of the back and stooping of the shoulders; yet he possessed a well-knit, vigorous, and not ungraceful figure, whose careless poise, and the ease with which he maintained his position, with his hands clasped behind his back, in spite of the rather heavy roll and pitch of the ship, in the very strong breeze, indicated long familiarity with the sea.

His naturally dark complexion was rendered extremely swarthy by the long exposure to weather, and tropic weather at that, which he had undergone. The expression of his face was of that abstract and thoughtful, nay, even melancholy, cast which we commonly associate with the student rather than the man of affairs. He was dressed in the prescribed uniform of a captain of the American navy, in the Revolutionary period: a dark blue cloth coat with red lapels, slashed cuffs, and stand-up collar, flat gold buttons (this last a piece of unusual extravagance); blue breeches, and a red waistcoat heavily laced; silk stockings and buckled shoes, with a curved cross-hilted sword and cocked hat, completed his attire. As the men came crowding aft to the main mast, the idlers tumbling up through the hatches in response to the command, his indifferent look gave way to one of quick attention, and each individual seaman seemed to be especially embraced in the severe scrutiny with which he regarded the mass. In truth, they were a crew of which any officer might well be proud; somewhat motley and nondescript as to uniform and appearance, perhaps, and unused to the strict discipline of men-of-war, but hardy, bold, resolute seamen, with whom, properly led, all things were possible,—men who would hesitate at nothing in the way of attack, and who were permeated with such an intensity of hate for England and for British men-of-war as made them the most dangerous foes that country ever encountered on the seas. Several of them, Bentley among the number, had been pressed, at one time or another, on English war vessels; and one or two had even felt the lash upon their backs, and bore shocking testimony, in deep-scarred wounds, to the barbaric method of punishment in vogue for the maintenance of discipline in the British navy, and, indeed, in all the great navies of the world,—a practice, however, but little resorted to by the American navy.

The officers, gathered in a little knot on the lee side of the quarter-deck, several midshipmen among them, were worthy of the crew and the commander.

"Men," said the captain, in a clear, firm voice, removing his cocked hat from his thick black hair, tied in a queue and entirely devoid of powder, as he looked down at them from the break of the poop with his piercing black eyes, "we are bound for English waters—"

"Hurrah, hurrah!" cried many voices from the crew, impetuously.

"We will show the new flag for the first time on the high seas," he continued, visibly pleased, and pointing proudly to the stars and stripes, which his own hand had first hoisted, fluttering gayly out at the peak; "and I trust we may strike a blow or two which will cause it, and us, to be long remembered. While you are under my orders I shall expect from you prompt, unquestioned compliance with my commands, or those of my officers, and a ready submission to the hard discipline of a ship-of-war, to which most of you, I suspect, are unfamiliar, unless you have learned it in that bitter school, a British ship. You will learn, however, while principles of equality are very well in civil life, they have no place in the naval service. Subordination is the word here; this is not a trading-vessel, but a ship-of-war, and I intend to be implicitly obeyed," he continued sternly, looking even more fiercely at them. "Nevertheless," he added, somewhat relaxing his set features, "although we be not a peaceful merchantman, yet I expect and intend to do a little trading with the ships of the enemy, and in any prizes which we may capture, you know you will all have a just, nay, a liberal, share. It must not be lost sight of, however, that the first business of this ship, as of every other ship-of-war of our country, is to fight the ships of the enemy of equal, or of not too great, force. Should we find such a one, as is most likely, in the English Channel, we must remember that the honor and glory of our flag are above prize money."

"Three cheers for Captain John Paul Jones!" cried one of the seamen, leaping on a gun and waving his hat; they were given with a mighty rush from nearly two hundred lusty throats, the ship being heavily overmanned for future emergencies.

"That will do, men," said the captain, smiling darkly. "Remember that a willing crew makes a happy cruise—and don't wake the sleeping cat![1] Mr. Seymour, have the boatswain pipe all hands to grog, then set the watches. Mr. Talbot," he added, turning to the young officer in the familiar buff and blue of the Continental army, who stood by his side, an interested and attentive spectator to all that had occurred, "will you do me the honor of taking a glass of wine with me in the cabin?—I should be glad if you would join us also, Mr. Seymour, after the watch has been called, and you can leave the deck. Let Mr. Wallingford have the watch; he is familiar with the bay. Tell him to take in the royal and the fore and mizzen topgallantsails if it blows heavily," he continued, after a pause, and then, bowing, he left the deck.

[1] The cat-o'-nine-tails, used for punishment by flogging.

Cyrus Townsend Brady

CHAPTER XII

AN IMPORTANT COMMISSION

Meanwhile, interesting conversations were going on forward, of which this is a sample.

"I 'm blest if I like this orderin' business," said one grizzled seaman; "they said he was h—l on orders, but what I shipped for was prize money and a chance to get a lick at them bloody Britishers; not for to clean brass work, an' scrape spars, an' flemish down, an' holy-stone decks, which he won't let us spit terbacker on. I don't call this no fighting fur liberty, not by a durn sight."

"Shut up, Bill," replied another; "you've got to obey orders. This yere ain't no old tea wagon, no fishing-boat, you old scowbanker, it's a wessel-o'-war; and may I never see Nantucket again if the old man," using a merchantman's expression, "ain't goin' to be captain of the old hooker while he's in it. And if you call this hard work and growl at this kind o' dissyplin'—well, all I got ter say, you'd oughter been on the old Radnor. Curse the British devils!" he cried, grinding his heel in the deck. "I'd give twenty years of my life to be alongside her in a ship half her size; yes, even in this one, and I tell ye yon's the man to put her there, if he gets a chance. Ain't that so, mates?"

"Ay, ay, Jack, 'tis true," came a deep-toned chorus of approval.

"Besides," went on the forecastle orator, "we all know'd wot kind of a officer he is. Fightin' and prize money is wot we all want; and here's where we'll git it, you'll see, eh, mates?"

"Ay, ay; Jack's right, Bill."

"Then blow the dissyplin', say I; I'll take orders from a man wot ain't afraid o' nothin', wot hates the red rag we knows of, wot won't send me where he won't go himself. Fightin' and prize money, he's our man. Besides, wot's the use o' kickin', we got to do it; we're bound by them articles of war we signed," continued this deep-sea philosopher. "Now, pass me my can o' grog, Tom, I 'm dry as a cod. Here's to America, and damn the British, too," continued this sea lawyer, drinking his toast amid shouts of approval from the men.

Left to himself, Seymour, after the men had received their grog, and other necessary duties had been attended to, turned the deck over to Lieutenant Wallingford, whose watch it was with Philip Wilton, and, descending the poop-deck ladder, disappeared through the same door which had received the two officers into the cabin.

Three weeks had elapsed since the raid upon the Wilton place, and the scene had shifted from Virginia to the sea, or rather to the great bay which gives entrance to it, from the Delaware River. It was a clear cold day in the early part of December, and the American Continental ship Ranger had just left her moorings off Philadelphia, with orders to proceed to English waters; stopping at Brest to receive the orders of the commissioners in Paris, and then, in case no better ship could be found, to ravage the English Channel and coast, as a warning that like processes, on the part of

Cyrus Townsend Brady

England on our own shores, should not go unpunished.

John Paul Jones, who had already given evidence, not only of that desperate courage and unyielding tenacity which had marked him as among the most notable of sea officers the world has seen,—lacking nothing but opportunity to have equalled, if not surpassed a Nelson—but of consummate seamanship and great executive ability as well, had been appointed to command the ship. Before proceeding on the mission, however, an important undertaking had been allotted to him. The commissioners had sent word from France, by a fast-sailing armed packet, of the near departure of a transport from England, called the Mellish, laden with two thousand muskets, twenty field-pieces, powder, and other munitions of war, and ten thousand suits of winter clothes, destined for the army that was assembling at Halifax and Quebec for the invasion of the colonies, by way of the St. Lawrence River and Lake Champlain.

Congress had transmitted the letter from France to Captain Jones, with directions that he endeavor to intercept and capture this transport. The destitution of the American army at this period of the war was frightful: devoid of clothes, arms, provisions, powder,—everything, in fact, which is apparently vital to the existence of an army; continually beaten, menaced by a confident, well-equipped, and disciplined enemy in overwhelming force, and before whom they had been habitually retreating, they were only held together by the indomitable will and heroic resolution of one man, George Washington. The fortunes of the colonies were never at a lower ebb than at that moment, and there was apparently nothing further to look forward to but a continuation of the disintegration until the end came. The meagre resources of the lax confederacy were already strained to the utmost, and the capture of a ship laden as this one was reported to be, would be of incalculable service.

Clothes and shoes to cover the nakedness of the soldiery and protect them from the inclemency of the winter, now fast approaching, and arms to put in their hands, by means of which they could assume the offensive and attack the enemy, or at least defend themselves—what more could they desire! The desperate nature of the situation, the dire need of just such additions to the equipment of the army, had been plainly communicated to Captain Jones, and he was resolved to effect the capture if it were humanly possible. The matter had also been reported to General Washington; and such was his opinion of the necessity of a prompt distribution and a speedy forwarding of the supplies, if they could be secured, by the blessing of Providence, and so little was his faith in the inefficient commissariat, which, moreover, had to endeavor to keep the balance between different colonies and different bodies of troops, more or less loosely coherent, that he had detailed one of his own staff officers to accompany the ship, with explicit instructions as to the exact distribution and the prompt forwarding which the needs of the troops rendered necessary, when the captured ship should reach port, which would probably be Boston, though circumstances might render it advisable to take the longer journey to Philadelphia. The officer to whom this duty had been allotted was Talbot, of whose capacity and energy General Washington already thought highly; the three weeks of their military association only confirming his previous opinion. It was understood that Seymour, who was Jones' first lieutenant, and would shortly be promoted to a captaincy, would bring back the transport if they were lucky enough to capture it. In case they were unsuccessful, Talbot was to report himself to the commissioners at Paris as military secretary, until further orders; and Seymour was to command the Ranger, when Jones should get a better ship in France.

The Ranger was a small sloop of war, a corvette of perhaps five hundred tons, with a raised poop and a topgallant forecastle, built at Portsmouth, New Hampshire; a new ship, and one of the first of those built especially for naval purposes. She was originally intended for twenty-six guns, but the number, through the wisdom of her captain, who had fathomed the qualifications of the ship, had been reduced to eighteen, four long twelves, and the rest six pounders, and smaller, with one long eighteen forward. She had been some days in commission, and the effect of Jones' iron discipline was already apparent in the absence of confusion and in the cleanness and order of the ship. The vessel had been very popular with the good people of Philadelphia, her commander and officers likewise, many of the latter, like Seymour, being natives of the town; and a constant stream of visitors had inspected her, at all permitted hours. The presence of these visitors, of course including many ladies, coupled with an inherent vanity and love of finery and neatness on the part of the captain,—and, to do him justice, his appreciation of the necessity for order and neatness,— had caused him to maintain his ship in the handsomest possible trim, and he had not scrupled to employ his private fortune to beautify the vessel in many small ways, the details of which would have escaped any eye but that of a seaman, though the general results were apparent.

That general appearance which should always distinguish a trim and well-ordered vessel of war from the clumsy and disorderly trader, was due entirely to his efforts. The crew, as we have seen, had chafed under the unusual restraints of this stern discipline; but they were unable, as, indeed, in the last resort they would have been unwilling, to oppose it. Some of the older men, too, and some of those who had sailed with Jones in his already famous cruises, held out the hope of large prize money, and, what was better with many of them, the chance of a blow at the enemy, if any of her cruisers of anything like equal force appeared,—a chance sure to come about in the frequented waters of the English Channel. The crew of an American man-of-war at that period, at least the native portion of it, always in overwhelming majority, was of much higher class than the general run of seafaring men. Among those in the Ranger were several who had been mates of merchantmen,—Bentley again among the number,—men of some education, and able to serve their country as officers with credit, had the navy been increased as it should have been, and whose subordinate positions only indicated their intense patriotism. The low and degraded element which sometimes is such a source of mischief and disaster in ships' crews, was conspicuous by its absence. The reputation of Captain Jones as a disciplinarian was very well known among sailors generally, and only his reputation as a fighter and a successful prize-taker would have enabled him to assemble the remarkable crew to which he had spoken, and which was to back him up so gallantly in many desperate undertakings and wonderful sea fights, of this and his succeeding phenomenal cruise.

Seymour had rapidly recovered from his wounds under Madam Talbot's careful nursing and ministrations, and when his orders reached him he had been ready, accompanied by Philip Wilton and Bentley, to join his ship at once.

He still carried the blood-stained handkerchief, and many and many a time had laid it, with its initials, "K. W.," embroidered by her own hand, upon his lips. This was not his only treasure, however. In a wallet in the breast pocket of his coat he carried and treasured a letter, only the veriest scrap of paper, with these few lines hastily written upon it.

These by a friendly hand. We are to accompany Lord Dunmore to England next week as prisoners in the ship Radnor. Both well, but very unhappy. I love you.— Katharine.

This note had been brought to him, the day before his departure from Fairview Hall, by one of the slaves from the Wilton place, who had in turn received it from a stranger who had handed it to him with the orders that it be given to Lieutenant Seymour if he were within the neighborhood; if not, it was to be destroyed. There was no address on the outside of the letter, which, indeed, was only a soiled and torn bit of paper, and unsealed. Seymour had hitherto communicated this news to no one, and was hesitating whether or no to tell Talbot, who had that day joined the ship.

Seymour found Talbot and the captain together, when, after giving his name to the negro boy, Joe, who waited in attendance, for Captain Jones was one of the most punctilious of men, he was ushered into the captain's cabin.

"Come in, Seymour," said the captain, genially, laying aside the formal address of the quarter-deck. "Joe, a glass of wine for Mr. Seymour. Has the watch been set?"

"Yes, sir, and Lieutenant Wallingford has the deck."

"Ah, that's well; he knows the channel like a pilot. Sit down, man."

"Thank you, captain. How do you like your first experience on a ship-of-war, Talbot?"

"Very much, indeed," answered the young officer; "and if we shall only succeed in capturing the transport I shall like it much better."

"Well, gentlemen," said Captain Jones, "I will give you a toast. Here's to a successful cruise, many prizes, good chances at the enemy, and, of course, first of all, the capture of the transport, though that will deprive me of the pleasure of your society. I intend to bear away to the northeast immediately we pass the Capes, and I count upon striking the transport somewhere off Halifax. If we should succeed in capturing her, I am of the opinion, if her cargo proves as valuable as reported, that my best course would be to convoy her to one of our ports, or at least so far upon her way as to insure her safe arrival. The cargo would be too important to be lost or recaptured under any circumstances," he continued meditatively. "Well, I think I would better go on deck for the present. You will excuse me, Mr. Talbot, I am sure. You will both dine with me to-night. Seymour, a word with you," he continued, opening the door and going out, followed by his executive officer.

CHAPTER XIII

A CLEVER STRATAGEM

Six days out from the Capes of Delaware Bay, and the Ranger was cruising between Halifax and Boston, about one hundred leagues east of Cape Sable. If there be truth in the maxim that a ship is never fit for action until she has been a week at sea, the Ranger might be considered as ready for any emergency now. The crew had thoroughly learned their stations; they and the officers had become acquainted with each other; the possibilities of the ship in different weather, and on various points of sailing, had been ascertained. The drill at quarters twice daily, and the regular target practice with great guns, and the exercises with small arms, had materially developed the offensive and defensive possibilities of the ship.

The already warm friendship between Seymour and Talbot, now thrown into close association by the necessary confinement of a small ship, had grown into an intimacy, and they held many discussions concerning their absent friends in the long hours of the night watches. Talbot had learned through common rumor before they sailed, that Colonel Wilton would probably be sent to England with Lord Dunmore, whose retirement, under the vigorous policy pursued by the Virginians under the leadership of Patrick

Henry, who had been elected governor, was inevitable; and he did not doubt but that Katharine would accompany her father. He had never told Seymour of the plans which had involved the destinies of Katharine and himself, and something had restrained him from mentioning either his hopes or his affection for her, though time and absence had but intensified his passion, until it was the consuming idea of his soul.

This reserve was matched by a similar reticence on the part of Seymour, who had said nothing of the note he had received, and had not communicated the news of his own successful suit to his unsuspecting rival. Seymour had a much clearer apprehension of the situation than Talbot, and, intrenched in Katharine's confession, could endure it without disquiet, magnanimously saying nothing which could disturb his less favored rival. The situation, however, was clearly an impossible one, and that there would be a sudden break in the friendship, when Talbot found out the true state of affairs, he did not doubt. This was a grief to him, for he really liked the young man, and would gladly have spared his friend any pain, if it were possible; however, since there was only one Kate in the world, and she was his, he saw no way out of the difficulty, and could only allow Talbot to drift along blindly in his fool's paradise, until his eyes were opened. Both the young men were favorites with Captain Jones, and he treated them in a very different manner from that he usually assumed to his subordinates, for Jones was a man to be respected and feared rather than loved.

Late in the afternoon, the ship being under all plain sail, on the port tack, heading due west, the voice of the lookout on the mainroyal-yard floated down to the deck in that hail which is always thrilling at sea, and was doubly so in this instance,—

"Sail ho!"

Motioning to the officer of the deck, Jones himself replied in his powerful voice,—

"Where away?"

"Broad off the lee-beam, sir."

"Can you make her out?"

"No, sir, not yet."

"Well, keep your eye lifting, my man, and sing out when you do. Mr. Simpson," he said, turning to the officer of the deck, "let her go off a couple of points."

"Ay, ay, sir. Up with the helm, quartermaster, round in the weather-braces, rise tacks and sheets."

The speed of the ship going free was materially increased at once, and in a few moments the lookout once more hailed the deck,—

"I can make her out now, sir."

"What is it?"

"A ship, sir, ay, and there is another one with her, and a third. I can't tell what she is, sir. The first one looks like a large ship."

"Mr. Wallingford, take the glass and go up the crosstrees and see what you make of them, sir," said the captain.

"Very good, sir," replied the lieutenant, springing into the main rigging and rapidly ascending to the crosstrees, glass in hand.

"Gentlemen, we will have a nearer look at these gentry," continued the captain, glancing back at the officers, who had all come up from below, while the men, equally interested, were crowding on the forecastle, and gazing eagerly in the direction of the reported sails, which were not yet visible from the deck.

"On deck, there."

"Ay, ay, what is it?"

"I can make out five ships, and two brigs, and a schooner, and some other sails just rising, all close hauled on the port tack. I think there are more of them, sir, but I can't say yet. We are rapidly drawing down on them, and shall be able to make them out in a minute. I think it is a convoy or a fleet."

"That will do, Mr. Wallingford; lay down on deck, sir; give the glass to the man on the royal-yard, though, before you come. Who is he?"

"It is me, sir, Jack Thompson."

"Keep a bright lookout then, Thompson, and if yon's an enemy's fleet or convoy, it means a glass of grog and a guinea for you when your watch is over."

"Thankee, sir," cried the delighted seaman.

"Mr. Wallingford, could you make anything out of the size of the ships?"

"One of them I should say was a large ship, a frigate or ship of the line possibly, the others were too far off."

"It can't be a fleet," replied Captain Jones; "there are not so many of the enemy's ships together in these waters, if we are correctly informed. I suspect it must be a lot of merchantmen and transports, convoyed by two or three men of war. Now is our opportunity, gentlemen," he continued, his eyes sparkling with delight. "They are apparently beating in for Halifax, and probably the Mellish, our transport, will be among them. We will pay them a visit to-night in any event. I would n't let them pass by without a bow or two, if they were a fleet of two deckers!"

Apparently this reckless bravado entirely suited the ship's company, for one of the men who had heard the doughty captain's speech called for three cheers, which were given with a will.

"Ay, that's a fine hearty crew, and full of fight. Call on all hands, Mr. Simpson."

This was more or less a perfunctory order, since every man from the jack-of-the-dust to the captain was already on deck.

"Mr. Seymour," said Jones to the first lieutenant, who had taken the trumpet at the call of all hands, "we must dress for the ball, and our best disguise for the present will be that of a merchantman. I don't suppose that the English imagine that we have a ship afloat in these waters, and possibly they can't see us, against this cloud bank in this twilight, as we can see them against the setting sun; but we will be on the safe side for the few moments of daylight left us. They may be looking at us over there, so we will hoist the English flag at once; and as we are nearing them a little too rapidly, better brail up the fore and main sails, and take in the royals and the fore and mizzen topgallantsails for the present, and slack off the running gear. Then beat to quarters, and have the guns run in and double shotted, close the ports, and have the arms distributed; clear the forecastle too, except of two or three men, and bid everybody observe the strictest quiet, especially when we get in among the convoy," he continued rapidly.

"You can see them now from the deck, sir," said Lieutenant Simpson, handing the glass to the captain.

"Ay, so you can, but not well. Mainroyal there! Can you make them out any better?"

"Yes, sir. There's eighteen sail of them; one is a frigate and one looks like a sloop of war, sir; the rest is merchantmen, some of 'em armed."

"Very good. Have they seen us yet?"

"Don't appear to take no notice on us so far, sir."

"Come down from aloft then, and get your grog and guinea, Jack; we won't need you up there any more; it is getting too dark to see anything there, anyway. Beat to quarters, Mr. Seymour. Ah, there go the lights in the convoy."

For the next few moments the decks presented a scene of wild confusion, which gradually settled down into an orderly quiet, the various directions of the captain were promptly carried out, and the ship was speedily prepared for the conflict, though outwardly she had lost her warlike appearance, and now resembled a peaceful trader.

While the Ranger had been slowly drawing nearer to the sluggish fleet of merchantmen and their convoy, the early twilight of the late season faded away and soon gave place to darkness; the night was cloudy, the sky being much overcast, and there was no moon, all of which was well for their present purpose.

The men thoroughly appreciated the hazardous nature of this advance upon the unsuspecting fleet, protected by two heavy vessels of war, either of which was probably much stronger than their own ship; but the very audacity and boldness with which the affair was being carried out thoroughly suited the daring crew.

Most of them had stripped to the waist in anticipation of the coming conflict, for they felt confident that the fleet would not escape without a battle; and during the next hour they clustered about the guns, quietly whispering among themselves, and eagerly waiting the events of the night. The nervous strain appeared to affect everybody except the imperturbable captain, but the deep silence was unbroken save by low-voiced commands from the first lieutenant. All sail had been made as soon as it had become thoroughly dark, the yards properly braced, and the guns run out again.

CHAPTER XIV

A SURPRISE FOR THE JUNO

The Ranger, a new and swift-sailing ship, and going free also, rapidly edged down upon the slow moving convoy on the wind. The frigate, it was noticed, was several miles ahead in the van; the other ships were carelessly strung out in a long line, probably not suspecting the existence of any possible enemy in those waters. The sloop of war appeared to be among the rear ships, while the nearest vessel to the Ranger was a large schooner, whose superior sailing qualities had permitted her to reach several miles to windward of the square-rigged ships; she appeared to be light in ballast also. All of the convoy showed lights. The Ranger, on the contrary, was as dark as the night, not even the battle lanterns being lighted. She rapidly overhauled the schooner, and almost before her careless people were aware of it, she was alongside.

"Schooner ahoy!" called out the captain of the ship, standing on the rail, trumpet in hand.

"Ahoy, there!" came back from the schooner; "what ship is that?"

"His Britannic majesty's sloop of war Southampton, Captain

Sir James Yeo. I have a message from the admiral for this convoy, which we have been expecting. Send a boat aboard."

"Ay, ay, sir. Will you heave to for us?"

"Yes, swing the main-yard there, Mr. Seymour, and heave to."

In a few moments the splash of oars was heard, and a small boat drew out of the darkness to the starboard gangway of the Ranger. A man stood up in the stern sheets, and seizing the man ropes thrown to him climbed up on the deck.

"Ah, Sir James," he commenced, taking off his hat, "how do you do? How dark you are! Why, what's all this?" he exclaimed in surprise and terror, as he made out the strange uniforms in the dim light. He hesitated a moment, and then stepped back hastily to the gangway, lifting his hand.

"Seize him," cried a stern voice, "shoot him if he makes a sound."

The captain of the unlucky schooner was soon dragged, struggling and astonished, to the break of the poop.

"Oh, Sir James, what is the meaning of this outrage, sir, on a British ship-master? I shall report—"

"Silence, sir, this is the American Continental ship Ranger, and you are a prisoner," replied the same voice. "Answer my questions now at once; your life depends on it. What are these ships to leeward?"

"Sixteen merchantmen from London, to Halifax, under convoy of two men-of-war, sir."

"And what are they?"

"The Acasta, thirty-six, and the Juno, twenty-two, sir."

"Very good; is the transport Mellish among them?"

The man made no reply.

"Answer me."

"Ye—yes, sir."

"Which is she?"

"Oh, sir, I can't tell you that, sir; she is the most valuable ship of them all," he said incautiously.

"You have got to tell me, my man, if you ever want to see daylight again; which is she?"

"No, sir, I can't tell you," he replied obstinately.

"Put the muzzle of your pistol to his forehead, Williams, and if he does not answer by the time I count ten, pull the trigger. One, two, three, four—"

"Mercy, mercy," cried the frightened skipper, as he felt the cold barrel of the pistol pressed against his temple.

"Eight, nine—" went on the voice in the darkness, imperturbably.

"I'll tell, I'll tell."

"Ah, I thought so; which one is she?"

"The last one, sir."

"And the Juno?"

"The fourth from the rear; the frigate's the first one, sir," he volunteered. "Oh, don't kill me, gentlemen."

"Have you told me the truth, sirrah? Williams, keep your pistol there."

"Oh, sir, yes, so help me; oh, gentlemen, for God's sake don't murder me. I've a wife and—"

"Peace, you fool! We won't hurt you if you've told the truth; you shall even be released presently and have your schooner again—we don't want her; but if you have lied to me, you shall hang from that yard-arm in the morning, as sure as my name is John Paul Jones."

"O Lord!" said the now thoroughly frightened man, looking up and meeting the gaze of two eyes which gleamed in the dim light from the deck above him, "I've told you the truth, sir."

"Very well. Go call your boat's crew on deck. Stand by to capture them as soon as they reach the gangway, some of you, then stow them all below; let their boat tow astern. And when that's done, you, sir, hail your schooner and tell her to heave to until your return. Say just what I tell you to and nothing more—the pistol at your head is loaded still. Watch him carefully, men, and then send him below with the rest. Fill away again, Mr. Seymour."

The ponderous yards were swung, and the Ranger soon gathered way again and rapidly overhauled the last of the fleet. The first trick had worked so well that it was worth trying again. As soon as she drew near the doomed ship, she showed lights like those of the frigate and sloop of war. Ranging alongside the weather quarter of the transport, the captain again hailed,—

"Ship ahoy!"

"Ahoy, what ship is that?"

Again the same deluding reply,—

"His Britannic majesty's sloop of war Southampton, Captain Sir James Yeo. What ship is that?"

"The transport Mellish."

"Very well, you are the one we want. I have a message for you. The Yankees are about, and the admiral has sent us to look up the convoy. Where is the Acasta?"

"In the van, Sir James, about two leagues ahead; the corvette is about a mile forward there, sir."

"Very good. Heave to and send a boat aboard and get your orders. Look sharp now, I must speak the corvette and the frigate as well."

"Ay, ay, sir," replied the Englishman, as his mainyard was promptly swung.

Immediately the Ranger was hove to as well, and on her weather side, which was that away from the transport, two well-manned boats, their crews heavily armed, one commanded by Seymour, who had Talbot with him, and the other by Philip Wilton, accompanied by Bentley, had been silently lowered into the water, and were pulling around the

Ranger with muffled oars; making a large detour not only to avoid the boat of the captain of the Mellish, but also to enable one of them to approach the unsuspecting ship on the lee side. The night was pitch dark, and the plan was carried out exactly as anticipated. The utterly unsuspecting captain of the Mellish was seized as he came on deck and nearly choked to death before he could make an outcry, then sent below with the rest; his boat's crew were tempted on deck also by an invitation to partake of unlimited grog, and treated in the same way, and the two boats of the Ranger reached the Mellish undiscovered. The watch on the deck of the transport, diminished by the absence of the boat's crew, were overwhelmed by the rush of armed men, from both sides of the ship, and after a few shots from two or three men on the quarter-deck, some yelling and screaming, and a brief scuffle, in which one man of the Mellish was killed, the ship was mastered. The hatches were at once secured, before the watch below scarcely knew of the occurrence. A company of soldiers, about seventy-five in number, of the Seaforth Highlanders, found themselves prisoners ere they awakened, the only resistance having come from the mate and two or three of their officers, who had not yet turned in.

"Have you got her, Mr. Seymour?" hailed the Ranger.

"Yes, sir."

"What is she?"

"She's the Mellish right enough, sir."

"Good. Anybody hurt?"

"One of the enemy killed, sir; all of ours are all right."

"What's her crew?"

"Fifteen men, they say, and seventy-five soldiers. We have the hatches battened down, and I think with the men we have, we can manage her all right."

"Very well, sir. I congratulate you. I am sending the second cutter off to you with the men's dunnage and your boxes. You have your orders. Present my compliments to General Washington, with that ship as a Christmas present, if you bring her in. God grant you get in safely. Good-by. Better put out that light; we will take your place in the fleet, and see what happens."

"Good-by, sir," cried the young lieutenant; "a prosperous cruise to you."

In a moment the boat from the Ranger was alongside, the bags and boxes were speedily shifted, and the cutter, with the other two boats in tow, dropped back to the Ranger, which by a shift of the helm had drawn much nearer. Then the Mellish filled away, and presently wearing round on her heel went off before the wind, and, all her lights having been extinguished, faded speedily away in the darkness. The boats were hoisted on the Ranger, she braced up on the port tack, and took the place vacated by the Mellish. But these things had not happened without attracting some attention.

The captain of the vessel next ahead of the Mellish had heard the pistol shots and shouting. Luffing up into the wind to check his own headway, he made out a second ship in the darkness alongside his next astern. In doubt as to what was happening, but certain that something was wrong, he acted promptly, and caused a blue light to be burned on his forecastle; this was the agreed signal of danger, and it immediately awakened the unsuspecting fleet into action. Several of the ships at different intervals in the long line repeated the signal, which was finally answered by the frigate, hull down ahead. The corvette, a half mile away perhaps, responded immediately, and wearing short round came to on the other tack, and headed for the last of the line, beating to quarters the while.

A less audacious man might have thought that he had done enough in cutting out with so little loss so valuable a transport from under the guns of two ships of war, either of greater force than his own, and therefore would have taken advantage of the night to effect his own escape. But this would not have suited the daring nature of Captain Jones, and he resolved to await the advent of the sloop of war, trusting that the advantage of a surprise might compensate for the great difference in the batteries of the two ships. Besides the natural desire to fight the enemy, there was a method in the apparent madness. If he could successfully disable the sloop before the arrival of the frigate, he would ensure the escape of the captured Mellish, for the sloop would be in no condition to pursue, and the frigate could not safely leave her convoy. So with rather a mixture of ideas, he trusted to the God of battles and the justice of his cause, and also to the darkness and his own mother-wit and great skill in seamanship, to make his own escape after the battle, resolutely putting out of his head the fact that the loss of a spar or two would in all probability result in the capture of his own ship. To sum it all up, Jones was not a man to decline battle when there was the slightest prospect of success, and the very audacity of the present situation enchanted him. All the lanterns of the Ranger were again extinguished, therefore, and the men sent quietly to their quarters, with the strictest injunctions not to make a sound or fire a gun until ordered, under pain of death. Every other preparation had long since been made for action, so the officers slipped on their boarding caps, loosened their swords in their sheaths, and looked to the priming of their pistols; then receiving their final commands, departed quietly to their several stations,—Simpson, now occupying the position of first lieutenant, vacated by Seymour, having charge of the batteries, and Wallingford, on deck with the captain, in command of the sail trimmers, who were clustered about the masts, the sloop being still heavily manned.

"Man the starboard battery," said the captain, in a low but distinct voice; "men, we've got our work cut out for us to-night. No cheering until the first shot is fired, and no firing till I give the order, and then, all together, give it to them. Do you understand?"

A chorus of subdued "Ay, ays" indicated that the orders were heard.

"Mr. Wallingford, do you stand ready to back the maintopsail when she is alongside, though if she attempts to pass in front of us we'll up helm and take her on the port side. Two of you after-guards go below and bring up the captain of the Mellish. Lively, we shall soon have the sloop down on us."

In a few moments the unfortunate British skipper was standing on the poop-deck beside Captain Jones.

"Now, my man, you are the master of the Mellish, are you not?"

"I was a few moments ago," replied the man, sullenly.

"Well, you are to stand right here, and answer hails just as I tell you; do you understand?"

"Yes."

"Williams, you and another hold him, and if he hesitates to answer, or answers other than I tell him, blow his brains out.

Now we have nothing to do but wait. Keep her a good full at the helm there."

"Ay, ay, sir," replied the veteran quartermaster, stationed at the con. Meanwhile the Juno had come abeam of the vessel next ahead of the Ranger, and the conversation which followed was as plainly audible in the latter ship as had been the beating to quarters just after she wore.

"Providence ahoy there!" came from the Juno. "What is the matter? What are you burning blue lights for?"

"Nothing is the matter with us, sir, but we heard pistol shots and cries on the Mellish astern, and thought we saw two ships instead of one. It's so beastly black to-night we could n't make out anything very well."

"All right; better keep off a little, out of the way. I will run down and see what's wrong."

The present course of the Juno would have brought her across the bows of the Ranger, but the ships were nearing so rapidly that a collision would have resulted, so the Juno was kept away a little, and soon ran down on the lee bow of the Ranger. The two ships were thus placed side by side, the Ranger on the port tack having the advantage of the weather gauge of the Juno, which had the wind free,—an advantage the captain of the English ship would never have yielded without an effort, had he imagined the character of the ship opposite him. The battle lanterns of the Juno were lighted, the ports triced up, and she presented a brilliant picture of a gallant ship ready for action. The Ranger, black as the night and silent as death, could barely be discerned in dim outline from the Juno.

"Mellish ahoy."

"Ahoy, the Juno."

"What's wrong on board of you?"

"Nothing, sir."

"Pistol shots and screams were heard by the ship ahead; but who hails—where is Captain Brent?"

"Answer him," hissed Jones, in the ear of the British captain; "tell him there were some drunken soldiers of the Highlanders in a row. Speak out, man," he continued threateningly.

"Why don't you answer?" came from the Juno. "I shall send a boat aboard. Call away the first cutter," the voice continued. But the British seaman on the Ranger's deck was made of sterner stuff than the other. By a violent and unexpected movement he wrenched his arm free from the grasp of one of the men, struck the other heavily in the chest, and before any one could seize him he leaped upon the rail, shouting loudly, "Treachery! You are betrayed. This is a Yankee pirate." Then he sprang into the water between the two ships. Williams raised his pistol.

"Let him go," cried Jones, "he is a brave fellow;" then lifting his powerful voice he shouted, "This is the American Continental ship Ranger. Stand by!"—the port shutters dropped or were pulled up with a crash, a moment's hasty aim was taken at the brilliantly lighted ship full abeam.— "Fire! Let them have it, men," he cried in a voice of thunder. Instantly the black side of the Ranger gave forth a sheet of flame, and the startling roar of the full broadside in the quiet night was followed by shrieks and cries and the crashing of woodwork, which told that the shots had taken effect. Three hearty British cheers rang out, however, in reply, and the broadside was promptly returned, but with nothing like the effect of that from the Ranger, for the first blow counts for as much at sea as in any other contest.

The next moment the maintopsail of the Juno was gallantly laid to the mast, that of the Ranger following suit, and the two ships, side by side, at half pistol-shot distance, continued the dreadful combat, both crews being encouraged and stimulated by their captains and other officers. A battle lantern or two, which had been hastily lighted here and there, shed a dim uncertain light over the decks of the Ranger. The men, half naked, covered with sweat and dust and powder stains, or splashed with blood from some more unfortunate comrade, some with heads tied up, fighting though wounded, served the guns. Several brave fellows were arranged on the weather side of the deck, dead, their battles ended; one or two seriously wounded men were lying groaning by the hatchway, waiting their turn to be carried below to the cockpit to be committed to the rough surgery of the period, while the fleet-footed powder boys were running to and fro from the different guns with their charges, leaping over the wounded and dying with indifference. The continuous roar of the artillery, for the guns were served with that steady, rapid precision for which the American seamen soon became famous, the crackling of musketry, from the men in the tops, with the yells and cheers and curses and groans of the maddened men, completed a scene which suggested a bit of hell.

"This is warm work, Wallingford," said the captain, coolly, though his eyes were sparkling with excitement. "Do we gain any advantage?"

"I think so; their fire does not seem to be so heavy. Does it not slacken a little, sir?"

"Ay, I think so too. I trust our sticks hold."

"I have not had any serious damage reported so far, sir."

"Well, we must end it soon, or that frigate will be down on us; in half an hour at most, I should say. Ha! what was that?" he said, as a loud crash from the Juno interrupted him.

"Their maintopmast's gone by the board, hurrah!" shouted Wallingford, looking toward the ship, after springing on the rail, from whence a moment later he fell back dead, with a bullet in his breast.

"Poor fellow!" murmured Jones, and then called out, "Give it to them, lads, they have lost their maintopmast." A cheer was the answer. But the matter must be ended at once.

"Johnson," said Jones, to the young midshipman by his side, "run forward and have the main-yard hauled; give her a good full, quartermaster," he said to the veteran seaman at the helm, and then watched the water over the side to see when she gathered headway through it. "Now! Hard up with the helm! Flatten in the head sheets! Round in the weather braces! Cease firing, and load all!"

The ship gathered way, forged ahead slowly, fell off when the helm was put up, and in a trice was standing across the stern of the Juno, which endeavored to meet the manoeuvre as soon as it was seen; but, owing to the loss of the jib and maintopsail and the fouling of the gear, she did not answer the helm rapidly enough to escape the threatening danger.

"Stand by to rake her! Ready! Fire! Stand by to board!"

The effect of this raking broadside delivered at short range was awful; the whole stern of the Juno was beaten in, and the deadly projectiles had free range the full length of the devoted ship, which reeled and trembled under the terrible shock. A moment of silence followed, broken by shrieks and groans and a few feeble cheers from some undaunted spirits. Then the Ranger, still falling off, a rank sheer of the helm brought her beam against the stern of the Juno, when eager hands hove the grapnels which bound the two ships together.

"Away, boarders!"

Certain of the men left their quarters at the guns, and cutlass and pistol in hand, led by Jones himself, swarmed over the rail and on the poop of the Juno. Two or three men were standing there among the dead and wounded men, half dazed by the sudden catastrophe, but they bravely sprang forward.

"Do you surrender?" cried Jones.

"No, you damned rebel!" answered the foremost, in the uniform of an officer, crossing swords with him gallantly; but in a moment the sword of the impetuous American beat down his guard and was buried in his breast. With a hollow groan, he fell dying on the deck of the ship he had so gallantly defended, while his men, borne back by the determined rush of the Rangers, after a feeble resistance, threw down their arms, crying, "Quarter, quarter!"

All this time the guns of that ship had been firing, one or two of them depressed by Simpson's orders so as to pierce the hull below the water-line, the rest sending their heavy shot ripping and tearing through the length of the Juno, which was unable to bring a single gun to bear in reply.

"Do you strike?" called Jones, from the break of the poop, his men massed behind him for a rush through the gangways, to one or two of the officers who were stationed there.

"Yes, yes, God help us," cried a wounded officer; "what else can we do?"

"Where's your captain?"

"Dead, sir," answered one of the seamen who had been seized by the boarders. "Him you killed when you boarded."

"Poor fellow, he was a brave man, and fought his ship well."

"Captain, the frigate is bearing down upon us!" cried one of the Ranger's men.

"Ay, ay. Well, gentlemen, we cannot take possession, so we will have to leave you to your consort," he said to the British officers. "Give the captain of the Acasta the compliments of Captain John Paul Jones, of the American Continental ship Ranger, and say that he will find me in the British Channel. Thank him for our entertainment to-night," he said, bowing courteously, and then—"Back to the ship, all you Rangers.— Let that man's sword alone, sirrah! He used it well, let it remain with him on his own ship; but first haul down and bring the Juno's flag with us."

The men hastily scrambled over the rails to their own ship, the grapnels were cut loose, and none too soon the ship slowly gathered way and slipped by the stern of the Juno, whose mizzenmast fell a moment after, and she lay rolling, a ghastly shattered hulk on the waters, fire breaking out forward.

The frigate, coming down rapidly on the starboard tack, luffed up into the wind, and fired a broadside at the rapidly disappearing Ranger, which, however, did no harm, and was only answered by a musket-shot in contempt, and then she ranged down beside her battered and shattered consort. As soon as she reached the side of the Juno she was hove to, and a boat was sent off at once. An officer stepped on board. He was horrified at the scene of carnage which presented itself. The ship aloft was a wreck, the decks were a perfect shambles, wounded and dying men lay around in every position. The masts were gone, the ship was full of shot-holes, the water was rushing and gurgling in through the shot-holes below the waterline, flames were breaking out forward.

"Where is Captain Burden?" cried the officer.

"Dead," replied the wounded first lieutenant, in a hollow voice.

"Did you strike?"

"Yes."

"What was the ship with which you fought?"

"The American ship Ranger, Captain John Paul Jones. He says he will see you in the English Channel. Oh, God, Lawless, isn't this awful? Three-fourths of ours are dead or wounded! The cursed rebel captured the Mellish, we ranged alongside at quarters; they got in the first broadside; the maintopmast went, then the jib; they fell off, raked us through the stern, boarded; Jones cut down Burden with his sword; we could not get a gun to bear, they were pounding through us. We could not keep the men at quarters, we struck; they took our flag too; then you came down, and he sheered off; then the mizzenmast went. I expect the fore will go next."

"What's his force? Was it a frigate?"

"I can answer that," said the brave master of the Mellish, who had gained the Juno and fought well in the fight; "she's a sloop of eighteen guns."

"Less than ours! We have twenty-two. Oh, Lawless, what a disgrace! I can't understand it. Our men did well. And she goes free, and look at us!"

"Ship is making water fast; we can't get at the fire forward either, sir," reported one of the Juno's officers.

"Good God, can't we save the ship?" queried Lieutenant Lawless, of the Acasta.

"No, it will be as much as we can do to get off the wounded, I fear."

"Back," cried Lawless, turning to the cutter in which they had come, "to the Acasta, and tell her to send all her boats alongside; this ship is a perfect wreck. She must sink in a few minutes. We have hardly time to get the wounded off. Lively, bear a hand for your lives, men."

However, in spite of all that could be done by willing and able hands, some of the helpless men were still on board when the Juno pitched forward suddenly and then sank bow foremost into the dark waters, carrying many of her gallant defenders into the deep with her. Among them on the quarter-deck lay the body of the dead captain, the sword which the magnanimity of his conqueror had left to him lying by his side.

And this is war upon the sea!

CHAPTER XV

CHASED BY A FRIGATE

Three days after the sinking of the Juno, the Mellish, which had escaped in the dark without pursuit from the fleet, after witnessing the successful termination of the action between the two sloops of war, was heading about northwest-by-west for Massachusetts Bay and Boston, with single reefs in her topsails and close hauled on the starboard tack. Seymour's orders had left him sufficient discretion as to his destination, but Boston being the nearest harbor held by the Americans, he had deemed it best to try to make that port rather than incur further risk of recapture by making the longer voyage to Philadelphia.

The weather had turned cloudy and cold; there was a decided touch of winter in the air. The men were muffled up in their pea-jackets, and the little squad of prisoners, tramping up and down, taking exercise and air under a strong guard, looked decidedly uncomfortable, not to say disgusted, with the situation.

It had been a matter of some difficulty to disarm the prisoners, especially the soldiers, and to feed and properly exercise them; but the end had been successfully arrived at through the prudence and ability of Seymour, who was well aided by Talbot and Wilton, and who profited much by many valuable suggestions born of the long experience of the old boatswain.

On this particular afternoon, about ten days before Christmas, the young captain, now confident of carrying his prize into the harbor, felt very much relieved and elated by his apparent command of the situation. He knew what a godsend the ship's cargo, which he and Talbot had ascertained to be even more valuable than had been represented, would be to the American army. It might be said without exaggeration, that the success of the great cause depended upon the fortune of that one little ship under his command. Talbot had properly classified and inventoried the cargo according to orders, and was prepared to make immediate distribution of it upon their arrival in port. Both of the young men were as happy as larks, and even the thought of their captured friends did not disquiet them as it might under less fortunate circumstances, for among the captives on the Mellish was a Colonel Seaton of the Highlanders, whom they trusted to be able to exchange for Colonel Wilton, and they did not doubt in that case that Katharine would return with her father.

While indulging themselves in these rosy dreams, natural to young men in the elation of spirit consequent upon the events of their short and exciting cruise,—the capture and successful escape of the transport, the apparent assurance of bringing her in, and the daring and brilliant night-action which they had witnessed,—they had neither of them ventured to touch upon the subject uppermost in each heart,—the love each bore for Katharine,—and the subject still remained a sealed book between them. The cruise was not yet over, however, and fate had in store for them several more exciting occurrences to be faced. Seymour, often accompanied by Talbot, and Wilton, always accompanied by

Bentley, kept watch and watch on the brief cruise of the transport. On the afternoon of the third day, about three bells in the afternoon watch, or half after one o'clock, Seymour, whose watch below it was, was called from the cabin by old Bentley, who informed him that a suspicious sail had been seen hull down to the northeast, and Wilton had desired that his commanding officer be informed of it. Seizing a glass and springing to his feet, he hastened on deck.

"Well, Mr. Wilton," he said to that young officer, proud of his responsibilities, "you keep a good lookout. Where away is the sail reported?"

"Broad off the weather bow, sir, due north of us. You can't see her from the deck yet," replied Wilton, flushing with pride at the compliment.

Seymour sprang into the main rigging, and rapidly ascended to the crosstrees, glass in hand. There he speedily made out the topgallantsails of a large ship, having the wind on the quarter apparently, and slowly coming into view. He subjected her to a long and careful scrutiny, during which the heads of her topsails rose, confirming his first idea that she was a ship-of-war, and if so, without doubt, one of the enemy. She was coming down steadily; and if the two vessels continued on their present courses they would pass each other within gun-shot distance in a few hours, a thing not to be permitted under any circumstances, if it could be avoided. He continued his inspection a moment longer, and then closing the glass, descended to the deck with all speed by sliding down the back-stay.

"Forward, there!" he shouted. "Call the other watch, and be quick about it! Philip, step below and ask Mr. Talbot to come on deck at once. Bentley, that seems to be a frigate or a heavy sloop going free; she will be down on us in a few hours if we don't change our course. Take a look at her, man," he said, handing him the glass, "and let me know what you think of her."

While the men were coming on deck, Bentley leaped into the mizzen rigging and ran up the shrouds with an agility surprising in one of his gigantic figure and advanced age. After a rapid survey he came down swiftly. "It's an English frigate, and not a doubt of it, sir, and rising very fast."

"I thought so. Man the weather braces! Up with the helm! Bear a hand now, my hearties! Now, then, all together! Brace in!" He himself set a good example to the short crew, who hastened to obey his rapid commands, by assisting the two seamen stationed aft to brail in the spanker, in which labor he was speedily joined by Talbot, who had come on deck. Young Wilton and Bentley lent the same assistance forward, and in an astonishingly brief time, considering her small crew, the Mellish, like the stranger, was going free with the wind on her quarter, her best point of sailing, her course now making a wide obtuse angle with that of the approaching ship.

"Now, then, men, lay aloft, and shake the reefs out of the topsails. Stand by to loose the fore and main topgallantsails as well."

"Why, what's wrong, Seymour?" said Talbot, in surprise. "I rather expected we should be in Massachusetts Bay this evening, and here we are, heading south again. Isn't that Cape Cod,—that blue haze yonder? Why are we leaving it? What's the matter?"

"Take the glass, man; there, aft on the starboard quarter, a sail! You should be able to see her from the deck now. Can you make her out?"

Cyrus Townsend Brady

"Yes, by heaven, it's a ship, and a large ship too! What is it, think you, Seymour?"

"An English ship, of course, a frigate; we have no ships like that in these waters, or in our navy, either—more's the pity."

"Whew! This looks bad for us."

"Well, we're not caught yet by a long sight, Talbot. A good many leagues will have to be sailed before we are overhauled, and there's many a slip 'twixt the cup and the lip, you know; that old stale maxim is truer on the sea than any place else, and truer in a chase, too; a thousand things may help us or hinder her. See, we are going better now that the reefs are out and the topgallantsails set. But it's a fearful strain on our spars. They look new—pray God they be good ones," he continued, gazing over the side at the masses of green water tossed aside from the bows and sweeping aft under the counter in great swirls.

The spars and rigging of the Mellish were indeed fearfully tested, the masts buckling and bending like a strained bow. The wind was freshening every moment, and there was the promise of a gale in the lowering sky of the gray afternoon. The ship felt the increased pressure from the additional sail which had been made, and her speed had materially increased, though she rolled and pitched frightfully, wallowing through the water and smashing into the waves with her broad, fat bows, and making rather heavy weather of it. In spite of all this, however, the chase gained slowly upon them, until she was now visible to the naked eye from the decks of the Mellish. Seymour, full of anxiety, tried every expedient that his thorough seamanship and long experience could dictate to accelerate the speed of his ship,—rather a sluggish vessel at best, and now, heavily laden, slower than ever. The stream anchors were cut away, and then one of the bowers also; all the boats, save one, the smallest, were scuttled and cast adrift; purchases were got on all the sheets and halliards, and the sails hauled flat as boards, and kept well wetted down; some of the water tanks were pumped out, to alter the trim and lighten her; the bulwarks and rails partly cut away, and, as a final resort, the maintopmast studdingsail was set, but the boom broke at the iron and the whole thing went adrift in a few moments. Talbot, anxious to do something, suggested the novel expedient of breaking out a field-piece from the fore hold and mounting it on the quarter-deck to use as a stern-chaser. This had been done, but the frigate was yet too far away for it to be of any service.

In spite of all these efforts, they were being overhauled slowly, but Seymour still held on and did not despair. There was one chance of escape. Right before them, not a half league away, lay a long shoal known as George's Shoal, extending several leagues across the path of the two ships; through the middle of this dangerous shoal there existed a channel, narrow and tortuous, but still practicable for ships of a certain size. He was familiar with its windings, as was Bentley, as they both had examined it carefully in the previous summer with a view to just such a contingency as now occurred. The Mellish was a large and clumsy ship, heavily laden, and drawing much water, but he felt confident that he could take her through the pass. At any rate the attempt was worth making, and if he did fail, it would be better to wreck her, he thought, than allow her to be recaptured. The English captain either knew or did not know of the shoal and the channel. If he knew it, he would have to make a long detour, for in no case would the depth of water in the pass permit a heavy ship as was the pursuing vessel to follow them; and, aided by the darkness rapidly closing down, the Mellish would be enabled to escape.

If the English captain were a new man on the station, and unacquainted with the existence of the shoal, as was most likely—well, then he was apt to lose his ship and all on board of her, if he chased too far and too hard. The problem resolved itself into this: if the Mellish could maintain her distance from the pursuer until it was necessary to come by the wind for a short tack, and still have sufficient space and time left to enable her to run up to the mouth of the channel without being sunk, or forced to strike by the batteries of the frigate, they might escape; if not—God help them all! thought Seymour, desperately, for in that event he resolved to run the vessel on the rocky edge of the shoal at the pass mouth and sink her.

They were rapidly drawing down upon the shoal at the point from which they must come by the wind, on the starboard tack. Some far-away lights on Cape Cod had just been lighted, which enabled Seymour to get his bearing exactly. He had talked the situation over quietly with Bentley, and they had not yet lost hope of escaping. The men had worked hard and faithfully, carrying out the various orders and lightening ship, and now, having done all, some few were lying about the deck resting, while the remainder hung over the rails gazing at their pursuer. One of the men, the sea philosopher Thompson, of the Ranger's crew, finally went aft to the quarter-deck to old Bentley, who was privileged to stand there under the circumstances, and asked if he might have a look through the glass for a moment at the frigate.

CHAPTER XVI

'TWIXT LOVE AND DUTY

"Ay, it's as I thought," he remarked, returning the glass after a long gaze; "that's the Radnor, curse her!"

"The Radnor, mate? Are you quite sure?"

"Bosun, does a man live in a hell like that for a year and a half, and forget how it looks? I'd know her among a thousand ships!"

"What's that you say, my man?" eagerly asked Seymour, stopping suddenly, having caught some part of the conversation as he was passing by.

"Why, that that 'ere ship is the Radnor, sir."

Talbot and his men were busy with the gun aft; no one heard but Seymour and Bentley.

"The Radnor! How do you know it, man?"

"I served aboard her for eighteen months, sir. I knows every line of her,—that there spliced fore shroud, the patch in the mainsail,—I put it on myself,—besides, I know her; I don't know how, but know her I do, every stick in her. Curse her—saving your honor's presence—I 'm not likely to forget her. I was whipped at the grating till I was nearly dead, just for standing up for this country, on board of her, and me a freeborn American too! I've got her sign manual on my back, and her picture here, and I'd give all the rest of my life to see her smashed and sunk, and feel that I'd had some hand in the doing of it. Ay, I know her. Could a man ever forget her!" continued the seaman, turning away white with passion, and shaking his fist in convulsive rage at the frigate, which made a handsome picture in spite of all. Seymour's face was as white as Thompson's was.

"The Radnor! The Radnor! Why, that's the ship Miss Wilton is on. Oh, Bentley, what can be done now?" he said, the whole situation rising before him. "If we lead that ship through the pass it means wreck for her. Dacres, who commands the Radnor, is a new man on this station. And if we don't try the pass, this ship is captured. And our country, our cause, receives a fatal blow! Was ever a man in such a situation before?"

Bentley looked at him with eyes full of pity. "We are approaching the shoal now, sir, and unless we would be on it, we will have to bring the ship by the wind at once."

This, at least, was a respite. Seymour glanced ahead, and at once gave the necessary orders. When the course was altered it became necessary to take in the fore and main topgallantsails, on account of the wind, now blowing a half gale and steadily rising. The speed of the ship, therefore, was unfortunately sensibly diminished, and she was soon pitching and heaving on the starboard tack, much to the astonishment of Talbot and the crew, who were ignorant of the existence of the shoal, and the latter of whom could see no necessity for the dangerous alteration in the course; they, however, of course said nothing, and Talbot, whose ignorance of seamanship did not qualify him to decide difficult questions, after a glance at Seymour's stern, pale face, decided to ask nothing about it. This present course being at right angles to that of their pursuer, whom neither Seymour nor Bentley doubted to be the Radnor, would speedily bring the two ships together. They had gained a small but precious advantage, however, as the frigate, apparently as much surprised by the unexpected manoeuvre as their own men, had allowed some moments to elapse before her helm was shifted and the wind brought on the other quarter; the courses of the two ships now intersected at an angle of perhaps seventy degrees, which would bring them together in a short time.

The people on the Mellish could plainly hear the drums of the frigate, now almost in range, beating to quarters. They were near enough to count the gunports; it was indeed a heavy frigate,—a thirty-six, just the rating of the Radnor. Talbot had made ready his field-piece, and in a moment the heavy boom of the gun echoed over the waters. The shot fell a little short, but was in good line. Much encouraged, the men hastened to load the piece again, while the Mellish crept along, all too slowly for the eager anxiety of her crew, toward the mouth of the channel, of which most of them, however, knew nothing. The frigate, partly because in order to bring a gun to bear on the chase it would have to luff up into the wind and thus lose valuable distance, and also because the rapidity with which the Mellish was being overhauled rendered it unnecessary, had hitherto refrained from using its batteries. The chances of escape under the present conditions were about even, had it not been for the complication introduced by the presence of Katharine and her father upon the frigate.

Seymour was in a painful and frightful state of indecision.

What should he do? The dilemma forced upon him was one of those which Katharine had foreseen, and of which they had talked together. He, apparently, must decide between his love and his country. If he held on when he reached the mouth of the channel and passed it by, the capture of the ship was absolutely inevitable. If he went through the channel and enticed the English ship after him, the death of his sweetheart was likewise apparently inevitable.

Chasing with the determination shown by the English captain, who had his topgallantsails still set, and with the little warning he would have of the existence of the shoal, owing to the rapid closing of the day, the frigate would have to attempt the channel, and in that way for that ship lay destruction.

Save Katharine—Lose the ship. Save the ship—Lose Katharine. Love or Duty—which should it be? The man was attacked in the two most powerful sources of human action. He saw on one side Katharine tossed about by the merciless waves, white-faced with terror, and stretching out her hands to him in piteous appeal from that angry sea in the horror of darkness and death. And every voice which spoke to the human heart was eloquent of her. And then on the other side there stood those grim and frozen ranks, those gaunt, hungry, naked men. They too stretched out hands to him. "Give us arms, give us raiment," they seemed to say. "You had the opportunity and you threw it away for love. What's love—to liberty?"

And every incentive which awakens the soul of honor in men appealed to him then. Behind him stood the destinies of a great people, the fate of a great cause; on him they trusted, upon his honor they had depended, and before him stood one woman. He saw her again as he had seen her before on the top of the hill on that memorable night in Virginia. What had she said?—

"If I stood in the pathway of liberty for one single instant, I should despise the man who would not sweep me aside without a moment's hesitation."

Oh, Katharine, Katharine, he groaned in spirit, pressing his hands upon his face in agony, while every breaking wave flung the words, "duty and honor," into his face, and every throb of his beating heart whispered "love—love."

CHAPTER XVII

AN INCIDENTAL PASSAGE AT ARMS

There were two entrances to the channel, lying perhaps a half mile apart, the first the better and more practicable, and certainly, with the frigate rapidly drawing near, the safer. They were almost abreast of the first one now. Bentley, who had been observing him keenly, came up to him.

"We are almost abreast the first pass, Mr. Seymour," he said respectfully.

Seymour turned as if he had been struck. Was the decision already upon him? He could not make it.

"We—we will try the second, Bentley."

"Sir," said the old man, hesitating, and yet persisting, "the frigate is coming down fast; we may not be able to make the second pass."

"We will try the second, nevertheless," said the young man, imperatively.

"But, Mr. John—"

"Silence, sir! When have you bandied words with me before?" shouted Seymour, in a passion of temper. "Go forward where you belong."

The old man looked at him steadily: "When, sir? Why, ever since I took you from your dead father's arms near a score of years ago. Oh, sir, I know what you feel, but you know what you must do. It's not for me to tell you your duty," said the old man, laying heavy emphasis upon that talismanic word "duty," which seems to appeal more powerfully to seamen than to any other class of men. "Love is a mighty thing, sir. I know it, yes, even I," he went on with rude eloquence, "ever since I took you when you were a little lad, and swore to watch over you, and care for you, and make a man of you— Ay, and I've done it too—and the love of woman, they say, is stronger than the love of man, though of that I know nothing, but honor and duty are above love, sir; and upon your honor, and your doing your duty, our country depends. Yes, love of woman, Mr. Seymour, but before that love of country; and now," said the old man, mournfully, "after twenty years of— of friendship, if I may say it, you order me forward like a dog. But that's neither here nor there, if you only save the ship. Oh, Mr. John, in five minutes more you must decide. See," pointing to the frigate, "how she rises! Think of it. Think of it once more before you jeopard the safety of this ship for any woman. Honor, sir, and duty—it's laid upon you, you must do it—they come before everything."

Seymour looked at the old man tenderly, and then grasped him by the hand. "You are right, old friend. Forgive my rough words. I will do it. It kills me, but I will do it—the country first of all. O God, pity me and help me!" he cried.

"Amen," said Bentley, his face working with grief, yet iron in its determination and resolution.

Cyrus Townsend Brady

Seymour turned on his heel and sprang aft, bringing his hand the while up to his heart. As he did so, his fingers instinctively went to the pocket of his waistcoat and sought the letter he carried there.

He took it out half mechanically and glanced at the familiar writing once more, when a sudden gust of wind snatched it out of his hand and blew it to the feet of Talbot.

"My letter!" cried Seymour, impulsively.

The soldier courteously stooped and picked it up and glanced down at the open scrap mechanically, as he extended his hand toward Seymour; then the next moment he cried,—

"Why, it's from Katharine!"

One unconscious inspection sufficed to put him in possession of the contents. "Where did you get this note, sir?" he exclaimed, his face flushing with jealousy and sudden suspicion; "it is mine, I am the one she loves. How came it in your possession?" he continued, in rising heat.

Seymour, already unstrung by the fearful strain he had gone through and the frightful decision he would have to make later on, nay, had made after Bentley's words, was in no mood to be catechized.

"I am not in the habit of answering such personal questions, sir. And I recognize no right in you to so question me."

"Right, sir! I find a letter in your possession with words of love in it, from my betrothed, a note plainly meant for me, and which has been withheld. How comes it so?"

"And I repeat, sir, I have nothing to say except to demand the return of my letter instantly; it is mine, and I will have it."

"Do you not know, Mr. Seymour, that we have been pledged to each other since childhood, that we have been lovers, she is to be my wife? I love her and she loves me; explain this letter then."

"It is false, Mr. Talbot; she has pledged herself to me,—yes, sir, to me. I care nothing for your childish love-affairs. She is mine, if I may believe her words, as is the letter which you have basely read. You will return it to me at once, or I shall have it taken from you by force."

"I give you the lie, sir, here and now," shrieked Talbot, laying his hand upon his sword. "It is not true, she is mine; as for the note—I keep it!"

Seymour controlled himself by a violent effort, and looked around for some of his men. Wilton and Bentley had come aft in great anxiety, and the whole crew were looking eagerly at them, attracted by the aroused voices and the passionate attitude of the two men. For a moment the chase was forgotten.

"Oh, Hilary," said Philip, addressing his friend.

"Hush, Philip, this man insults your sister. I am defending her honor."

The lad hesitated a moment; discipline was strong in his young soul. "That is my duty—Mr. Seymour," he said.

Seymour turned swiftly upon him. "What are you doing here, Mr. Wilton? All hands are called, are they not? Your station is on the forecastle, then, I believe," he said with deadly calm. "Oblige me by going forward at once, sir."

"Go, Philip," cried Talbot; "I can take care of this man."

"Aft here, two or three of you," continued Seymour, his usually even voice trembling a little. "Seize Lieutenant Talbot. Arrest him. Take his sword from him, and hand me the letter he has in his hand, and then confine him in his cabin."

Two or three of the seamen came running aft. Talbot whipped out his sword.

"The first man that touches me shall have this through his heart," he said fiercely. But the seamen would have made short work of him, if it had not been for the restraining hand of Bentley.

"Gentlemen, gentlemen!" he said.

"Out of the way, Bentley. You have changed my plans once. I will not be balked again. I am the captain of this ship, and I intend to be obeyed."

"'T is well that Mr. Seymour is on his ship and surrounded by his bullies. He dare not meet me man to man, sword to sword. Would we were on shore! You coward!" screamed Talbot, advancing toward him, "shall I strike you?"

"You will have it then, sir," said Seymour, at last giving way. "No man so speaks to me and lives. Back, men!" and white with passion and rage he drew his own sword and sprang forward. No less resolutely did Talbot meet him. Their blades crossed and rang against each other. Bentley wrung his hands in dreadful indecision, not knowing what to do; he dared not lay hands upon his superior officer, yet this combat must cease. But the fierce sword-play, both men being masters of the weapon, as was the habit of gentlemen of that day, was suddenly interrupted.

CHAPTER XVIII

DUTY WINS THE GAME

A booming roar came down upon them from the frigate, which had fired a broadside, which was followed presently by the whistling of shot over their heads. Great rents were seen in the canvas, pieces of running gear fell to the deck, there was a crashing, rending sound, and a part of the rail, left standing abaft the mizzen shrouds, smashed into splinters and drove inboard under the impact of a heavy shot.

One splinter struck the man at the helm in the side; he fell with a shriek, and lay white and still by the side of the wheel, which, no longer restrained by his hand, spun round madly. Another splinter hit the sword of Talbot, breaking the blade and sweeping it from his hands, and the unlucky scrap of paper was blown into the sea. The spanker sheet was cut in two, and the boom swept out to windward, knocking one of the men overboard. There was neither time nor opportunity to pick him up, and he went to his death unheeded.

Seymour dropped his sword, every instinct of a sailor aroused, and sprang to the horse-block. The ship, left to itself, fell off rapidly before the wind. Bentley jumped to seize the helm.

"Flow the head sheets there!" cried the lieutenant; "lively! Aft here and haul in the spanker! Brail up the foresail! Down, hard down with the helm!"

There was another broadside from the heavy guns of the frigate. Talbot replied with his stern-chaser, and a cloud of splinters showed that the shot took effect, whereat the men at the gun cheered and loaded, and then crash went the mizzen topgallant mast above their heads!

"Lively, men!" shouted Seymour, "we must get on the wind again or we are lost."

"Breakers on the starboard bow!" shrieked the lookout on the forecastle suddenly. "Breakers on the port bow!" His voice ran aft in a shrill scream, fraught with terror, "Breakers ahead!"

"Down, hard down with the helm, Bentley," said Seymour, himself springing over to assist the old man at the wheel.

But Bentley raised his hand and kept the wheel steady. "Too late, sir, for that," he cried, "we are in the pass. God help us now, sir. Mr. Seymour, look to the ship, sir, look to the ship!"

The young officer sprang back on the horse-block, his soul filled with horror. So fate had decided for him at last, and duty, not love, had won the mighty game. A third broadside passed harmlessly over the ship, doing little damage, the rough weather making aiming uncertain. Again the field-piece replied. Seymour never turned his head in the direction of the frigate. He could not look upon the catastrophe; besides, the exigency of the situation demanded that he give his whole mind to conning the ship through the narrow pass. Bentley himself, assisted by a young sailor, kept the helm;

the oldest seamen had charge of the braces. The wreck of the mizzen topgallant mast was allowed to hang for the present.

The white water dashed about the ship in sheets of foam; they were well in the breakers now, and the most ignorant eye could see the danger. One false movement meant disaster for the ship for whose safety Seymour had sacrificed so much. He did not make it. To his disordered fancy Katharine's white face looked up at him from every breaking wave. He steeled his heart and gave his orders with as much ease and precision as if it had been a practice cruise. To the day of his death he could not account for his ability to do so. He made a splendid figure, standing on the horse-block, his hair flowing out in the wind, his face deadly pale; calm, cool, steady; his voice clear and even, but heard in every part of the ship. The heart of the old sailor at the helm yearned toward him, and the seamen looked at him as if he had been a demigod. He never once looked back, but from the cries of the men he could follow every motion of the frigate behind him. The frigate, the unsuspicious frigate, had followed the course of the transport exactly, and was coming down to the deadly rocks like a hurricane.

Talbot, his quarrel forgotten for the moment, ceased firing, and stood, with all of the men who could be spared from their stations, looking aft at the tremendous drama being played.

"The frigate! Look at the frigate! She's going to strike, sir!" cried one of the seamen, excitedly,—old Thompson, who had sailed upon her. "See, they see the breakers. Now there go the head yards. It won't do. It's too late. My God, she strikes, she strikes! I'll have one more shot at her before she goes," he shrieked, taking hasty aim over the loaded field-piece and touching the priming. "Ay, and a hit too. Hurrah! hurrah! To h—l with ye, where you belong, ye—"

"Silence aft!" shouted Seymour, in a voice of thunder. "Keep fast that gun; and another cheer like that, and I put you in irons, Thompson."

The water in the front of the Mellish suddenly became darker, the breakers disappeared, the ship was in deep water again; she had the open sea before her, and was through the channel.

"We are through the pass, sir," said Bentley.

"I know it," answered Seymour, at last. "I suppose there is no use beating back around the shoal, Bentley?" he said tentatively.

"No, sir, no use; and besides in this wind we could not do it; and, sir, you know nothing will live in such a sea. Look at the Englishman now, sir."

The captain turned at last. The frigate was a hopeless wreck. All three of her masts had gone by the board; she had run full on the rocky ledge of the shoal at the mouth of the channel. The wind had risen until it blew a heavy gale; no boat, no human being, could live in such a sea. The waters rushed over her at every sweep, and she was fast breaking up before them. Night had fallen, and darkness at last enshrouded her as she faded out of view. A drop of snow fell lightly upon the cold cheek of the young sailor, and the men gazed into the night in silence, appalled by the awful catastrophe. Bentley, understanding it all, laid his hand lightly on Seymour's arm, saying softly,—

"Better clear the wreck and get the mizzen topsail and the fore and main sail in, sir, and reef the fore and main topsails; the spars are buckling fearfully. She can't stand much more."

"Oh, Bentley," he said with a sob, and then, mastering himself, he gave the necessary orders to clear away the wreck and take in the other sails, and close reef the topsails, in order to put the ship in proper trim for the rising storm; after which, the wind now permitting, the ship was headed for Philadelphia.

As Seymour turned to go below, he came face to face with Talbot. The two men stood gazing at each other in silence.

"We still have an account to settle, Mr. Talbot," he said sternly.

"My God," said Talbot, hesitatingly, "was n't it awful? How small, Seymour, are our quarrels in the face of that!" pointing out into the darkness,—"such a tremendous catastrophe as that is."

Seymour looked at him curiously; the man had not yet fathomed the depth of the catastrophe to him, evidently.

"As for our quarrel," he continued in a manly, generous way, "I—perhaps I was wrong, Mr. Seymour. I know I was, but I have loved her all my life. I am sorry I spoke so, and I beg your pardon; but—won't you tell me about the note now?"

A great pity for the young man filled Seymour's heart in spite of his own sorrow. "I loved her too," he said quietly. "The note was sent to me from Gwynn's Island, where they were confined. I had offered myself to her the night of the raid,— just before it, in fact,—and she accepted me. The note was mine. Where is it?"

"Oh!" said Talbot, softly, lifting his hand to his throat, "and I loved her too, and she is yours. Forgive me, Seymour, you won her honorably. I was too confident,—a fool. The note is gone into the sea. We cannot quarrel about it now."

"There can be no quarrel between us now, Talbot. She is mine no more than she is yours. She—she—" He paused, choking. "She—"

"Oh, what is it? Speak, man," cried Talbot, in sudden fear which he could not explain. Philip Wilton had drawn near and was listening eagerly.

"That ship there—the Radnor, you know—is lost, and all on board of her must have perished long since."

"Yes, yes, it's awful; but what of that? what of Katharine?"

"Don't you remember the note? Colonel Wilton and she were on the Radnor."

The strain of the last hour had undermined the nervous strength of the young soldier. He looked at Seymour, half dazed.

"It can't be," he murmured. "Why did you do it? How could you?" The world turned black before him. He reeled as if from a blow, and would have fallen if Seymour had not caught him. Philip strained his gaze out over the dark water.

"Oh, my father, my father!" he cried. "Mr. Seymour, is there no hope, no chance?"

"None whatever, my boy; they are gone."

"Oh, Katharine, Katharine! Why did you do it, Seymour?" said Talbot, again.

Seymour turned away in silence. He could not reply; now

that it was done, he had no reason.

The dim light from the binnacle lantern fell on the face of Bentley; tears were standing in the old man's eyes as he looked at them, and he said slowly, as if in response to Talbot's question,—

"For love of country, gentlemen."

And this, again, is war upon the sea!

BOOK III

THE LION AT BAY

CHAPTER XIX

THE PORT OF PHILADELPHIA

The day before Christmas, the warden of the port of Philadelphia, standing glass in hand on one of the wharves, noticed a strange vessel slowly coming up the bay. This in itself was not an unusual sight. Many vessels during the course of a year arrived at, or departed from, the chief city of the American continent. Not so many small traders or coasting-vessels or ponderous East Indiamen, perhaps, as in the busy times of peace before the war began; but their place was taken by privateers and their prizes, or a ship from France, bringing large consignments of war material from the famous house of Rodrigo Hortalez & Co., of which the versatile and ingenuous [Transcriber's note: ingenious?] M. de Beaumarchais was the *deus ex machina*; and once in a while one of the few ships of war of the Continental navy, or some of the galleys or gunboats of Commodore Hazelwood's Pennsylvania State defence fleet. But the approaching ship was evidently neither a privateer nor a vessel of war, neither did she present the appearance of a peaceful merchantman. There was something curious and noteworthy in her aspect which excited the attention of the port warden, and then of the loungers along Front Street and the wharves, and speedily communicated itself to the citizens of the town, so that they began to hasten down to the river, in the cold of the late afternoon. Finally, no less a person than the military commander of the city himself appeared, followed by one or two aids, and attended by various bewigged and beruffled gentlemen of condition and substance; among whose finery the black coat of a clergyman and the sober attire of many of the thrifty Quakers were conspicuous. Here and there the crowd was lightened by the uniform of a militiaman or home guard, or the faded buff and blue of some invalid or wounded Continental. In the doorways of some of the spacious residences facing the river, many of the fair dames for which Philadelphia was justly famous noted eagerly the approaching ship. As she came slowly up against the ebb tide, it was seen that her bulwarks had been cut away, all her boats but one appeared to be lost, her mizzen topgallant mast was gone, several great patches in her sails also attracted attention; there too was a field-piece mounted and lashed on the quarter-deck as a stern-chaser. The fore royal was furled, and two flags were hanging limply from the masthead; the light breeze from time to time fluttering them a little, but not sufficiently to disclose what they were, until just opposite High Street, where she dropped her only remaining anchor, when a sudden gust of wind lifted the two flags before the anxious spectators, who saw that one was a British and the other their own ensign. As soon as the eager watchers grasped the fact that the red cross of St. George was beneath the stars and stripes, they broke into spontaneous cheers of rejoicing. Immediately after, the field-gun on the quarterdeck was fired, and the report reverberated over the water and across the island on the one side, and through the streets of the town on the other, with sufficient volume to call every belated and idle citizen to the river-front at once.

Immediately after, a small boat was dropped into the water and manned by four stout seamen, into which two officers rapidly descended,—one in the uniform of a soldier, and the other in naval attire. When they reached the wharf at the foot of High Street, they found themselves confronted by an excited, shouting mass of anxious men, eager to hear the news they were without doubt bringing.

"It's Lieutenant Seymour!" cried one.

"Yes, he went off in the Ranger about two weeks ago," answered another.

"So he did. I wonder where the Ranger is now?"

"Who is the one next to him?" said a third.

"That's the young Continental from General Washington's staff, who went with them," answered a fourth voice.

"Back, gentlemen, back!"

"Way for the general commanding the town!"

"Here, men, don't crowd this way on the honorable committee of Congress!" cried one and another, as a stout, burly, red-faced, honest, genial-looking man, whose uniform of a general officer could not disguise his plain farmer-like appearance, attended by two or three staff-officers and followed by several white-wigged gentlemen of great dignity, the rich attire and the evident respect in which they were held proclaiming them the committee of Congress, slowly forced their way through the crowd.

"Now, sir," cried the general officer to the two men who had stepped out on the wharf, "what ship is that? We are prepared for good news, seeing those two flags, and the Lord knows we need it."

"That is the transport Mellish, sir; a prize of the American

Continental ship Ranger, Captain John Paul Jones."

"Hurrah! hurrah!" cried the crowd, which had eagerly pressed near to hear the news.

"Good, good!" replied the general. "I congratulate you. How is the Ranger?"

"We left her about one hundred leagues off Cape Sable about a week ago; she had just sunk the British sloop of war Juno, twenty-two guns, after a night action of about forty minutes. We left the Ranger bound for France, and apparently not much injured."

"What! what! God bless me, young men, you don't mean it! Sunk her, did you say, and in forty minutes! Gentlemen, gentlemen, do you hear that? Three cheers for Captain John Paul Jones!"

Just then one of the committee of Congress, and evidently its chairman,—a man whose probity and honor shone out from his open pleasant face,—interrupted,—

"But tell me, young sir,—Lieutenant Seymour of the navy, is it not? Ah, I thought so. What is her lading? Is it the transport we have hoped for?"

"Yes, sir. Lieutenant Talbot here has her bills of lading and her manifest also."

"Where is it, Mr. Talbot?" interrupted the officer; "let me see it, sir. I am General Putnam, in command of the city."

The general took the paper in his eagerness, but as he had neglected to bring his glasses with him, he was unable to read it.

Cyrus Townsend Brady

"Here, here," he cried impatiently, handing it back, "read it yourself, or, better, tell us quickly what it is."

"Two thousand stand of arms, twenty field-pieces, powder, shot, and other munitions of war, ten thousand suits of winter clothes, blankets, shoes, Colonel Seaton and three officers and fifty men of the Seaforth Highlanders and their baggage, all *en route* for Quebec," said Talbot, promptly.

The crowd was one seething mass of excitement. Robert Morris turned about, and lifting his hat from his head waved it high in the air amid frantic cheers. Putnam and his officers and the other gentlemen of the committee of Congress seized the hands of the two young officers in hearty congratulation.

"But there is something still more to tell," cried Mr. Morris; "your ship, her battered and dismantled condition, the rents in the sails—you were chased?"

"Yes, sir," replied Seymour, "and nearly recaptured. We escaped, however, through a narrow channel extending across George's Shoal off Cape Cod, with which I was familiar; and the English ship, pursuing recklessly, ran upon the shoal in a gale of wind and was wrecked, lost with all on board."

"Is it possible, sir, is it possible? Did you find out the name of the ship?"

"Yes, sir; one of our seamen who had served aboard her recognized her. She was the Radnor, thirty-six guns."

"That's the ship that Lord Dunmore is reported to have returned to Europe in," said Mr. Clymer, another member of the committee. A shudder passed over the two young men at this confirmation of their misfortunes. Seymour continued with great gravity,—

"We have reason to believe that some one else in whom you have deeper interest than in Lord Dunmore was on board of her,—Colonel Wilton, one of our commissioners to France, and his daughter also. They must have perished with the rest."

There was a moment of silence, as the full extent of this calamity was made known to the multitude, and then a clergyman was seen pushing his way nearer to them.

"What! Mr. Seymour! How do you do, sir? Did I understand you to say that all the company of that English ship perished?"

"Yes, Dr. White."

"And Colonel Wilton and his daughter also?"

"Alas, yes, sir."

"I fear that it is as our young friend says," added Robert Morris, gloomily. "I remember they were to go with Dunmore."

"Oh, Mr. Morris, our poor friends! Shocking, shocking, dreadful!" ejaculated the saintly-looking man; "these are the horrors of war;" and then turning to the multitude, he said: "Gentlemen, people, and friends, it is Christmas eve. We have our usual services at Christ Church in a short time. Shall we not then return thanks to the Giver of all victory for this signal manifestation of His Providence at this dark hour, and at the same time pray for our bereaved friends, and also for the widows and orphans of those of our enemies who have been so suddenly brought before their Maker? I do earnestly invite you all to God's house in His name."

The chime of old Christ Church ringing from the steeple near by seemed to second, in musical tones, the good man's invitation, as he turned and walked away, followed by a number of the citizens of the town. General Putnam, however, engaged Talbot in conversation about the disposition of the stores, while Robert Morris continued his inquiries as to the details of the cruise with Seymour. The perilous situation of the shattered American army was outlined to both of them, and Talbot received orders, or permission rather, to report the capture of the transport to General Washington the next day. Seymour asked permission to accompany him, which was readily granted.

"If you do not get a captain's commission for this, Mr. Talbot," continued Putnam, as they bade him good-night, "I shall be much disappointed."

"And if you do not find a captain's commission also waiting for you on your return here, Lieutenant Seymour, I shall also be much surprised," added Robert Morris.

"Give my regards to his excellency, and wish him a merry Christmas from me, and tell him that he has our best hopes for success in his new enterprise. I will detach six hundred men from Philadelphia, to-morrow, to make a diversion in his behalf," said the general.

"Yes," continued Robert Morris, "and I shall be obliged, Lieutenant Seymour, if you will call at my house before you start, and get a small bag of money which I shall give you to hand to General Washington, with my compliments. Tell him it is all I can raise at present, and that I am ashamed to send him so pitiable a sum; but if he will call upon me again, I shall, I trust, do better next time."

Bidding each other adieu, the four gentlemen separated, General Putnam to arrange for the distribution and forwarding of the supplies to the troops at once; Robert Morris to send a report to the Congress, which had retreated to Baltimore upon the approach of Howe and Cornwallis through the Jerseys; and Seymour and Talbot back to the ship to make necessary arrangements for their departure.

Seymour shortly afterward turned the command of the Mellish over to the officer Mr. Morris designated as his successor; and Talbot delivered his schedule to the officer appointed by General Putnam to receive it. Refusing the many pressing invitations to stay and dine, or partake of the other bounteous hospitality of the townspeople, the young men passed the night quietly with Seymour's aunt, his only relative, and at four o'clock on Christmas morning, accompanied by Bentley and Talbot, they set forth upon their long cold ride to Washington's camp,—a ride which was to extend very much farther, however, and be fraught with greater consequences than any of them dreamed of, as they set forth with sad hearts upon their journey.

CHAPTER XX

A WINTER CAMP

About half after one o'clock in the afternoon of Wednesday, December 25th, being Christmas day, and very cold, four tired horsemen, on jaded steeds, rode up to a plain stone farmhouse standing at the junction of two common country roads, both of which led to the Delaware River, a mile or so away. In the clearing back of the house a few wretched tents indicated a bivouac. Some shivering horses were picketed under a rude shelter, formed by interlacing branches between the trunks of a little grove of thickly growing trees which had been left standing as a wind-break. Bright fires blazed in front of the tents, and the men who occupied them were enjoying an unusually hearty meal. The faded uniforms of the men were tattered and torn; some of the soldiers were almost barefoot, wearing wretched apologies for shoes, which had been supplemented when practicable by bits of cloth tied about the soles of the feet. The men themselves were gaunt and haggard. Privation, exposure, and hard fighting had left a bitter mark upon them. Hunger and cold and wounds had wrestled with them, and they bore the indelible imprint of the awful conflict upon their faces. It was greatly to their credit that, like their leader, they had not yet despaired. A movement of some sort was evidently in preparation; arms were being looked to carefully, haversacks and pockets were being filled with the rude fare of which they had been thankful to partake as a Christmas dinner; ammunition was being prepared for transportation; those who had them were wrapping the remains of tattered blankets about them, under the straps of their guns or other equipments; and the fortunate possessors of the ragged adjuncts to shoes were putting final touches to them, with a futile hope that they would last beyond the first mile or two of the march; others were saddling and rubbing down the horses.

A welcome contribution had been made to their fare in a huge steaming bowl of hot punch, which had been sent from the farmhouse, and of which they had eagerly partaken.

"What's up now, I wonder?" said one ragged veteran to another.

"Don't know—don't care—couldn't anything be worse than this," was the reply.

"We've marched and fought and got beaten, and marched and fought and got beaten again, and retreated and retreated until there is nothing left of us. Look at us," he continued, "half naked, half starved, and we're the best of the lot, the select force, the picked men, the head-quarters guard!" he went on in bitter sarcasm.

"Yes, that's so," replied the other, laughing; then, sadly, "Those poor fellows by the river are worse off than we are, though. What would n't they give for some of that punch? My soul, wasn't it good!" he continued, smacking his lips in recollection.

"Where are we going, sergeant?" asked another.

"Don't know; the command is, 'Three days' rations and light marching order.'"

"Well, we're all of the last, anyway. Look at me! No stockings, leggings torn, no shirt; and you'd scarcely call this thing on my back a coat, would you? What could be lighter? So comfortable, too, in this pleasant summer weather!"

"Oh, shut up, old man; you're better off than I am, anyway; you've got rags to help your shoes out, and just look at mine," said another, sticking out a gaunt leg with a tattered shoe on the foot, every toe of which was plainly visible through the torn and worn openings. "And just look at this," he went on, bringing his foot down hard on the snow-covered, frost-bound soil, making an imprint which was edged with blood from his wounded, bruised, unprotected feet. "That's my sign-manual; and it's not hard to duplicate in the army yonder, either."

"That's true; and to think that the cause of liberty's got down so low that we are its only dependence. And they call us the grand army!"

"Well, as you say," went on another, recklessly, "we can't get into anything worse, so hurrah for the next move, say I."

"Three days' rations and light marching order, meaning, I suppose, that we are to leave our heavy overcoats and blankets and foot stoves and such other luxuries behind; that rather indicates that we are going to do something besides retreat; and I should like to get a whack at those mercenary Dutchmen before I freeze or starve," was the reply.

"Bully for you!"

"I'm with you, old man."

"I, too."

"And I," came from the group of undaunted men surrounding the speaker.

"And to think," said another, "of its being Christmas day, and all those little children at home—oh, well," turning away and wiping his eyes, "marching and fighting may make us forget, boys. I wouldn't mind suffering for liberty, if we could only do something, have something to show for it but a bloody trail and a story of defeat. I 'm tired of it," he continued desperately. "I'd fight the whole British army if they would only let me get a chance at them."

"We're all with you there, man, and I guess this time we get a chance," replied one of the speakers, amid a chorus of approval which showed the spirit of the men.

While the men were talking among themselves thus, the four riders on the tired horses had ridden up to the farmhouse. A soldier dressed no better than the rest stood before the door.

"Halt! Who are you?" he cried, presenting his musket.

"Friends. Officers from Philadelphia, with messages for his excellency," replied the foremost. "Don't you recognize me, my man?"

"Why, it's Lieutenant Talbot! Pass in, sir, and these other gentlemen with you," answered the soldier, saluting. "It's glad the general will be to see you."

Without further preliminaries the young man opened the door and entered, followed by his three companions. A cheerful fire of logs was blazing and crackling in the wide fireplace in the long low room. On the table before it stood a great bowl of steaming punch, and several officers were sitting or standing about the room in various positions. The uniforms of all save that of one of them were scarcely less worn and faded, if not quite so tattered, than were those of the escort; the same grim enemies had left the same grim marks upon them as upon the soldiers. The only well-dressed person in the room was a bright-eyed young man, a mere boy, just nineteen, wearing the brilliant uniform of an officer of the French army. He was tall and thin, red-haired, with a long nose and retreating forehead; his bright eyes and animated manner expressed the interest he felt in a conversation carried on in the French language with his nearest neighbor, another young man scarcely a year his senior. The contrast between the new and gay French uniform of the one and the faded Continental dress of the other was not less startling than that suggested by the difference in their size. The American officer was a small, a very small man; but, in spite of his insignificant stature, the whole impression of the man was striking, and even imposing. In contrast to the other, his face was very hand-some, the head finely shaped, the features clear-cut and regular; he had a decisive mouth, bespeaking resolution and firmness, and two piercing eyes out of which looked a will as hard and imperious as ever dwelt in mortal man.

In front of the fire were two older men, each in the uniform of a general officer, one of thirty-five or six years of age, the other perhaps ten years older. The younger of the two, a full-faced, intelligent, active, commanding sort of man, whose appearance indicated confidence in himself, and the light of whose alert blue eyes told of dashing brilliancy in action and prompt decision in perilous moments, which made him one of those who succeed, would have been more noticed had not his personality been so overshadowed by that of the officer who was speaking to him. The latter was possessed of a figure so tall that it dwarfed every other in the room: he was massively moulded, but well proportioned, with enormous hands and feet, and long, powerful limbs, which indicated great physical force, and having withal an erect and noble carriage, easy and graceful in appearance, which would have immediately attracted attention anywhere, even if his face had not been more striking than his figure. He had a most noble head, well proportioned, and set upon a beautiful neck, with the brow broad and high, the nose large and strong and slightly aquiline; his large mouth, even in repose, was set in a firm, tense, straight line, with the lips so tightly closed from the pressure of the massive jaws as to present an appearance almost painful, the expression of it bespeaking indomitable resolution and unbending determination; his eyes were a grayish blue, steel-colored in fact, set wide apart, and deep in their sockets under heavy eyebrows. He wore his plentiful chestnut hair brushed back from his forehead, and tied with a black ribbon in a queue without powder, as was the custom in the army at this juncture,—a fashion of necessity, by the way; and his ruddy face was burned by sun and wind and exposure, and slightly, though not unpleasantly, marked with the smallpox.

There was in his whole aspect evidence of such strength and force and power, such human passion kept in control by relentless will, such attributes of command, that none looked upon him without awe; and the idlest jester, the lowest and most insubordinate soldier, subsided into silence before that noble personality, realizing the ineffable dignity of the man. The grandeur of that cause which perhaps even he scarcely realized while he sustained it, looked out from his solemn eyes and was seen in the gravity of his bearing. His was the battle of the people of the future, and God had marked him deeply for His own. And yet it was a human man, too, and none of the immortal gods standing there. On occasion his laugh rang as loudly, or his heart beat as quickly as that of the most careless boy among his soldiers. He was fond of the good things of life too,—loving good wine, fair women, a well-told story, a good jest, pleasant society, and delighting in struggle and contest as well. He preserved habitually the just balance of his strong nature by the exercise of an unusual self-control, and he rarely allowed himself to step beyond that mean of true propriety, so well called the happy, except at long intervals through a violent outbreak of his passionate temper, rendered more terrible and blasting from its very infrequency. And this was the man upon whom was laid the burden of the war of the Revolution, and to whom, under God, were due the mighty results of that epoch-making contest. Seldom, if ever, do we see men of such rare qualities that when they leave their appointed places no other can be found to fill them; but if such a one ever did live, this was he.

CHAPTER XXI

THE BOATSWAIN TELLS THE STORY

One or two other men were writing at a table, and another stalwart officer of rank was sitting by the fire reading. None of the four men coming into the room had seen the general before, except Talbot. As the door opened, his excellency glanced up inquiringly, and, recognizing the first figure, stepped forward quickly, extending his hand, all the other officers rising and drawing near at the same time.

"What, Talbot! I trust you bring good news, sir?"

"I do, sir," said the young officer, saluting.

"The transport?" said the general, in great anxiety.

"Captured, sir."

"Her lading?"

"Two thousand muskets, twenty field-pieces, powder, shot, intrenching tools, other munitions of war; ten thousand suits of winter clothes, blankets, and shoes; and four officers and fifty soldiers; all bound for Quebec, where the British army is assembling."

"Now Almighty God be praised!" exclaimed the general, with deep feeling. "From whence do you come now?"

"From Philadelphia, sir."

"Ah! You thought best to take your prize there instead of Boston. It was a risk, was it not? But now that you are there, it is better for us here. Who are your companions, sir? Pray present them to me."

"Lieutenant Seymour, sir, of the navy, who brought in the prize."

"Sir, I congratulate you. I am glad to see you."

"And this is Philip Wilton, a midshipman. I think you know him, general."

"Certainly I do; the son of my old friend the commissioner, Colonel Wilton of Virginia, now unhappily a prisoner. You are very welcome, my boy. And who is this other man, Talbot?"

"William Bentley, sir, bosun of the Ranger, at your honor's service," answered the seaman himself.

"Well, my man," said the general, smiling, "if the Ranger has many like you in her crew, she must show a formidable lot of men. I am glad to see you all. These are my staff, gentlemen, the members of my family, to whom I present you. General Greene, General Knox; and these two boys here are Captain Alexander Hamilton and the Marquis de La Fayette, a volunteer from France, who comes to serve our country without money or without price, for love of liberty. This is Major Harrison, this Captain Laurens, this Captain Morris of the Philadelphia troop, our only cavalry; they serve like the marquis, for love of liberty. I know not how I could dispense with them." The gentlemen mentioned bowed ceremoniously, and some of them shook hands with the newcomers.

"Billy," continued Washington, turning to his black servant, "I wish you to get something to eat for these gentlemen. It's only bread and meat that we can offer you, I am sorry to say; we are not living in a very luxurious style at present,—on rather short rations, on the contrary. But meanwhile you will take a glass of this excellent punch with us, and we will drink to a merry Christmas. Fill your glasses, gentlemen all. Your news is the first good news we have had for so long that we have almost forgot what good news is. It is certainly very pleasant for us, eh, gentlemen? Now give us some of the details of the capture of the transport. How was it? You, Mr. Seymour, are the sailor of the party; do you tell us about it."

Then, in that rude farmhouse among the hills on that bitter winter day, Seymour told the story of the sighting of the convoy, and the ruse by which the capture of the two ships had been effected, at which General Washington laughed heartily. Then he described in a graphic seamanlike way the wonderful night action; the capture of the Juno by the heroic captain of the Ranger, the successful escape of that ship from the frigate, and the sinking of the Juno. He was interrupted from time to time by exclamations and deep gasps of excitement from the officers crowding about him; even Billy bringing the dinner put it down unheeded, and listened with his eyes glistening. And then Seymour delivered Jones's message to General Washington.

"Wonderful man! wonderful man!" he said. "We shall hear of him, I think, in the English Channel; and the English also, which is more to the point. But your own ship—had you an eventless passage, Mr. Seymour? And, gentlemen, you look as solemn as if you were the bearers of bad news instead of good tidings, or had been retreating with us for the past six months. Thank goodness, that's about over tonight. Fill your glasses, gentlemen. 'T is Christmas day. Now for your own story. Did you meet an enemy's ship?"

"We did, sir.—Talbot, you tell the story."

"No, no, I cannot; 't is your part, Seymour."

Here, in the presence of friends, and friends who knew and loved Colonel Wilton and his daughter, neither of the young men felt equal to the tale. Each day brought home to them their bitter sorrow more powerfully than before, and each hour but deepened the anguish in their hearts.

"Why, what is this? What has happened? The transport is safe, you said," continued the general, in some anxiety. "What is it?"

"I can tell, if your honor pleases, sir," said the deep voice of Bentley.

"Speak, man, speak."

"It happened this way, sir: we were off Cape Cod, heading northwest by west for Boston, about a week ago, close hauled on the starboard tack in a half gale of wind. Your honor knows what the starboard tack is?"

"Yes, yes, certainly; go on."

"When about three bells in the afternoon watch,—your honor knows what three bells—Ay, ay, sir," continued the seaman, noting the general's impatient nod. "Well, sir, we spied a large sail coming down on us fast; we ran off free, she following. Pretty soon we made her out a frigate, a heavy frigate of thirty-six guns, and a fast one too, for she rapidly overhauled us. We cracked on sail, even setting the topmast stunsail, till it blew away. Then we cut away bulwarks and rails, flattened the sails by jiggers on the sheets and halliards until they set like boards, pumped her out, cast adrift the boats, cut away anchors, but it was n't any use; she kept a-gaining on us. By and by we came to George's Shoal extending about three leagues across our course to the southeast of Cape Cod. There is a pass through the shoal; Lieutenant Seymour knows it, we surveyed it this last summer. We brought the ship to on the wind on the same tack again, near the shoal, and ran for the mouth of the pass. The frigate edged off to run us down. Lieutenant Talbot broke out a field-piece from the hold and mounted it as a stern-chaser, and used it too—"

"Good! well done!" said the general, nodding approvingly. "Go on."

"We came to the mouth of the pass. The frigate fired a broadside. One shot carried away the mizzen topgallant mast; another sent a shower of splinters inboard, killing the man at the wheel. The ship falls off and enters the pass. I seize the helm. Mr. Seymour conned us through. The frigate chased madly after us. She sees the breakers; she can't follow us, draws too much water; she makes an effort to back off. It is too late; she strikes. The wind rises to a heavy gale. We see her go to pieces, and never a soul left to tell the story, never a plank of her that hangs together. She's gone, and we go free. That's all, your honor, and may God have mercy on their souls, say I," added the solemn voice of the boatswain in the silence.

"A frightful catastrophe, indeed, and a terrible one! I do not wonder at your sadness. But, young gentlemen, do not take it so to heart. It is the fate of war, and war is always frightful."

"Did you find out the name of the ship, boatswain?" asked General Greene.

"Yes, your honor; the Radnor, thirty-six."

"Could no one have been saved?" queried General Knox.

"No one, sir. No boat could have lived in that sea a moment. We could n't put back, could do no good if we had, and so we came on to Philadelphia, and that's all."

"No, general," cried Seymour; "it's not all. We will tell the general the whole story, Talbot. You remember, sir, the raid on the Wilton place and the capture of the colonel and his daughter?" The general nodded. "Well, sir, before the Ranger sailed, I received a note from Miss Wilton saying they were to be sent to England in the Radnor."

"You received the note? I thought she was Mr. Talbot's betrothed, Mr. Seymour!"

"I thought so too, general; but it seems that we are both wrong. Lieutenant Seymour captured her during his visit there with Colonel Wilton," said Talbot, with a faint smile.

"I am very sorry for you, Talbot, and you are a fortunate man, Mr. Seymour. But go on; we are all friends here. Did you say they were to go on the Radnor?"

"Yes, sir. The pursuing frigate was recognized by one of my men who had been pressed and flogged while on her, as the Radnor, the ship on which they were. I heard the man say so just as we neared the reef. To go through the pass was to lead the English ship to destruction and cause the death of those we—of the colonel, sir," continued Seymour, in some confusion. "To refrain from attempting the pass was to lose the ship and all it meant for our cause. I could not decide. I say frankly I could not condemn those I—our friends to death, and I could not lose the ship either. This old man knew it all. He has known me from a child. He spoke out boldly, and laid my duty before me, and pleaded with me—"

"He did not need it, your honor. No, sir; he would have done it anyway," interrupted Bentley.

The general took the hand of the embarrassed old boatswain and shook it warmly; then, fixing his glowing eyes upon the two young men, said,—

"Continue, Mr. Seymour."

"I know not what I might have done, but the old seaman's appeal to my honor decided me. I went aft with horror in my heart, but resolved to do my duty. On my way there I took out of my pocket the little note received from Miss Wilton; a gust of wind blew it to the hand of Mr. Talbot. It was only a line. As he picked it up, he read it involuntarily. We had some words. I drew on him, sir. It was my fault."

"No, no, general, the fault was mine!" interrupted Talbot. "I said it was my letter, refused to give it up, insulted him. He would have arrested me. Bentley and Philip interfered. I taunted him, advanced to strike him. He had to draw or be dishonored."

"Nay, general, but the fault was mine. I was the captain of the ship; the safety of the ship depended on me."

"Go on, go on, Mr. Seymour," said the general; "this dispute does honor to you both."

"The rest happened as has been told you. One of the splinters struck Mr. Talbot's sword and swept it into the sea; the note went with it, and then the frigate was wrecked, and Colonel Wilton and his daughter, with all the rest, lost."

It was very still in the room.

"My poor friend, my poor friend," murmured the general, "and that charming girl. Without a moment's warning! Young gentlemen," taking each of the young men by the hand, "I honor you. You have deserved well of our country,—for the frankness with which one of you admits his fault, for it was a fault, and takes the blame upon himself, and for the heroic resolution by which the other sacrifices his love for his duty. Laurens, make out a captain's commission for Mr. Talbot. Hamilton, I wish you would write out a general order declaring the capture of the transport and her lading, and the sinking of the Juno and the wreck of the English frigate; it will hearten the men for our enterprise to-night. As for you, Mr. Seymour, I shall use what little influence I may be able to exert to get you a ship at once; meantime, as we contemplate attacking the enemy at last, I shall be glad to offer you a position as volunteer on my staff for a few days, if your duties will permit. And to you, Philip, let me be a father indeed—my poor boy! As for you, boatswain, what can I do for you?"

"Nothing, your honor, nothing, sir. You have shaken me by the hand, and that's enough." The old man hesitated, and then, seeing only kindness in the general's face, for the old sailor attracted and pleased him, he went on softly: "Ay, love's a mighty thing, your honor; we knows it, we old men. And love of woman's strong, they say, but these boys have shown us that something else is stronger."

"And what is that, pray, my friend?"

"Love of country, sir," said Bentley, in the silence.

CHAPTER XXII

WASHINGTON—A MAN WITH HUMAN PASSIONS

Half an hour later, after the four travellers had taken some refreshment, hasty steps were heard outside the door, followed by the sentry's hail.

"Ah!" said the general, looking up eagerly from the book he had been reading, "perhaps that is Mr. Martin with news from the enemy." Then laying aside his book, he rose to his feet to meet the new-comer, who proved to be the man he had expected. The young man stood at attention and saluted, while the general addressed him sharply,—

"Well, sir, what have you learned?"

The young officer appeared extremely embarrassed. "I— well, the fact is, sir, nothing at all," he stammered.

"Nothing!" said the general, loudly, with rising heat, "nothing, sir! Did you not cross the river as I directed you?"

"No, sir. That is, I tried to, but there was so much floating ice, and it was so difficult to manage a boat that I thought it would be hardly worth while to attempt it, sir. In fact, the crossing is impracticable for troops," he went on more confidently; but his face changed as he looked up at his infuriated superior. The general was a picture of wrath; the lines in his forehead standing out plainly, his mouth shut more tightly and grimly than ever. It was evident that he was furiously angry, and his face had in it something terrible from his rage. The young officer stood before him now, white and frightened to death.

"I saw him this way at Kip's Landing," whispered Hamilton to Seymour. "Look! he has lost control of himself completely, there will be an explosion sure."

The general struggled for a moment, and then broke away.

"Impracticable, sir! impracticable!" he roared out in a voice of thunder. "How dare you say what this army can or can not do! And what do you mean by not crossing the river and ascertaining the facts I desire to know!" The next moment he stepped forward and, seizing a heavy leaden inkstand from the table near him, threw it with all his force full at the man, crying fiercely,—

"Damnation, sir! Be off and send me a *man*."

The officer dodged the missile, which struck the wall with a crash, saluted, and ran out of the door as if his life depended on it; feeling in his heart that he would face any danger rather than brave another storm of wrath like that he had just sustained. The general continued to pace up and down the room restlessly for a few moments, until he recovered his composure.

"I depended upon that information, and I must have it," he soliloquized. "If that man does not bring it back to us before we cross the river, I'll have him cashiered. Shall I send another man? No, I'll give him another chance."

Seymour picked up the book the general had been reading. It was the Bible, and open at the twenty-second chapter of the Book of Joshua. His eye fell full upon the twenty-second verse, which was marked. "The Lord God of gods, the Lord God of gods, he knoweth, and Israel he shall know; if; *it be* in rebellion, or if in transgression against the Lord, (save us not this day.)"

Just then the little daughter of Keith, the owner of the farmhouse at which they were staying, entered the room. As the little miss came up fearlessly to the general, he stopped and smiled down at her.

"Father and mother wish to know if you will want supper to-night, sir?"

"No, my little maid," he replied; "not here, at any rate. And which do you like the better now, the Redcoats or the Continentals?"

"The Redcoats, sir, they have such pretty clothes," said the nascent woman.

"Ah, my dear," he replied blithely, catching her up in his arms and kissing her the while, "they look better, but they don't fight. The ragged fellows are the boys for fighting."

"Singular man!" mused Seymour, contrasting the outbreak of wrath at the recalcitrant officer, the open Bible he had been reading, and the last merry, tender greeting to the child. But his musings were interrupted by the general himself, speaking.

"General Greene, you would better ride over to the landing and place the different brigades; take Hamilton with you, and perhaps General Knox will go also to look out for the artillery. The brigades were to start at three o'clock for McConkey's Ford, and the nearest of them should be there now. We shall move in two divisions after we leave Birmingham on the other side. I wish you to command the first one, which will comprise the brigades of Sterling, Mercer, and De Fermoy, with Hand's riflemen and Hausegger's Germans and Forest's battery. I shall accompany your column. General Sullivan will take the second division, with Sargeant's and St. Clair's brigades, and Glover's Marblehead men, and Stark's New Hampshire riflemen. The two columns will divide at Birmingham. You will take the east, or inland road, and Sullivan that by the river. Have you that order I spoke of for the troops, Mr. Hamilton? If so, you will give a copy of it to General Greene, who will publish it to the troops as soon as they arrive. Captain Morris, I think you would better go also. You will muster your troop; the men will have returned from carrying my orders to the different brigades, and can be assembled once more. I desire you to attend my person to-night as our only cavalry. Talbot, you would better go with General Greene; you also, marquis, so that you can be with your friend Captain Hamilton. The rest of us will follow you shortly."

The officers designated bowed, and in a few moments were on the road. The officers left at the headquarters were speedily busy with their necessary duties, and Seymour and his two companions, one of whom, the boatswain, was most unfamiliar with and uncomfortable upon a horse, were able to get a couple of hours of needed rest before starting out upon what they felt would be an arduous journey. About half after six o'clock the signal to mount was given, and the whole party, led by the general himself, and followed by the ragged guard, was soon upon the road.

It was intensely cold, and the night bade fair to be the

Cyrus Townsend Brady

severest of the winter. The sky was cloudless, however, and there was a bright moon.

CHAPTER XXIII

LIEUTENANT MARTIN'S LESSON

As they rode along slowly, the general explained his plans. General Howe had pursued him relentlessly through the Jerseys, until he had crossed into Pennsylvania, only escaping further pursuit and certain defeat because he had had the forethought to seize every boat upon the Delaware and its tributaries for miles in every direction, and bring them with his army to the west bank of the river, so that Howe was unable to cross. The English general had threatened, however, to wait until the river was frozen and then cross on the ice, and after brushing aside the miserable remains of Washington's army, march on to Philadelphia and establish himself in the rebel capital. Making that most serious of mistakes for a military man of despising his opponents, Howe had scattered his army, for convenience in quartering, in various small detachments along the river. The small American army, supplemented by the Pennsylvania militia, had been placed opposite the different fords from Yardley to New Hope, to hold the enemy in check in case an attempt should be made to force a crossing.

The fortunes of the country were at the lowest ebb. But there was to be a speedy reversal of conditions, and the world was to learn how dangerous a man was leading the Continental troops. Washington, to whom a retreat was as hateful as it had been necessary, had long meditated an attack whenever any chance whatever of success might present itself. The necessity for a change was apparent, not merely for the material result which would flow from a victory, but for the moral effect as well. The fancied security of the enemy, their exposed positions, disconnected from each other, and the contempt they felt for his own troops, were large factors in determining him to strike then; but another factor had still more weight, and that was the fact that the time of the enlistment of nearly the whole of his own army expired with the end of the year, and whatever was to be done must be done quickly. He therefore conceived the daring and brilliant design of suddenly collecting his scattered forces, crossing the river, and falling upon his unsuspecting enemy at Trenton, where a small brigade of Hessians, under Colonel Rahl, was stationed.

It would be a piece of unparalleled audacity. To turn, as it were, just before the dissolution of his army, and cross a wide and deep river full of ice, in the dead of winter, and strike, like the hammer of Thor, upon his unwary foe, rudely disturbing his complacent dreams, was a conception of exceeding brilliancy, and it at once stamped Washington as a military genius of the first order. And with such an army to make such an attempt! Said one of the officers of the period in his memoirs: "An army without cavalry, partially provided with artillery, deficient in transportation for the little they had to carry; without tents, tools, or camp equipage,— without magazines of any kind; half clothed, badly armed, debilitated by disease, disheartened by misfortune." But their leader was a Lion, and the Lion was at last at bay! There was another factor which contributed greatly to the efficiency of the army, and that was the high quality and overwhelming number of the American officers.

Orders had been given to the brigades and troops mentioned to concentrate at McConkey's Ferry, about nine miles above Trenton. Another division under Ewing was to cross a mile below Trenton and seize the bridge and fords across the Assunpink, to check the retreat of the enemy and co-operate with the main attack.

Cadwalader's Pennsylvania militia under Gates were to cross at Bristol or below Burlington, and attack Von Donop at that point, while Putnam, in conjunction with him, was to make a diversion from Philadelphia. The movements were to be simultaneous, and the result it was hoped would accord with the effort. The main column, and the one upon which the most dependence was to be placed, was that which Washington himself was to accompany, which was composed of veteran Continentals, to the number of twenty-four hundred, with eighteen pieces of artillery.

All this was briefly explained by the general to Seymour and the staff, while they rode slowly along the frozen road. About eight o'clock they arrived at the ford, near which the troops who had arrived before them now stood shivering on the high ground by the river. A few fires were burning in the ravines back of the banks, around which the men took turns in warming themselves, as they munched their frugal fare from the haversacks. A large number of boats had been collected for their transportation, but the river itself was in a most unpromising condition, full of great cakes of ice which the swift current kept churning and grinding against each other.

The general surveyed the scene in silence, as his staff and the general officers gathered about him.

"There is something moving in the river, general," suddenly said Seymour, pointing, his practised eye detecting a dark object among the cakes of ice. "It is a boat, sir!"

"Ah," replied the general, "you have sharp eyes. Where is it?"

"There, sir, coming nearer every minute; there is a man in it."

"I see now. So there is. Who can it be?"

"Probably it is Lieutenant Martin," remarked General Greene, quietly. "You know you sent him back."

"Oh, so I did," replied the general, nodding sternly at the recollection. Meanwhile the man in the boat was skilfully making his way between the great cakes of ice, which threatened every moment to crush his frail skiff. He rapidly drew near until he finally jumped ashore, and, having tied his boat, hastened up to where the general sat on his horse. He stopped.

"I have been across, general," he said, saluting.

"So I perceive, sir. How did you get across?"

"When I left you, sir, this afternoon," went on the young man, gravely, "I was in such a hurry that I did not wait for anything. I swam it, sir, with my horse."

"Swam it!"

"Yes, sir."

"Very well done, indeed! Was it cold?"

"Not very, sir. At least I was too excited to feel it, and a good hard gallop on the other side soon warmed me up."

"Where did your ride take you?"

"Almost to Trenton, sir."

"And what is the situation there?"

"Very confident, the guard very negligent, the men carousing in the houses. I examined both roads, and neither of them is well picketed. I should think a surprise would not be very difficult, sir."

"Humph! Where's your horse?"

"He fell dead on the other side just as I got back. I found that leaky skiff, and came over to report, sir."

"You have done well, Mr. Martin, very well indeed! I think you must have found that man I sent you for!" continued the general, smiling grimly, while the young soldier blushed with pleasure. "Meanwhile we must get you another horse. Who has a spare one?"

"May it please your honor," spoke out Bentley, who had attached himself to Seymour, "he can have mine. I am as much at sea on him as you would be on the royal yard, begging your honor's pardon, and I'll feel better carrying a gun or pulling an oar with the men there than here."

The general laughed.

"There's your horse, Mr. Martin. Where do you belong, sir?"

"To Colonel Stark's regiment, sir."

"Good! Keep at it as you have begun and you will meet with a better reception when you call upon me again. Now God grant that fortune may favor us. Gentlemen, if the brigades are all up, we will undertake the crossing. It looks dangerous, but it can be done—it must be done. Who will lead us?"

"I will, sir, with your permission, with my Marblehead fishermen," said Colonel Glover, stepping out.

"Ah, gentlemen, this is our marine regiment. Go on, sir! You shall have the right of way across the river. I think none will dispute it with you. Mr. Seymour, as a seaman, perhaps you can render efficient service, and your boatswain will find here more opportunities for his peculiar talents than in carrying a musket. General Greene, will you and your staff go over with the first boat to make proper disposition of the brigades as they arrive? I shall come over after the first division has passed. Then General Sullivan, and lastly our friend General Knox with his artillery. I expect we shall have to wait for him. Well, we cannot dispense with either him or the guns."

"You won't have to wait any longer than is absolutely necessary to get the guns and horses over, general."

"I know that, Knox, I know that. Now, gentlemen, forward! and may God bless you!"

In a few moments the terrible passage began.

CHAPTER XXIV

CROSSING THE DELAWARE

The men, divided into small squads, marched down to the boats,—large unwieldy scows, which had been hauled up against the shore,—and each boat was speedily filled to its utmost capacity. The most experienced seized the oars; three or four Marblehead fishermen armed with long poles took their stations forward and aft along the upper side of the boat, with one to steer and one to command; and then, seizing a favorable opportunity, the boat was pushed off from the shore, and threading its way in and out between the enormous ice-cakes grinding down upon her, the difficult and dangerous passage began. Should the heavily laden boat be overturned, very few of its occupants would be able to reach the shore. Once on the other side, the fishermen took the boat back, and the weary process was gone over again. Fortunately it was yet bright moonlight, though ominous clouds were banking up in the northeast, and everything could be clearly seen; each boat was perfectly visible all the way across to the eager watchers on the shore, and a sigh of relief went up after each fortunate passage. In this labor Seymour and Bentley, and in a less degree Philip Wilton, aided Colonel Glover's men; Seymour having the helm of one boat continuously, Bentley that of another.

About half-past nine it was reported to General Washington that all of the first division had crossed, and the boat was now ready for him according to his orders. The largest and best boat had been selected for the commander-in-chief, one sufficiently capacious to receive his horses and those of his staff who accompanied him. Seymour was to steer the boat; Bentley stood in the bow; Colonel Glover stationed himself amidships, with three or four of his trustiest men, to superintend the crossing, and all the oars were manned by the hardy fishermen instead of the soldiers. The general dismounted and walked toward the boat, leading his horse. Just as he was about to enter, an officer on a panting steed rode up rapidly, and saluted.

"General Washington?"

"Yes, sir."

"A letter, sir!"

"What a time is this to hand me letters!"

"Your excellency, I have been charged to do so by General Gates."

"By General Gates! Where is he?"

"I left him this morning in Philadelphia, sir."

"What was he doing there?"

"I understood him that he was on his way to Congress."

"On his way to Congress!" said the general earnestly, with much surprise and disgust in his tone. And then, after a pause, he broke the seal and read the letter, frowning; after which he crumpled the paper up in his hand, and then turned again to the officer. "How did you find us, sir?"

"I followed the bloody footprints of the men on the snow, sir."

"Poor fellows! Did you learn anything of General Ewing or General Cadwalader?"

"No, sir."

"And General Putnam?"

"He bade me say that there were symptoms of an insurrection in the city, and he felt obliged to stay there. He has detached six hundred of the Pennsylvania militia, however, under Colonel Griffin, to advance toward Bordentown."

"'T is well, sir. Do you remain to participate in our attack?"

"Yes, sir, I belong to General St. Clair's brigade."

"You will find it over there; it has not yet crossed. Now, gentlemen, let us get aboard."

The general stepped forward in the boat, where Bentley, an enormous pole in his hands, was stationed, and the remainder of the party soon embarked. The order was given to shove off. The usual difficulties and the usual fortune attended the passage of the boat with its precious freight, until it neared the east bank, when one of the largest cakes that had passed swiftly floated down upon it.

"Pull, men, pull hard!" cried Colonel Glover, as he saw its huge bulk alongside. "Head the boat up the stream, Mr. Seymour. Forward, there—be ready to push off with your poles." As the result of these prompt manoeuvres, the oncoming mass of ice, which was too large to be avoided, instead of crashing into them amidships and sinking the boat, struck them a quartering blow on the bow, and commenced to grind along the sides of the boat, which heeled so far over that the water began to trickle in through the oar-locks on the other side.

"Steady, men," said Glover, calmly. "Sit still, for your lives."

Bentley had thrown his pole over on the ice-cake promptly, and was now bearing down upon it with all the strength of his powerful arms. But the task was beyond him; the ice and the boat clung together, and the ice was reinforced by several other cakes which its checked motion permitted to close with it. The vast mass crashed against the side of the boat; the oar of the first rower was broken short off at the oar-lock; if the others went the situation of the helpless boat would be, indeed, hopeless. The general himself came to the rescue. Promptly divining the situation, he stepped forward to Bentley's side, and threw his own immense strength upon the pole. Great beads of sweat stood out on Bentley's bronzed forehead as he renewed his efforts; the stout hickory sapling bent and crackled beneath the pressure of the two men, but held on, and the boat slowly but steadily began to swing clear of the ice. These two Homeric men held it off by sheer strength, until the boat was in freewater, and the men, who had sat like statues in their places, could once more use their oars. The general stepped back into his place, cool and calm as usual, and entirely unruffled by his great exertions. Bentley wiped the sweat from his face, and turned and looked back at him in admiration.

"Friend Bentley," he said quietly, "you are a man of mighty thews and sinews. Had it not been for your powerful arms, I fear we would have had a ducking—or worse."

"Lord love you, your honor," said the astonished tailor, "I've met my match! It was your arm that saved us. I was almost done for. I never saw such strength as that, though when I was younger I would have done better. What a man you would be for reefing topsails in a gale o' wind, your honor, sir!" he continued, thrusting his pole vigorously into a small and impertinent cake of ice in the way. The general was proud of his great strength, and not ill pleased at the genuine and hearty admiration of this genuine and hearty man.

A few moments later they stepped ashore, and a mighty cheer went up from the men who had crowded upon the banks, at the safety of their beloved general. Greene met him at the landing, and the two men clasped hands. The general immediately mounted his powerful white horse, and stationed himself on a little hillock to watch the landing of the rest of the men, engaging General Greene in a low conversation the while.

"Do you know, Greene, that Gates has refused my entreaty to stop one day at Bristol, and take command of Reed's and Cadwalader's troops and help us in the attack! I did not positively order him to do so; only requested him to delay his journey by a day or two. I can't understand his action. A letter was handed me just before we crossed by Wilkinson, telling me that he had gone on to Congress."

"To Congress! What wants he there? Oh, general, it seems as if you had to fight two campaigns,—one against the enemy, and the other against secret, nay open, attempts to minimize your authority and check your plans."

"It seems so, Greene; but with a just cause to sustain, and the blessing of God to help our efforts, we cannot ultimately fail, though, indeed, it may be better that I give place to another man, more able to save the country," went on the general, solemnly.

"Forbid it, Heaven!" cried Greene, passionately. "We, at least, in the army, know to whom has been committed this work; ay, and who has done it, and will do it, too! We will stand by you to the last. Could you not feel in the cheers of those frozen men, when you landed, the love they bear you?"

"Yes, I know that you are with me, and they too. 'T is that alone that gives me heart. Did you publish the orders about the capture of the transport?"

"Yes, sir, and it put new heart in the men, I could see. I wish we had the supplies, the clothing especially, now. It grows colder every moment."

"Ay, and darker, too; I think we shall have snow again before we get through with the night. I wonder how the others down the river have got along. But who comes here?" continued the general, as two men walked hastily up to him and saluted.

"Well, sir?" he said to the first.

"Message from General Ewing, sir."

"Did he get across?"

"No, sir, the ice was so heavy he bade me say he deemed it useless to try it."

"One piece removed from the game, General Greene," said Washington, smiling bitterly. "Now your news, sir?" to the other.

"General Cadwalader got a part of his men across, but the ice banks so against the east side that not a single horse or piece of artillery could be landed, so he bade me say he has recrossed with his men, sir."

"And there's the other piece gone, too! Now, what is to be done?"

General Sullivan, having crossed with the last of his division, at this moment rode up.

"The troops are all across, general," he said.

"Well done! What time is it, some one?"

"Half after eleven, sir," answered a voice.

"Very well, indeed! We have now only to wait for the guns. But, gentlemen, I have just heard that Ewing made no attempt to cross, and that Cadwalader, having tried it, failed. He could get his men over, but no horses and guns, on account of the ice on the bank, and therefore he returned, and we are here alone. What, think you, is to be done now?"

There was a moment's silence.

"Perhaps we would better recross and try it again on a more favorable night," finally said De Fermoy, in his broken accents.

"Yes, yes, that might be well," said one or two others, simultaneously. The most of them, however, said nothing. The general waited a moment, looking about him.

"Gentlemen, it is too late to retreat. I promised myself I would not return without a fight, and I intend to keep that promise. We will carry out the plan ourselves, as much of it at least as we can. I trust Putnam got Griffin off, and that his skirmishers may draw out Von Donop. But be that as it may, we will have a dash at Trenton, and try to bag the game, and get away before the enemy can fall upon us in force. General Greene, you, of course have sent out pickets?"

"Yes, sir, the first men who crossed over, a mile up the road, on the hill yonder."

"Good! Ha, what was that? Snow, as I live, and the moon's gone, too! How dark it has grown! I think you might allow the men to light fires in those hollows, and let them move about a little; they will freeze to death standing still—I wonder they don't, anyway. How unfortunate is this snow!"

"Beg pardon, your excellency?" said the first of the two messengers.

"What is it, man? Speak out!"

"Can we stay here and take part in your attack, sir?"

"Certainly you may. Fall in with the men there. Where are your horses?"

"We left them on the other side, sir."

"Well, they will have to stay there for this time, and you'll have to go on foot with the rest."

"Thank you, sir," said the men, eagerly, darting off in the darkness.

"That's a proper spirit, isn't it? Well, to your stations, gentlemen! We have nothing to do now but wait. Don't allow the men to lie down or to sleep, on any account."

And wait they did, for four long hours, the general sitting motionless and silent on his horse, wrapped in his heavy cloak, unheeding, alike, the whirling snow or the cutting sleet of the storm, which grew fiercer every moment. He strained his eyes out into the blackness of the river from time to time, or looked anxiously at the troops, clustered about the fires, or tramping restlessly up and down in their places to ward off the deadly attack of the awful winter night, while some of them sought shelter, behind trees and hillocks, from the fury of the storm. Filled with his own pregnant thoughts, and speaking to no one, he waited, and no man ventured to break his silence. At half after three General Knox, whose resolute will and iron strength had been exerted to the full, and whose mighty voice had been heard from time to time above the shriek of the fierce wind, was able to report that he had got all the artillery over without the loss of a man, a horse, or a gun, and was ready to proceed. The men were hastily assembled, and, leaving a strong detail to guard the boats, at four o'clock in the morning the long and awful march to Trenton was begun, the general and his staff, escorted by the Philadelphia City Troop, in the lead. The storm was at its height. All hopes of a night attack and surprise had necessarily to be abandoned. Still the general pressed on, determined to abide the issue, and make the attack as soon as he reached the enemy. It was the last effort of liberty, conceived in desperation and born in the throes of hunger and cold! What would the bringing forth be?

CHAPTER XXV

TRENTON—THE LION STRIKES

The route, for the first mile and a half, lay up a steep hill, where the men were much exposed and suffered terribly; after that, for three miles or so, it wound in and out between the hills, and through forests of ash and black oak, which afforded some little shelter. The storm raged with unabated fury, and the progress of the little army was very slow. The men were in good spirits, however, and they cheerfully toiled on over the roads covered with deep drifts, bearing as best they might the driving tempest. It was six in the morning when they reached the little village of Birmingham, where the two columns divided: General Greene's column, accompanied by Washington, taking the longer or inland road, called the Pennington road, which entered the town from the northeast; while Sullivan's column followed the lower road, which entered the town from the west, by way of a bridge over the Assunpink Creek. As Greene had a long detour to make, Sullivan had orders to wait where the cross-road from Rowland's Ferry intersected his line of march, until the first column had time to effect the longer circuit, so that the two attacks might be delivered together. General Washington himself rode in front of the first column. It was still frightfully cold.

About daybreak the general spied an officer on horseback toiling through the snowdrifts toward him. As the horseman drew nearer, he recognized young Martin.

"What is it now, sir?"

"General Sullivan says that the storm has rendered many of his muskets useless, by wetting the priming and powder. He wishes to know what is to be done, sir?"

"Return instantly, and tell him he must use the bayonet! When he hears the firing, he is to advance and charge immediately. The town must be taken, and I intend to take it."

"Very good, sir," said the young man, saluting.

"Can you get through the snow in time?"

"Yes, sir," he replied promptly. "I can get through anything, if your excellency will give the order."

The general smiled approvingly. It was evident that young man's first lesson had been a good one; his emphasis, he was glad to see, had not been misapplied.

When Martin rejoined Sullivan's column, which had been halted at the cross-roads, the men who had witnessed his departure were eagerly waiting his return. As he repeated the general's reply, they began slipping the bayonets over the muzzles of their guns without orders. So eager were they to advance, that Sullivan had difficulty in restraining them until the signal was given. Such was their temper and spirit that, in the excitement of the moment, they recked little of the freezing cold and the hardships of their terrible march. The retreating army was at last on the offensive, they were about to attack now, and no attack is so dangerous as that delivered by men from whom the compelling necessity of retreat has been suddenly removed.

It was about eight o'clock in the morning when they came in sight of the town. The village of Trenton then contained about one hundred houses, mostly frame, scattered along both sides of two long streets, and chiefly located on the west bank of the Assunpink, which here bent sharply to the north before it flowed into the Delaware. The Assunpink was fordable in places at low water, but it was spanned by a substantial stone bridge, which gave on the road followed by Sullivan, at the west end of the village. Washington came down from the north, and entered the village from the other side. About half a mile from the edge of the town, the column led by him came abreast of an old man, chopping wood in a farm-yard by the roadside.

"Which is the way to the Hessian picket?" said the general.

"I don't know," replied the man, sullenly.

"You may tell," said Captain Forest, riding near the general, at the head of his battery, "for this is General Washington."

The man's expression altered at once.

"God bless and prosper you!" he cried eagerly, raising his hands to heaven. "There! The picket is in that house yonder, and the sentry stands near that tree."

The intense cold and heavy snow had driven the twenty-five men, who composed the advance picket, to shelter, and they were huddled together in one of the rude huts which served as a guard-house. The snow deadened the sound of the American advance, and the careless sentry did not perceive them. No warning was given until the lieutenant in command of the guard stepped out of the house by chance, and gave the alarm in great surprise. The picket rushed out, and the men lined up in the road in front of the column, the thick snow preventing them from forming a correct idea of the approaching force. The advance guard of the Continentals, led by Captain William A. Washington and Lieutenant James Monroe, instantly swept down upon them. After a scattered volley which hurt no one, they fled precipitately back toward the village, giving the alarm and rallying on the main guard, posted nearer the centre of the town, which had been speedily drawn up, to the number of seventy-five men. Meanwhile Sullivan's men, with Stark at the head, had routed the pickets on the other road in the same gallant style. This picket was composed of about fifty Hessian chasseurs, and twenty English light dragoons, under command of Lieutenant Grothausen of the chasseurs. They all fled so precipitately that they did not stop to alarm the brigade which they had been stationed to protect, but rapidly galloped down the road, and, crossing the bridge over the Assunpink, made good their escape toward Bordentown. Grave suspicions of cowardice attached thereafter to their commanding officer. Had Ewing performed his part in the plan, the bridge would have been held, and they would have been captured with the rest. Stark's men, followed by the rest of Sullivan's division, were now pushed on rapidly for the town, and the cheers of the New England men were distinctly heard by Washington and his men on the main road. The main guard on the upper road, almost as completely surprised as the other by the dashing onslaught of the Americans, made another futile attempt at resistance to Greene's column, but they soon fell back in great disorder upon the main body.

It was broad daylight now, and the violence of the storm had somewhat abated. In the town, where the firing had been heard, the drums of the three regiments were rapidly beating the assembly. Colonel Rahl was in bed, sleeping off the effects of his previous night's indulgences, when he heard the commotion. Jumping from the bed and running rapidly to the window, still undressed, he thrust out his head and asked the acting brigade adjutant, Biel,—who was hurriedly galloping past,—what it was all about. There was a total misapprehension on all sides, even at this hour, as to the serious nature of the attack; so the confused colonel, satisfied with Biel's surmise that it was a raid, ordered him to take a company and go to the assistance of the main guard, in the supposition that it was only a skirmishing party, and never dreaming of a general attack. Nevertheless he then dressed rapidly, and, running down to the street, mounted his horse, which had been brought around. The three regiments which comprised his brigade and command were already forming; they were the regiment Rahl, the regiment Von Lossburg, and the regiment Von Knyphausen. At this moment the advance party and the main guard came running through the streets in great confusion, crying that the whole rebel army was down upon them. The regiment Rahl and the regiment Von Lossburg at once began retreating to an apple orchard back of the town; firing ineffectively in their excitement, as they ran, from behind the houses, at the head of the column, which had now appeared in the street; while the regiment Von Knyphausen, under the command of Major Von Dechow, the second in command of the brigade, separated from the two others and made for the bridge over the Assunpink.

King and Queen streets run together at the east end of the town. There Washington stationed himself, on the left of Forest's battery, which was immediately unlimbered and opened up a hot fire. The general's position was much exposed, and after his horse had been wounded, his officers repeatedly requested him to fall back to a safer point, which he peremptorily refused to do. The joy of battle sparkled in his eyes; he had instinctively chosen that position on the field from whence he could best see and direct the conflict, and nothing but a successful charge of the enemy upon them could have moved him to retire.

A few of the cooler-headed men among the Hessians had rallied some of the Lossburg regiment, and two guns had been run out into the street and pointed up toward the place where Washington stood, to form a battery, which might, could it have been served, have held the American army in check until such time as the startled Germans could recover their wits and make a stand. General Washington pointed them out to the officer of the advance guard, which had already done such good service, with a wave of his sword. The little handful of men, led by Captain Washington and Lieutenant Monroe, charged down upon the guns, which the party had not had time to load. A scattering volley received them. Captain Washington and Monroe and one of the men were wounded, another fell dead; the men hesitated. Talbot sprang to the head of the column, in obedience to the general's nod, and they rallied, advanced on the run, and the guns were immediately captured.

Meanwhile the fire of Stark's riflemen could be heard at the other end of the town. St. Clair's brigade held the bridge; the regiment Von Knyphausen lost a few precious moments endeavoring to extricate its guns, which had become mired in the morass near the bridge, and then charged upon St. Clair. But it was too late; Von Dechow was seriously wounded, and when the regiment saw itself taken in the flank by Sargeant's brigade, it retired in disorder, though some few men escaped by the fords.

At this juncture Rahl re-formed his scattered troops in the apple orchard. He seems to have had an idea of retreating toward Princeton at first, with the two regiments still under his command; at any rate, he also lost precious moments by hesitation. It was even then too late to effect a successful retreat, for Washington, foreseeing the possibility, had promptly sent Hand's Pennsylvania riflemen along the Pennington road back of the town to check any move in that direction. As fast as the other brigades of Greene's column came up, they were sent down through the streets of the town, until Stirling, in the lead, joined Sullivan's men. Rahl's brigade was practically surrounded, though he did not know it. The commander completely lost his head, though he was a courageous man, brave to rashness, and a veteran soldier who had hitherto distinguished himself in this and many other wars. The town was full of plunder gathered by the troops, the Hessians having been looting the country for weeks; and he could not abandon it without a struggle. The idea of flying from a band of ragged rebels whom he had scouted, was intolerable. He had been, he now felt, more than culpable in neglecting many warnings of attack, and had lamentably failed in his duty as a soldier, in refraining from taking the commonest precautions against surprise. He had refused to heed the urgent representations of Von Dechow, and other of his high officers. Now his honor was at stake; so he rashly made up his mind to charge.

"We will retake the town. All who are my grenadiers— forward!" he cried intrepidly.

The men, with fixed bayonets, advanced bravely, and he led them gallantly forward, sword in hand. The Americans fired a volley; Forest's battery, which enfiladed them, poured in a deadly fire. Rahl in the advance, upon his horse, received a fatal wound and fell to the ground. The Continentals, cheering madly, charged forward with fixed bayonets. The Hessians stopped—hesitated—wavered—their chief was gone —the battle was lost—they broke and fled! Disregarding the commands and appeals of their officers, they turned quickly to the right, and ran off into the face of Hand's riflemen, who received them with another volley. Many of them fell. A body of Virginia troops led by Talbot now gained their left flank, the Philadelphia City Troop encircled their rear. The helpless men stopped, completely bewildered, huddled together in a confused mass. Washington, seeing imperfectly, and thinking they were forming again, ordered the guns from Forest's battery, which had been loaded with canister, to be discharged upon them at once.

"Sir, they have struck!" cried Seymour the keen-eyed, preventing the men from firing.

"Struck!" cried the general, in surprise.

"Yes, sir; their colors are down."

"So they are," said Washington, clasping his hands and raising his eyes to heaven; then, putting spurs to his horse, he galloped over toward the men. The firing had ceased in every direction, and the day was his own; the three regiments were surrendering at discretion, two to him and the other to Lord Stirling. As Major Wilkinson galloped up from the lower division for instructions, Colonel Rahl, pale and bleeding, and supported by two sergeants, presented his sword, which Washington courteously declined to receive. The general then gave orders that every care and assistance should be afforded the unfortunate soldier, who died the next day in a room in Potts' Tavern.

"This is indeed a glorious day for our country," said the general to Seymour.

It was in fact the turning-point in the history of the nation. The captives numbered nearly one thousand men, with twelve hundred stand of arms, six field-pieces, twelve drums, and four colors, including the gorgeous banner of the Anspachers, the Von Lossburg regiment.

Of the Continentals, only two were killed and four wounded, while upward of one hundred of the Hessians were killed and wounded, among the killed being Rahl and Von Dechow, the first and second in command. The whole of this brilliant affair scarcely occupied an hour.

As none of the other divisions had got across, it was scarcely safe for Washington to remain on the east side of the river in the presence of the vastly superior forces of the enemy, which would be concentrated upon him without delay. So that, after giving the men a much needed rest, securing their booty, and burying the dead, the evening found the little army, with its prisoners, retracing its steps toward the ford and its former camping-ground.

But with what different feelings the hungry, worn-out, tattered mass of men marched along in the bitter night! The contrast between the well-clothed and well-fed Hessians and their captors was surprising, but not less striking than that between their going out and coming in. Little recked the frozen men of the hardships of the way. They had shown the world that they possessed other capabilities than facility in retreating, and no American army, however small or feeble, would ever again be despised by any foe.

The return passage was made without incident, save that just on the crest of the hills leading down to the Ford, the general, who was in advance again, noticed a suspicious-looking, snow-covered mound by the roadside. Riding up to it, one of his aids dismounted and uncovered the body of a man, a Continental soldier, frozen to death. The cold weapon was grasped tightly in the colder hand. A little farther on there was another body asleep in the snow,—another soldier! The last was that man of the headquarters guard who had spoken of his little children at home on Christmas day. They would wait a long time before they saw him again. He had been willing to fight the whole English army! Ah, well, a sterner foe than any who marched beneath the red flag of Great Britain had grappled with him, and he had been defeated,—but he had won his freedom!

For forty hours now that little band of men had marched and fought, and when it reached its camp at midnight the whole army was exhausted. The only man among them all who preserved his even calmness, and was apparently unaffected by the hardships of the day, was the commander himself,— the iron man. Late into the night he dictated and wrote letters and orders, to be despatched in every direction in the morning. The successful issue of his daring adventure entailed yet further responsibilities, and the campaign was only just begun. As for himself, the world now knew him for a soldier. And a withered old man in the palace of the Sans Souci in Berlin, who had himself known victories and defeats, who had himself stood at bay, facing a world in arms so successfully that men called him "The Great," called this and the subsequent campaign the finest military exploit of the age!

Cyrus Townsend Brady

CHAPTER XXVI

MY LORD CORNWALLIS

And so the departure of my Lord Cornwallis was necessarily deferred. The packet upon which he had engaged passage, and which had actually received his baggage, sailed without him. It would be some days before he would grace the court of St. James with his handsome person, and a long time would elapse before he would once more rejoice in the sight of his beloved hills; when he next returned it would not be with the laurels of a conqueror either! He was to try conclusions once and again with the gentleman he had so assiduously pursued through the Jerseys; and this time, ay, and in the end too, the honors were to be with his antagonist. The Star and Order of the Bath, which his gracious and generous Britannic majesty had sent over to the new Caesar, General Howe, with so much laudation and so many words of congratulation, was to have a little of its lustre diminished, and was destined to appear not quite so glorious as it had after Long Island; in fact, it was soon to be seen that it was only a pyrotechnic star after all, and not in the order of heaven! Both of these gentlemen were to learn that an army—almost any kind of an army—is always dangerous until it is wiped out; and it is not to be considered as wiped out as long as it has any coherent existence at all, even if the coherent existence only depends upon the iron will of one man,—which is another way of saying the game is never won until it is ended.

There was mounting in hot haste in New York, and couriers and orders streamed over the frozen roads, and Lord Cornwallis himself galloped at full speed for Princeton. The calculations of a certain number of his majesty's faithful troops were to be rudely disturbed, and the comfortable quarters in which they had ensconced themselves were to be vacated forthwith. Concentration, aggregation, synthesis, were the words; and this time the reassembled army was not to disintegrate into winter quarters until this pestilent Mr. Washington was attended to, and attended to so effectually that they could enjoy the enforced hospitality of the surly but substantial Jerseymen through the long winter nights undisturbed. For his part, Mr. Washington, having tasted success, the first real brilliant offensive success of the campaign, was quite willing to be attended to. In fact, in a manner which in another sex might be called coquettish, he seemed to court attention. Having successfully attacked with his frost-bitten ragged regiments a detachment, he was now to demonstrate to the world that not even the presence of an army could stop him.

Things were not quiet on the Pennsylvania side of the river either; there were such comings and goings in Newtown as that staid and conservative village had never before seen. Our two friends, the sad-hearted, were both busily employed. Talbot had galloped over the familiar road, and had electrified the good people of Philadelphia with his news, and then had hastened on to Baltimore to reassure the spirits of the frightened Congress. Honest Robert Morris was trotting around from door to door upon New Year's morning, hat in hand, begging for dollars to assist his friend George Washington, and the cause of liberty, and the suffering army; and Seymour, become as it were a soldier, and with Philip for esquire, was waiting to take what he could get, be the amount ever so little, back to General Washington. The sailor had been granted a further leave of absence by the naval committee, at the general's urgent request, and was glad to learn that he should soon have command of the promised ship of war, which was even then making ready in the Delaware. Honest Bentley—beloved of the soldiery in spite of his genuinely expressed contempt for land warriors—was lending what aid he could in keeping up the spirits of the men, and in other material ways in the camp. Some of the clothing, some of the guns from the Mellish, some of the material captured from the Hessians had gone into the hands and over the backs and upon the feet of the men. But the clothed and the naked were equally happy, for had they not done something at last? Ay! they had given assurance that they were men to be reckoned with.

Fired by the example set them by the Continentals, the Pennsylvania militia, under Cadwalader and Ewing and Mifflin, had at last crossed the Delaware and joined Griffin's men. Washington had followed them, and the twenty-ninth of December found him established in new headquarters at Trenton. A number of mounds in the fields, covered with snow, some bitter recollections and sad stories of plunder, robbery, rapine, and worse, told with gnashing teeth or breaking heart by the firesides, were all that remained of their strange antagonists in the town. But the little town and the little valley were to be once more the scene of war. The great game was to be played again, and the little creek of the Assunpink was to run red under its ice and between its banks.

On the twenty-ninth, Washington's troops began to cross the river again. Two parties of light dragoons were sent on in advance under Colonel Reed, assisted by parties of Pennsylvania riflemen despatched by Cadwalader. They clung tenaciously to the flanks of Von Donop. That unfortunate commander had been led away from his camp at Burlington in pursuit of Griffin's gallant six hundred. When he returned, unsuccessful, the news from Trenton had so alarmed him that he fled precipitately, abandoning his heavy baggage and some of his artillery. It was a work of joy for the pursued to pursue, a reversal of conditions which put the heavy German veterans at a strange disadvantage compared with their alert and active pursuers. They had marched through that country with a high hand, plundering and abusing its inhabitants in a frightful way, and they were now being made to experience the hatred they themselves had enkindled. The country people rose against them, and cut them off without mercy.

It took two days to get the troops across, on account of the ice in the river. And now came another difficulty. The time of the major part of the Americans had expired on the last day of the year, but Washington had them paraded and had ridden up and addressed them in a brilliant, soldier-like fashion, and they had to a man volunteered to remain with him for six weeks longer, or as much more time as was necessary to enable him to complete his campaign before he went into winter quarters. He was at last able to pay them their long deferred salary out of the fifty thousand dollars sent him by Robert Morris, which Seymour and Talbot that day had brought him; and for their future reward he cheerfully pledged his own vast estate, an example of self-sacrifice which Greene, Stark, Talbot, Seymour, and others of the officers who possessed property, at once emulated. The men were put in good spirits by a promise of ten dollars' bounty also, and they were ready and eager for a fight.

Reed, attended by six young gentlemen of the Philadelphia Troop, had been sent out to reconnoitre. Up toward Princeton they had surprised a British outpost composed of a sergeant and twelve dragoons; the sergeant escaped, but the twelve dragoons, panic-stricken, were captured after a short resistance; and Reed and his gallant young cavaliers returned in triumph to headquarters. Valuable information was gained from this party. Cornwallis had joined Grant at Princeton, and with seven or eight thousand men was assembling wagons and transportation, preparing for a dash on Trenton. Confirmation of this not unexpected news came by a student from the college, who had escaped to Cadwalader and been sent up to General Washington. The situation of Washington was now critical, but he took prompt measures to relieve it. Cadwalader from the Crosswicks, and Mifflin from Bordentown, with thirty-six hundred men, were ordered forward at once. They promptly obeyed orders, and by another desperate night march reached Trenton on the morning of the first day of the year.

There was heavy skirmishing all day on the second. Cornwallis, advancing in hot haste from Princeton with eight thousand men, was checked, and lost precious time, by a hot rifle fire from the wood on the banks of the Shabbakong Creek, near the road he followed in his advance. The skirmishers under Greene, seconded by Hand, after doing gallant service and covering themselves with glory by delaying the advance for several hours, giving Washington ample time to withdraw his army across the Assunpink and post it in a strong defensive position, had retired in good order beyond the American line. In the skirmish Lieutenant Von Grothausen, he who had galloped away with the dragoons at Trenton and had been under suspicion of cowardice ever since, had somewhat redeemed his reputation in that he had boldly ridden down upon the riflemen, and had been killed. It was late in the evening when the advance parties crossed the bridge over the creek and sought safety behind the lines. Indefatigable General Knox had concentrated thirty pieces of cannon at the bridge—"A very pretty battery," he called it.

It was dusk when the eager Americans saw the head of the British army coming through the streets. They remained silent while the enemy formed, and advanced to attack the bridge and the fords in heavy columns at the same time. The men came on in a solid mass for the bridge head, cheering gallantly. They were met by Knox's artillery and a steady fire from the riflemen. Three times they crashed on that bridge like a mighty wave, and three times like a wave broken they fell back before an awful storm of fire. General Washington himself, sitting on his white horse, gave the orders at the bridge, and the brave enemy were repulsed. The position was too strong to be taken by direct assault without great loss; besides, it was not vital after all—so reasoned Cornwallis. The British soldiery were weary, they had marched all day at a hot pace and were exhausted. They had not lived in a chronic state of exhaustion for so long that they never gave it a thought; they were not used to it, as were the Continentals, and when the British were tired they had to rest. They would be in better spirit on the morrow. The creek was fordable in a dozen places, but Cornwallis resisted the importunities of some of his officers, who wished to ford it and attack at once; he sent urgent messengers off to Princeton to bring up the two thousand men left there with Von Donop, and to hurry up Leslie with the rear guard, six miles away; when they arrived they could turn the right flank of the Americans, and it would be all up with them then. He thought he had Washington at such a disadvantage that he could not escape, though the small advantage of position might enable him to make a desperate resistance, even with his inferior forces.

"We will wait," he said to Erskine, "until Von Donop comes up, and Leslie, and then we'll bag the 'old fox' in the morning!"

So, after brisk firing on both sides until night closed down, the camp-fires were lighted on both sides of the creek; and the British officer went to sleep, calmly confident that he had held the winning cards, and all that was necessary was that the hand should be played out in the morning, to enable him to take the game again. He did indeed hold the higher cards, but the "old fox" showed himself the better player.

On the other side of the creek, in the house of good Mistress Dagworthy, anxious hearts were debating. General Washington had summoned a council of war, which expressed the usual diversity of opinion on all subjects, except an unwillingness to fight, upon which, like every other council of war, it was agreed. Indeed the odds were fearful! Ten thousand seasoned, well-equipped, well-trained, veteran troops, ably led, and smarting with the late defeat and the check of the day against five thousand or six thousand wretchedly provided soldiers, three-fifths of whom were raw militiamen, who had never heard a shot fired in anger!

Not even a leader like Washington, and officers to second him like Greene, Sullivan, Knox, St. Clair, Stephen, Stirling, Cadwalader, Sargeant, Mercer, Mifflin, Reed, Stark, Hand, Glover, and the others, could overcome such a disparity and inequality.

Cornwallis had only to outflank them, crumple them up, roll them back on the impassable Delaware, and then—God help them all!

There was no disguising the critical nature of their situation, and the army had never before been in so desperate a position. It needed no great skill to see the danger now to be faced, but the mistake of Cornwallis gave them a brief respite, of which they promptly availed themselves.

Washington was not a man before whom it was ever safe to indulge in mistakes, and the more difficult his position, the more dangerous he became. Trial, danger, hazard, seemed to bring out all of the most remarkable qualities of the man in the highest degree. Nothing alarmed him, nothing dismayed him, nothing daunted him; the hotter the conflict, the more pressing the danger, the cooler he became. No man on earth was ever more ready and quick to avail himself of time and opportunity, once he had determined upon a course of action. This campaign was the most signal illustration, among many others, which his wonderful career affords. Action, prompt, bold, decisive, was as the breath of life to him; but before coming to a decision, contrary to the custom of great commanders generally, he usually called a council of war, which, on account of his excessive modesty, he sometimes allowed to overrule his own better judgment, to the great detriment of the cause. Alone he was superb! Given equal resources, the world has not seen a general with whom he could not successfully be matched. In this particular juncture, fortunately for the country, he insisted upon having his own way.

There were apparently but three alternatives before the council. The first was a retreat with all speed down the river, leaving the heavy baggage and artillery, and then crossing at Philadelphia if they could get there in time. But this would be to abandon the whole colony of New Jersey, to lose the results of the whole campaign, and leave the enemy in fine position to begin again in the spring; and if this were the end, they might better have stayed on the west side of the river. Besides, successes were vital and must be had. Another retreat meant disintegration and ruin, in spite of the lucky stroke at Trenton. The second alternative was a battle where they stood, and that meant total defeat,—a thing not to be considered a moment. The army must win or die; and as dying could do no good, it had to win. A brilliant idea, however, had occurred to the commander-in-chief, the man of brilliant ideas. He communicated it to the council, where it instantly found adherents, and objectors, too. It was the third alternative. A circuitous road called the Quaker road, recently surveyed and just made, led in a roundabout way from the rear of the camp toward the Princeton road, which it entered two miles from that town. Washington's plan was to steal silently away in the night by this road, leaving bright fires burning to deceive the confident enemy, and press with all speed toward Princeton, strike Cornwallis' rear-guard there at daybreak with overwhelming force, crush it before that general could retrace his steps, and then make a dash for the British supplies at New Brunswick. If it were not practicable to reach that point, Washington could take a position on the hills above Morristown, on the flank of the British, and, by threatening their communications, force the superior army to retreat and abandon the field, or else attack the Americans in their intrenchments in the hills, with a probable result even more disastrous to the attacking party than at Bunker Hill. It was a conception as simple and beautiful as it was bold, brilliant, and practicable.

But now the objectors began; it had been snowing, sleeting, and raining for several days; the roads were impassable, they had no bottom. Objections were made on all sides: the artillery could not possibly be moved, no horses could pull the wagons through the mud, the troops could not march in it. But Washington, with true instincts, held to his carefully devised plan with an unusual resolution. Arguing, explaining, suggesting, convincing, persuading, the hours slipped away, until at ten o'clock at night there came a sudden change in the weather, perceptible even to those in the house. Washington ran eagerly to the door and opened it. Followed by the general officers, he stepped out into the night. It was dark and cloudy, no moon or stars even, and growing colder every moment under the rising northeast wind.

"Gentlemen," he cried gayly, "Providence has decided for us. The wind has shifted. The army will move in two hours."

At the time specified by the commander, the muddy roads were frozen hard. The heavy baggage was sent down to Burlington, and a strong party of active men was left to keep bright fires burning, and charged to show themselves as much as possible and make a great commotion by throwing up fortifications and loud talking, with instructions to slip away and join the main body early next day as best they could. At one o'clock in the morning the astonished army started out upon their adventurous journey,—another long cold night march. The untravelled roads were as smooth and hard as iron. With muffled wheels they succeeded in stealing away undetected.

CHAPTER XXVII

THE LION TURNS FOX

The Quaker road led southeast from Trenton until it reached the village of Sandtown, where it turned to the northwest again, and it was not until that point was reached that the surprised soldiers realized the daring nature of the manoeuvre, and the character of that night march, which they had at first considered another hopeless retreat. It was astonishing, then, with what spirit and zeal the soldiers tramped silently over the frozen roads; the raw, green militia vied with the veterans, in the fortitude with which they sustained the dreadful fatigue of the severe march. The long distance to be traversed, on account of the detour to be made, rendered it necessary that the men be moved at the highest possible speed. The road itself being a new one, lately cleared, the stumps and roots of trees not yet grubbed up, made it difficult to transport the artillery and the wagons: but the tired men cheerfully assisted the tired horses, and the little army made great progress. The morning of Friday, January the 5th, dawned clear and cold, with the ground covered with hoar frost. About sunrise the army, with Washington again in the lead, reached the bridge over Stony Brook about three miles from the village of Princeton. Leading the main body across the bridge, they struck off from the main highway through a by-road which was concealed by a grove of trees in the lower ground, and afforded a short cut to the town.

General Mercer was an old friend and comrade of the commander-in-chief; he had been a companion of Prince Charles Edward in his romantic invasion of England in '45, a member of Braddock's unfortunate expedition, and wounded when that general's army was annihilated; and sometime commander of Fort Du Quesne, after its capture by General Forbes. He was detailed, with a small advance party comprising the remnants of Smallwood's Marylanders, Haslet's Delawareans, and Fleming's Virginians, and a small body of young men from the first families of Philadelphia, to the total number of three hundred, to continue up the road along the brook until he reached the main road, where he was to try and hold the bridge in order to intercept fugitives from Princeton, or check any retrograde movement of the troops which might have advanced toward Trenton. The little band had proceeded but a short distance on their way, when they unexpectedly came in sight of a column of the enemy.

It was the advance of the British, a part of Von Donop's leading brigade, *en route* for Trenton to assist Cornwallis in bagging the "old fox" according to orders,—the Seventeenth Regiment, under Colonel Mawhood. Mercer's troops being screened by the wood, their character was not visible to Mawhood, who conjectured that they must be a body of fugitives from the front. Under this impression, and never dreaming of the true situation, Mawhood promptly deployed his regiment and moved off to the left to intercept Mercer, at the same time despatching messengers to bring up the other two regiments, the Fortieth and Fifty-fifth, which had not yet left Princeton. Both parties rushed for a little rising ground on the edge of a cleared field, near the house of a peaceful Quaker named Clark. The Americans were nearer the goal than their opponents, and reached it first. Hastily deploying his column, Mercer sought shelter behind a hedge fence which crowned the eminence, and immediately opened up a destructive fire from his riflemen, which temporarily checked the advancing enemy. The British, excellently led, returned the fire with great spirit, and with such good effect that, after a few volleys, Mercer's horse was wounded in the leg and his rider thrown violently to the ground, Talbot's was killed under him, and several of the officers and men fell,— among them the brave Colonel Haslet, who was mortally wounded. In the confusion thus unfortunately caused, the Americans could hear sharp commands of the English officers, then the rattling of steel on the gun-barrels, and the next moment the red-coated men broke out of the smoke and, unchecked by a scattering fire from the Americans, gallantly rushed up at them with fixed bayonets. There were unfortunately no bayonets in this small brigade of the Continental army. A few of the men clubbed their muskets resolutely as the two lines met, and made a stout resistance; but the oncoming British would not be denied, and, as the charge was pressed home, the Americans wavered, broke, and fell back in some disorder before the vigorous onslaught of the veteran troops. Mercer, filled with shame, strove in vain to rally his men. Disdaining himself to retreat, and gallantly calling upon them to advance, he threw himself upon the advancing British line, sword in hand, followed by his officers, and for a brief space there was an exciting melee on the hill. A blow from the butt end of a musket felled the general to the ground. Talbot sprang to his side, and swept the bayonet away from his heart by a blow of his sword delivered with a quick movement of his powerful arm. Mercer profited by the moment's respite to leap to his feet.

"Thank you, my lad," he said.

"Do you get to the rear and rally the men, general," cried Talbot, firing a pistol at short range into the midst of the crowding enemy. "I'll hold these men in play." But the fighting blood of the old Scotchman was up, and for answer he struck boldly at the man opposite him.

"Surrender, you damned rebels!" cried an officer near them.

"Never!" replied Mercer, cutting down the man with whom he was engaged, while Talbot did the like to the one next him. With a roar of rage the British sprang on the two men. In a trice one of the bayonets got past Mercer's guard and grazed his arm, another buried itself in his bosom, a third struck him in the breast. The old man struck out weakly, dropped his sword and fell, pierced by a dozen wounds, but still breathing. Talbot, who was as yet unharmed, though covered with blood and dust, his hat gone, stepped across his body.

He might have retreated, being young and active; but that was not the custom of his family, neither would he abandon the body of his brave commander; besides, every moment of delay was precious. Surely they would be reinforced and rallied; he knew the promptness of Washington too well to doubt it for a moment; and, last of all, what was life without Kate? One glance he cast to the bright sky, flushed with the first rays of the rising sun, and then he stood on guard. The young man's eyes were burning with the intoxication of the fight, and his soul filled with great resolve; but his sword-play was as cool and as rapid as it had been in the Salle des Armes at Paris, where few could be found to master him. The little group of British paused a moment in admiration of his courage.

"One at a time, gentlemen," he cried, smiling, and warding off a vicious bayonet thrust. "Are there none here who will cross swords with me, for the honor of their flag?"

The young lieutenant in command of that part of the line promptly sprang forward and engaged; the two blades rang fiercely together, and grated along each other a moment later. The men stepped back. But the brave lieutenant had met his match, and, with set lips and iron arm, Talbot drove home his blade in the other's heart. Ere he could recover himself or withdraw his sword, he was beaten to his knees by a blow from a gun-barrel; the blood ran down over his face.

"Surrender! surrender!" they cried to him, "and we will spare your life."

For answer his hand sought his remaining pistol. The first one of his opponents fell dead with a bullet through his heart, and the next moment the deadly steel of a bayonet was buried in Talbot's throat.

"Kate—Kate!" he cried in agony, the blood bubbling from his lips, and then another bayonet found his gallant heart; and he sank down on his face, at the foot of the dying officer, his lips kissing the soil of that country in defence of whose liberties he had fallen.

As was customary with his family, he had died on the field, grimly facing fearful odds to the last. The last of his line, he had made a good ending, not unworthy his distinguished ancestry; for none of the proud and gallant race had ever died in the service of a better cause, be it that of king or Parliament, than this young soldier who had just laid down his life for love of his country!

The slight check afforded by the interposition of the Americans was over. The British were sweeping everything before them, when Colonel Mawhood, the cool-headed officer, who had been sitting on a little brown pony, with a small switch in his hand, directing the combat, became aware of a large body of men coming up on his right flank through the wood. With the readiness of a practised soldier, he instantly stopped the advance of his men, wheeled them about, brought up his guns, and prepared to open fire. The American officers had time to mark with admiration the skill with which the manoeuvre was effected, and the beautiful precision with which the men carried out their orders. Then the force, a large body of Pennsylvania militia which Washington had despatched at the first sound of firing in the direction of Mercer, broke out of the wood, and advanced rapidly. The muskets of the redcoats were quickly brought to the shoulder, and at the word of command the British line was suddenly tipped with fire and then covered with smoke. Many of the militia fell at this volley delivered at close range; some of the fallen lay still and motionless, while others groaned with pain; the raw troops fired hastily into the smoke, then hesitated and stopped uncertainly as the volley was repeated. It was another critical moment, and the hour brought the man.

Washington himself had most opportunely arrived on the field in advance of the troops, attended by Seymour. One glance showed him Mercer's broken retreating column and the hesitating Pennsylvania militia! Everything was at stake. It was not a time for strategic manoeuvres now, but for men—nay, there were men there as good as ever fought—but for a man then. Providentially one was at hand. Putting spurs to his gallant white horse, he rode down the line in front of the Pennsylvania militia, waving his hat and cheering them on.

"An old-fashioned Virginia fox-hunt, gentlemen!" he cried gayly, giving the view halloo! Galloping forward under the fire of the British battery, he called to Mercer's shattered men. They halted and faced about; the Seventh Virginia broke through the wood on the flank of the British;

Hitchcock's New Englanders came up on the run with fixed bayonets; Moulder's Philadelphia battery opened fire from the hill on the opposing guns.

The fire of a warrior had now supplanted the coolness of a general. Dashing boldly forward, reckless of the storm of bullets, to within thirty yards of the British line, and smiling with stern pleasure in the crisis which seemed to develop and bring out every fibre of his deep nature, he called upon his men to come on. Recovering themselves, they responded with the utmost gallantry. Mawhood was surrounded and outnumbered, his victory suddenly changed to defeat; but, excellent soldier that he was, he fought on with desperate resolution, and the conflict was exceedingly hot. Washington was in the thick of it. Seymour, who had followed him closely until the general broke away in the smoke to lead the charge, lost sight of him for a moment, enveloped as he was in the dust and smoke of the battle. When he saw him emerge from the cloud, waving his sword, and beheld the enemy giving way on every side, he spurred up to him.

"Thank God!" he said; "your excellency is safe."

"Away! away! my dear Seymour," he cried, "and bring up the troops. The day is our own!"

To the day of his death Seymour never lost the splendid impression of that heroic figure, the ruddy face streaked with smoke and dust, the eyes blazing with the joy of battle, the excitement of the charge, the mighty sweep of the mighty arm! Mawhood's men were, indeed, routed in every direction; most of them laid down their arms. A small party only, under that intrepid leader, succeeded in forcing its way through the American ranks with the bayonet, and ran at full speed toward Trenton under the stimulus of a hot pursuit.

Meanwhile the Fifty-fifth Regiment had been vigorously attacked by St. Clair's brigade, and, after a short action, those who could get away were in full retreat towards New Brunswick. The last regiment, the Fortieth, had not been able to get into action at all; a part of it fled in a panic, with the remains of the Fifty-fifth, towards New Brunswick, hotly pursued by Washington with the Philadelphia City Troop and what cavalry he could muster, and the rest took refuge in the college building in Princeton, from which they were dislodged by artillery and compelled to surrender. The British loss was about five hundred in killed and wounded and prisoners, the American less than one hundred; but among the latter were many valuable officers,—Colonels Haslet and Potter, Major Morris, Captains Shippen, Fleming, Talbot, Neal, and General Mercer.

After following the retiring and demoralized British for a few miles, Washington determined to abandon the pursuit. The men were exhausted by their long and fatiguing marches, and were in no condition to make the long march to New Brunswick; most of them were still ill equipped and entirely unfitted for the fatigue and exposure of a further winter campaign,—even those iron men must have rest at last. The flying British must have informed Leslie's troops, six miles away, of the situation; they would soon be upon them, and they might expect Cornwallis with his whole force at any time. He drew off his troops, therefore, and, leaving a strong party to break down the bridge over Stony Brook and impede the advance of the English as much as possible, he pushed on towards Pluckamin and Morristown, officers and men thoroughly satisfied with their brilliant achievements.

Early in the morning the pickets of Cornwallis' army discovered that something was wrong in the American camp; the guard had been withdrawn, the fires had been allowed to die away, and the place was as still as death. A few adventurous spirits, cautiously crossing the bridge, found that the guns mounted in front of it were only "quakers," and that the whole camp was empty,—the army had decamped silently, and stolen away before their eyes! My Lord Cornwallis, rudely disturbed from those rosy dreams of conquest with which a mocking spirit had beguiled his slumber, would not credit the first report of his astonished officers; but investigation showed him that the "old fox" was gone, and he would not be bagged that morning—nor on any other morning, either! But where had he gone? For a time the perplexed and chagrined commander could not ascertain.

The Americans had vanished—disappeared—leaving abso-lutely no trace behind them, and it was not until he heard the heavy booming of cannon from the northeast, borne upon the frosty air of the cold morning about sunrise, that he divined the brilliant plan of his wily antagonist and discovered his whereabouts. He had been outfought, outmanoeuvred, outflanked, and outgeneralled! The disgusted British were sent back over the familiar road to Princeton, now in hotter haste than before. His rear-guard menaced, perhaps over-whelmed, his stores and supplies in danger, Cornwallis pushed on for life this time. The English officer conceived a healthy respect for Washington at this juncture which did not leave him thereafter.

The short distance between Trenton and Princeton on the direct road was passed in a remarkably short time by the now thoroughly aroused and anxious British. A little party under command of Seymour and Kelly, which had been assi-duously engaged in breaking down the bridge over Stony Brook, was observed and driven away by two field-pieces, which had been halted and unlimbered on a commanding hill, and which opened fire while the troops advanced on a run; but the damage had been done, and the bridge was already impassable. After a futile attempt to repair it, in which much time was lost, the indefatigable earl sent his troops through the icy water of the turbulent stream, which rose breast-high upon the eager men, and the hasty pursuit was once more resumed. A mile or so beyond the bridge the whole army was brought to a stand by a sudden discharge from a heavy gun, which did some execution; it was mounted in a breastwork some distance ahead. The army was halted, men were sent ahead to reconnoitre, and a strong column deployed to storm what was supposed to be a heavy battery. When the storming party reached the works, there was no one there! A lone thirty-two-pounder, too unwieldy to accompany the rapid march of the Americans, had been left behind, and Philip Wilton had volunteered to remain, after Seymour's party had passed, and further delay the British by firing it at their army as soon as they came in range. These delays had given Washington so much of a start that Cornwallis, despairing of ever overtaking him, finally gave up the pursuit, and pushed on in great anxiety to New Brunswick, to save, if possible, his magazines, which he had the satisfaction in the end of finding intact.

To complete this brief *resume* of one of the remarkable campaigns of history, Washington strongly fortified himself on Cornwallis' flank at Morristown, menacing each of the three depots held by the British outside New York; Putnam advanced from Philadelphia to Trenton, with the militia; and Heath moved down to the highlands of the Hudson. The country people of New Jersey rose and cut off scattered detachments of the British in every direction, until the whole of the field was eventually abandoned by them, except Amboy, Newark, and New Brunswick. The world witnessed the singular spectacle of a large, well-appointed army of veteran soldiery, under able leaders, shut up in practically one spot, New York and a few near-by villages, and held there inexorably by a phantom army which never was more than half the size of that it held in check! The results of the six months' campaign were to be seen in the possession of the city of New York by the British army. That army, which had won, practically, all the battles in which it had engaged, which had followed the Americans through six months of disastrous defeat and retreat, and had overrun two colonies, now had nothing to show for all its efforts but the ground upon which it stood! And this was the result of the genius, the courage, the audacity of one man,—George Washington! The world was astounded, and he took an assured place thenceforward among the first soldiers of that or any age.

Even the English themselves could not withhold their admiration. The gallant and brave Cornwallis, a soldier of no mean ability himself, and well able to estimate what could be done with a small and feeble force, never forgot his surprise at the Assunpink; and when he congratulated Washington, at the surrender of Yorktown years after, upon the brilliant combination which had resulted in the capture of the army, he added these words: "But, after all, your excellency's achievements in the Jerseys were such that nothing could surpass them!" And the witty and wise old cynic, Mr. Horace Walpole, with his usual discrimination, wrote to a friend, Sir Horace Mann, when he heard of the affair at Trenton, the night march to Princeton, and the successful attack there: "Washington, the dictator, has shown himself both a Fabius and a Camillus. His march through our lines is allowed to have been a prodigy of generalship!"

CHAPTER XXVIII

THE BRITISH PLAY "TAPS"

The day after the battle Washington sent his nephew, Major Lewis, under protection of a flag of truce, to attend upon the wounded General Mercer; the exigency of his pursuit of the flying British and their subsequent pursuit of him having precluded him from giving to his old friend that personal attention which would have so accorded with his kindly heart and the long affection in which he had held the old Scotchman. Seymour received permission to accompany Lewis, in order to ascertain if possible what had become of Talbot.

The men of Mercer's command reported that they had seen the two officers dismounted and fighting bravely, after having refused to retreat. The two young officers were very melancholy as they rode along the familiar road. Lewis belonged to a Virginia regiment, and had known both Mercer and Talbot well, and in fact all the officers who had been killed. The officers of that little army were like a band of brothers, and after every battle there was a general mourning for the loss of many friends. The casualties among the officers in the sharp engagement had been unusually severe, and entirely disproportioned to the total loss; the bulk of the loss had fallen upon Mercer's brigade.

They found the general in Clark's farmhouse, near the field of battle, lingering in great pain, and slowly dying from a number of ferocious bayonet wounds. He was attended by his aid, Major Armstrong, and the celebrated Dr. Benjamin Rush came especially from Philadelphia to give the dying hero the benefit of his skill and services. He had been treated with the greatest respect by the enemy, for Cornwallis was always quick to recognize and respect a gallant soldier. The kindly Quakers had spared neither time nor trouble to lighten his dying hours, and the women of the household nursed him with gentle and assiduous care. He passed away ten days after the battle, leaving to his descendants the untarnished name of a gallant soldier and gentleman, who never faltered in the pursuit of his high ideals of duty. Brief as had been his career as a general in the Revolution, his memory is still cherished by a grateful posterity, as one of the first heroes of that mighty struggle for liberty.

Details of the British were already marching toward the field of action to engage in the melancholy work of burying the dead, when Seymour, under Major Armstrong's guidance, went over the ground in a search for Talbot. He had no difficulty in finding the place where his friend had fallen. The field had not been disturbed by any one. A bloody frozen mass of ice and snow had shown where Mercer had fallen, and across the place where his feet had been lay the body of Talbot. In front of him lay the lieutenant with whom he had fought, the sword still buried in his breast; farther away were the two men that the general and he had cut down in the first onslaught, and at his feet was the corpse of the man he had last shot, his stiffened hands still tightly clasping his gun. Around on the field were the bodies of many others who had fallen. Some of the Americans had been literally pinned to the earth by the fierce bayonet thrusts they had received in the charge; some of the British had been frightfully mangled and mashed by blows from the clubbed rifles of the Americans before they had retreated. Off to the right a long line of motionless bodies marked where the Pennsylvania militia had advanced and halted; there in the centre, lying in heaps, were the reminders of the fiercest spot of the little conflict, where Moulder's battery had been served with such good effect; here was the place where Washington had led the charge.

In one brief quarter of an hour nearly three hundred men had given up their lives, on this little farm, and there they lay attesting in mute silence their fidelity to their principles, warm red coat and tattered blue coat side by side, peace between them at last; indifferent each to the severities of nature or the passions of men; unheeding alike the ambitions of kings, the obstinacy of parliaments, or the desire of liberty on the part of peoples. Some were lying calmly, as if their last moments had been as peaceful as when little children they laid themselves down to sleep; others twisted and contorted with looks of horror and anguish fixed upon their mournful faces, which bespoke agonies attending the departure of life like to the travail pains with which it had been ushered into existence. Seymour with a sad heart stooped and turned over the body of his friend, lifting his face once more to that heaven he had gazed upon so bravely a few hours since—for it was morning again, but oh, how different! The face was covered with blood from the wound in the forehead, by which he had been beaten down. Sadly, tenderly, gratefully, remembering an hour when Talbot had knelt by his side and performed a similar service, he endeavored to wipe the lurid stains from off his marble brow. Then a thought came to him. Taking from his breast Katharine's handkerchief, which had never left him, he moistened it in the snow, and finding an unstained place where her dainty hand had embroidered her initials "K. W.," he carefully wiped clean the white face of his dead friend. There was a little smile upon Talbot's lips, and a look of peace and calm upon his face, which Seymour had not seen him wear since the sinking of the frigate. His right hand, whiter than the lace which drooped over it, was pressed against his heart, evidently as the result of his last conscious movement. Seymour bent down and lifted it up gently; there was something beneath it inside his waistcoat. The young sailor reverently inserted his hand and drew it forth. It was a plain gold locket. Touching the spring, it opened, and there were pictured the faces of the two women Talbot had loved,—on the one side the mother, stately, proud, handsome, resolute, the image of the man himself; on the other, the brown eyes and the fair hair and the red lips of beautiful Katharine Wilton. There was a letter too in the pocket. The bayonet thrust which had reached his heart had gone through it, and it, and the locket also, was stained with blood. The letter was addressed to Seymour; wondering, he broke the seal and read it. It was a brief note, written in camp the night of the march. It would seem that Talbot had a presentiment that he might die in the coming conflict; indeed the letter plainly showed that he meant to seek death, to court it in the field. His mother was to be told that he had done his duty, and had not failed in sustaining the traditions of his honorable house; and the honest soldierly little note ended with these words,—

As for you, my dear Seymour, would that fate had been kinder to you! Were Katharine alive, I would crave your permission to say these words to her: 'I love you, Kate,—I've always loved you—but the better man has won you.' My best love to the old mother. Won't you take it to her? And good-by, and God bless you!—Hilary Talbot.

The brilliance went out of the sunshine, the brightness faded out of the morning, and Seymour stood there with the tears running down his cheeks,—not ashamed to weep for his friend. And yet the man was with Kate, he thought, and happy,—he could almost envy him his quiet sleep. The course of his thoughts was rudely broken by the approach of a party of horsemen, who rode up to where he stood. Their leader, a bold handsome young man, of distinguished appearance, in the brilliant dress of a British general officer, reined in his steed close by him, and addressed him.

"How now, sir! Weeping? Tears do not become a soldier!"

"Ah, sir," said Seymour, saluting, and pointing down to Talbot's body at the same time, "not even when one mourns the death of a friend?"

"Your friend, sir?" replied the general officer, courteously, uncovering and looking down at the bodies with interest; his practised eye immediately taking in the details of the little conflict.

"He did not go to his death alone," he said meaningly. "'Fore Gad, sir, here has been a pretty fight! Your name and rank, sir?"

"Lieutenant John Seymour, of the American Continental navy, volunteer aid on his excellency General Washington's staff."

"And what do you here? Are you a prisoner?"

"No, sir, I came with Major Lewis to visit General Mercer, and to look for my friend, under cover of a flag of truce."

"Ha! How is General Mercer?"

"Frightfully wounded; he cannot live very long now."

"He was a gallant fellow, so I am told, sir, and fought the

father of his majesty in the '45."

"Yes," said Seymour, simply; "this is where he fell."

The general looked curiously about him.

"And who was your dead friend?" he continued.

"Captain Hilary Talbot, of Virginia, of General Washington's staff."

"What! Not Talbot of Fairview Hall on the Potomac?" said one of the officers.

"The same, sir."

"Gad, my lord, Madam Talbot's a red-hot Tory! She swears by the king. I've been entertained at the house,—not when the young man was there, but while he was away,—and a fine place it is. Well, here's a house divided truly!"

"Is it indeed so, Mr. Seymour?"

The young man nodded affirmatively.

"What were you proposing to do with the body?"

"Bury it near here, sir, in the cemetery on the hill by the college. We have no means of transporting it hence."

"Well, you shall do so, and we will bury him like a soldier. I remember the family now, in England, very well. Don't they call them the Loyal Talbots? Yes, I thought so. He was a rebel, and so far false to his creed, but a gentleman nevertheless, and a brave one too. Look at the fight he made here, gentlemen! Damme, he shall have an escort of the king's own troops, and Lord Cornwallis himself and his staff for his chief mourners! eh, Erskine?" said the gallant earl, turning to the officer who rode near him.

"How will that suit you, Mr. Seymour? You can tell that to his poor old mother too, when you see her once again. Some of you bring up a company of troops and get a gun carriage,—there's an abandoned one of Mawhood's over there,—and we'll take him up properly. Have you a horse, sir? Ah, that's well, and bring a Prayer Book if you can find one,—I doubt if there be any in my staff. I presume the man was a Churchman, and he shall have prayers too. We have no coffin for him, either; but stay—here's my own cloak, a proper shroud for a soldier, surely that will do nicely; and now let us go on, gentlemen."

In a short time the martial cortege reached the little Presbyterian cemetery. The young man wrapped in the general's cloak was soon laid away in the shallow grave, which had hastily been made ready for him. Seymour, attended by the two other American officers, Armstrong and Lewis, after cutting off a lock of Talbot's dark hair for his mother, read the burial service out of the young soldier's own little Prayer Book, which he had found in the pocket of his coat; as the earth was put upon him, Cornwallis and his officers stood about reverently uncovered, while the sailor read with faltering lips the old familiar words, which for twenty centuries have whispered of comfort to the heart-broken children of men, and illumined the dark future by an eternal hope—nay, rather, fixed assurance—of life everlasting.

There was one tender-hearted woman there too, one of the sweet-faced daughters of the kindly Quaker, Miss Clark. She had taken time to twine a hasty wreath from the fragrant ever-verdant pine; when the little mound of earth was finished, softly she laid it down, breathing a prayer for the mother in far-off Virginia as she did so.

Then they all drew back while the well-trained soldiers fired the last three volleys, and the drummers beat the last call. 'T was the same simple ending which closes the career of all soldiers, of whatever degree, when they come to occupy those narrow quarters, where earthly considerations of rank and station are forgot.

"Sir, I beg to thank you for this distinguished courtesy," said Seymour, with deep feeling, extending his hand to the knightly Briton.

"Do not mention it, sir, I beg of you," replied Cornwallis, shaking his hand warmly. "You will do the same for one of us, I am sure, should occasion ever demand a like service at your hands. I will see that your other men and officers are properly buried. Do you return now?"

"Immediately, my lord."

"Pray present my compliments to Mr.—nay, General—Washington," said the generous commander, "and congratulate him upon his brilliant campaign. Ay, and tell him we look forward eagerly to trying conclusions with him again. Good-by, sir. Come, gentlemen," he cried, raising his hat gracefully as he mounted his horse and rode away, followed by his staff.

CHAPTER XXIX

THE LAST OF THE TALBOTS

It was with a sinking heart that Seymour rode up the hill toward Fairview Hall a few days later. There had been a light fall of snow during the preceding night, and the brilliant sun of the early morning had not yet gained sufficient strength to melt it away. There was a softening touch therefore about the familiar scene, and Seymour, who had never viewed it in the glory of its summer, thought he had never known it to look so beautiful. Heartily greeted as he passed on by the various servants of the family, with whom he was a great favorite, he finally drew rein and dismounted before the great flight of steps which led up to the terrace upon which the house stood. His arrival had not been unnoticed, and Madam Talbot was standing in the doorway to greet him. He noticed that she looked paler and thinner and older, but she held herself as erect and carried herself as proudly as she had always done. Grief and disappointment and broken hope might change and destroy the natural tissues and fibres of her being, but they could not alter her iron will. Tossing the bridle to one of the attendant servants, Seymour, hat in hand, walked slowly up the steps and across the grass plat, and stepped upon the porch. She watched him in silence, with a frightful sinking of the heart; the gravity of his demeanor and the pallor of his face, in which she seemed to detect a shade of pity which her

Cyrus Townsend Brady

pride resented, apprised her that whatever news he had brought would be ill for her to hear, but her rigid face and composed manner gave no indication of the deadly conflict within. Seymour bowed low to her, and she returned his salute with a sweeping courtesy, old-fashioned and graceful.

"Lieutenant Seymour is very welcome to Fairview Hall, though I trust it be not the compelling necessity of a wound which makes him seek our hospitality again," she said, faintly smiling.

"Oh, madam," said Seymour, softly, yet in utter desperation as to how to begin, "unfortunately it is not to be cured of wounds, but to inflict them that this time I am come. I—I am sorry—that I have to tell you that—I—" he continued with great hesitation.

"You are a bearer of ill tidings, I perceive," she continued gravely. "Speak your message, sir. Whatever it may be, I trust the God I serve to give me strength to bear it. Is it—is it—Hilary?" she went on, with just a suggestion of a break in her even, carefully modulated tones.

"Yes, dear madam. He—he—"

"Stop! I had almost forgotten my duty. Tell me first of the armies of my king. The king first of all with our house, you know."

Poor Seymour! he must overwhelm her with bad news in every field of her affection. For a moment he almost wished the results had been the other way. The perspiration stood out upon his forehead in spite of the coldness, and he felt he would rather charge a battery than face this terrible old woman who put the armies of a king—and such a king too—before the fate of her only son! And yet he knew that what he had to tell her would break down even her iron will, and reaching the mother's heart beating warm within her in spite of her assumed coldness and self-repression, would probably give her a death-blow. He felt literally like a murderer before her, but he had to answer. Talbot's own letter, General Washington's command, and the promptings of his own affection had made him an actor in this pathetic drama. He had no choice but to proceed. The truth must be told. Nerving himself to the inevitable, he replied to her question,—

"The armies of the king have been defeated and forced to retire. General Washington has outmanoeuvred and out-fought them; they are now shut up in New York again. The Jerseys are free, and we have taken upward of two thousand prisoners, and many are killed and wounded among them,—on both sides, in truth," he added.

"The worst news first," she replied. "One knows not why these things are so. It seems the God of Justice slumbers when subjects rebel against their rightful kings! But I have faith, sir. The right will win in the end—must win."

"So be it," he said, accepting the implied challenge, but adding nothing further. He would wait to be questioned now, and this strange woman should have the story in the way that pleased her best. As for her she could not trust herself to speak. Never before had her trembling body, her beating heart escaped from the domination of her resolute will. Never before had her mobile lips refused to formulate the commands of her active brain. She fought her battle out in silence, and finally turned toward him once more.

"There was something else you said, I think. My—my son?" Her voice sank to a whisper; in spite of herself one hand went to her heart. Ah, mother, mother, this was indeed thy king! "Is—is he wounded?—My God, sir! Not dead?"

His open hand which he had extended to her held two little objects. What were they? The bright sunlight was reflected from one of them, the locket she had given him. There was a dark discoloration on one side of it which she had never seen before. The other was his Prayer Book. O God—prayer! Was there then a God, that such things could happen? Where was He that day? She had given that book to him when he was yet a child. "Dead,"—she whispered,—"dead," shrinking back and staring at him.

"Would God I had died in his place, dear madam!" he said with infinite pity.

"How—how was it?" she went on, dry-eyed, in agony, moistening her cracking lips.

"Fighting like a hero over the body of General Mercer at Princeton. His men retreated and left them—"

"The rebel cowards," she interrupted.

"Nay, not cowards, but perhaps less brave than he. The British charged with their bayonets; our men had not that weapon, they fell back."

"Were you there, sir?"

"Surely not! Should I be here now if I had been there then, madam?" he replied proudly.

"True, true! you at least are a gentleman. Forgive the question."

"General Mercer and some of his officers sprang at the line. I had it from his own lips. Some one cut the general down; Hilary interposed, and enabled him to rise to his feet; they were attacked, fought bravely until—until—they died."

Stricken to the death at least, but determined to die as the rest had died, fighting, she drew herself up resolutely, and lifted her hand to that pitiless heaven above her. "So—be—it—unto—all—the—enemies—" When had he heard her say that before, he wondered in horror. She stopped, her face went whiter before him, the light went out of it.

"Oh, my son, my son—O God, my son, my son—Oh, give him back, my son—my son!" She reeled and fell against him, moaning and beating the air with her little feeble hands. The break had come at last; she was no longer a Talbot, but a woman. With infinite pity and infinite care he half led, half carried her into the house, and then, after being bidden not to summon assistance, he sank down on his knees by her side, where she lay on the sofa in the parlor, crushed, broken, feeble, helpless, old. With many interruptions he told her the sad story. He laid the long dark lock of hair he had cut from her son's head in her hand. There was a letter from George Washington which he read to her, in which, after many tender words of consolation, he spoke of Talbot as "one who would have done honor to any country." He told her of that military funeral, the kind words of Cornwallis, the guard of honor, the soldiers of the king, and then he put Talbot's own letter to him before her, and she must be told of the loss of the frigate. Kate dead too, and Colonel Wilton. Alas, poor friends! But all her plans and hopes were gone; what mattered it—what mattered anything now!

"Oh, what a load must those unrighteous men bear before God who have inaugurated this wicked war!" she cried; but no echo of her reproach was heard in the houses of

Parliament in London, or whispered in the antechamber of the king, to whom, assuredly, they belonged.

And by and by he left her. It wrung his heart so to do, but the call of duty was stronger than her need. His ship was ready, or would be in a short time, and he had snatched a few days from his pressing work to fulfil this task. His presence was absolutely necessary on the vessel, and he must go. Saying nay to her piteous plea that he should stay, and most reluctantly refusing her proffers of hospitality, after leaving with her the letters and the pictures, he left the room. But in the doorway he looked back at her. The tears had come at last. Moved by a sudden impulse, he ran back and knelt down by her, and took her old face between his hands and kissed her.

"Good-by, dear madam," he whispered; "would it had been I!"

She laid her thin hands upon his head.

"Good-by," she whispered; "God bless you. Oh, my boy— my boy!" She turned her face to the wall in bitterness, and so he fled.

On the brow of the hill one could see, if he were keen-eyed, the Wilton place. There was the boat-house. There she had said she loved him. He struck spurs to his horse and galloped madly away. Was there nothing but grief and sorrow, then, under the sun?

The lawyer and the doctor and the minister were with Madam Talbot all that day, but it was little they could do. She added a codicil to her will with the lawyer, submissively took the medicine the doctor left her, and listened quietly to the prayers of the priest. In the morning they found her whiter, stiller, calmer than ever. She had gone to meet her son in that new country where none rebel against the King!

Cyrus Townsend Brady

BOOK IV

A DEATH GRAPPLE ON THE DEEP

CHAPTER XXX

A SAILOR'S OPINION OF THE LAND

It was a delightful morning in February. The Continental ship Randolph, a tight little thirty-two-gun frigate, the first to get to sea of those ordered by Congress in 1775, was just leaving the beautiful harbor of Charleston, South Carolina, by way of the main ship channel, on her maiden cruise, under the command of Captain John Seymour Seymour, late first lieutenant of the Ranger. This was the second departure she had taken from that port. Forced by severe damages, incurred in an encounter with a heavy gale shortly after leaving Philadelphia, to put into that harbor for needed repairs to the new and unsettled vessel, she had put to sea again after a short interval, and in one week had taken six valuable prizes, one of them, an armed vessel of twenty guns, after a short action. After this brief and brilliant excursion she had put back to Charleston to dispose of her prizes, re-collect her prize crews, and land her prisoners.

There was another motive, however, for the sudden return. From one of the prizes it had been learned that the English thirty-two-gun frigate Carrysford, the twenty-gun sloop Perseus, the sixteen-gun sloop Hinchinbrook, with several privateers, had been cruising off the coast together, and the commander of the Randolph was most anxious to get the help of some of the South Carolina State cruisers to go in search of the British ships. The indefatigable Governor Rutledge, when the news had been communicated to him, had worked assiduously to provide the State ships, and the young captain of the Randolph speedily found himself at the head of a little fleet of war vessels outward bound.

The departure of the squadron, the Randolph in the lead, the rest following, and all under full sail, made a pretty picture to the enthusiastic Carolinians, who watched them from the islands and fortifications in the harbor, and from a number of small boats which accompanied the war ships a short distance on their voyage. Besides Seymour's own vessel, there were the eighteen-gun ship General Moultrie, the two sixteen-gun ships Notre Dame and Polly, and the fourteen-gun brig Fair American; the last commanded by a certain master, Philip Wilton. They made officers of very young men in those days, and mere boys often occupied positions of trust and responsibility apparently far beyond their years,—even Seymour himself, though now a commodore or flag officer by courtesy, was very young for the position; and Governor Rutledge, moved by a warm friendship of long standing for old Colonel Wilton, and upon Seymour's own urgent recommendation, had intrusted the smallest vessel to young Captain Philip. We shall see how he showed himself worthy of the trust reposed in him in spite of his tender years.

All of these ships were converted merchantmen, hastily fitted out, poorly adapted for any warlike purpose, and, with the exception of the Fair American, exceedingly slow and unwieldy; but the heart of the young commander filled with pride as he surveyed the little squadron, which followed in his wake, looking handsome enough under full sail. It was a great trust and responsibility reposed in his skill and experience; doubtless it was the only fleet the country had assembled, or could assemble, at that time; the ships were certainly not as he would have desired them, but they were the best that could be got together; and manned and officered by devoted men, they could at least fight ships of their own size when the time came, and he trusted to be able to give a good account of the enemy, should they be so fortunate as to fall in with them. As for his own vessel, as his practised and critical eye surveyed the graceful proportions of the new and well-appointed ship, Seymour felt entirely satisfied with her. He regarded with pleasant appreciation the decks white as constant holy-stoning could make them, the long rows of grim black guns thrusting out their formidable muzzles on either side, and the lofty spars covered with clouds of new and snowy canvas. Everything was as neat and trim, and as ready, as ardor, experience, and ability, coupled with a generous expenditure from his own purse, could make them. He was satisfied with his officers and crew too. Seymour's reputation, his recent association with Paul Jones, the romantic story of his last successful cruise, the esteem in which he was held by Washington, and his own charming personality had conspired to render him a great favorite, and he had had the pick of Philadelphia's hardy seamen and gallant officers ere he sailed away. The three hundred and odd seamen and marines who comprised the crew were as fit and capable a body of men as ever trod the deck of a ship. Constant exercise and careful instruction, and drill and target practice, had made them exceedingly able in all the necessary manoeuvres, and in the handling of the guns.

Forward on the forecastle old Bentley was planted, surrounded by such of the older and more experienced petty officers and men as he permitted to associate with him on terms of more or less familiarity. Not only the position he occupied, that of boatswain of the frigate, gave him a vast importance with the men, but his age and experience, his long association with the captain, as well as some almost incredible tales of his familiar companionship with certain men of awe-inspiring name and great renown, with various mighty feats of arms in recent campaigns, vaguely current, conduced to make him the monarch of the forecastle, and the arbiter of the various discussions and arguments among the men, who rarely ventured to dispute the dictum of their oracle.

"Well, here we are pointing out again, thank the Lord!" he said to his particular friend and crony among the crew, the carpenter, Richard Spicer, a battered old shell-back, like himself. "There is only one place from which I like to see the land, Richard!"

"And where is that, bosun?"

"Over the stern, as now, mate, when we're going free with a fair wind, and leaving it fast behind. I feel safer then. A time since and I felt as if I never wanted to see it again from any place. To think of me, a decent God-fearing, seafaring man, at my time of life, turning soldier!" It is not in the power of written language to express the peculiar intonation of contempt which the old man laid upon that inoffensive word, "soldier." No one venturing to interrupt him, after staring at his particular aversion for a few moments, he went on more mildly, and in a reflective tone,—

"Not but what I have seen some decent soldiers—a few. There was old Blodgett, and young Mr. Talbot, ay, and General Washington too! Now there's a man for you, ship-mates. Lord, what a sailorman he would have made! They tell me he had a midshipman's warrant offered him when he was a lad once, and actually refused it—refused it! preferred to be a soldier, and what a chance he lost! Might have been an admiral by now!"

"I've heard tell as how 't was his mother that prevented him from goin' to sea—when he was ready an' willin' an' waitin' to get aboard," returned one of the men.

"May be, may be. The result's the same. You never can tell what women, and 'specially mothers, will do. They're necessary, of course, leastways it's generally believed we all had 'em, though I remember none myself, nor Captain Seymour neither, and he's a pretty good sort of a man—let alone me—but they've no place aboard ship. Now look what this one did,—spoiled a man that had the makin's of a first-class sailor in him, and turned him into a soldier!"

"But where would we be in this country of ours now, bosun, if it were not for the soldiers? No, no, don't be too hard on this man, Captain Washington; he's done his duty, and is doing it very well, too, so I 'm told, accordin' to your own account, matey," replied the old carpenter; "and soldiers is good too—in their places, that is, of course," he went on deprecatingly. "There are two kinds of men, as I take it, William, to do the fightin' in this world, sailormen and soldiermen; each has a place, a station to fill, and something to do, and one can't do t' other's work. Look at that there blasted marine, aft there in the gangway, for instance; he's a good man, I make no manner o' doubt, and he has got his place on this barkey, even if he is only a kind of a soldier and no sailorman at all."

"Now I asks you, Chips, what particular good are soldiers, anyway, leaving marines out of the question, for they do live on ships," said the old sailorman. "What can they do that we can't? They can fight, and fight hard—I've seen 'em, but so can we," he continued, extending his brawny arm; "and they can march, too,—I've seen their bloody footmarks in the snow; but there were sailormen there that kept right alongside of 'em and did all that they could do. Oh, I forgot one thing—they can ride horses, that's one thing I could never learn at all! You'd ought to seen me on one of the land-lubberly brutes. A horse has no place on shipboard, no more than a woman, and I've no use for either of 'em. But if this country would spend all its money buying ships, and man 'em with real first-class sailormen, why, d'ye see, King George's men could never land on our shores at all. We'd keep 'em off, and then there'd be no use for the soldiers; they could all go a-farming. No, give me ships every time, they always win. I know what I am talking about; I have been on the shore for a month at a time until I thought I would turn into mud itself. No, 't is not even a fit place to be buried in; 'earth to earth' won't do for me when I die; I just want to be dropped overboard—there."

"There is one time ships didn't win," said the carpenter, persisting in the argument, and pointing aft to the low mounds of sand backed by the rudely interlaced palmetto logs, behind which the gallant Moultrie had fought Barker's fleet six months before, until the ships had been driven off in defeat.

"Those were British ships, man," said the old sailor, with contempt. "I meant Americans, of course; it makes all the difference in the world. But as for land—I hate it. It's only good to grow vegetables, and soft tack, and fresh water, and tar, and timber, and breed children to make sailormen out of—why, it's a sort of a cook's galley, a kitchen they call it there, for the sea at best! Give me the sight of blue water, and let me have the solid feel of the deck beneath my feet; no unsteady earth for me!"

"Well, that's my own opinion, too, bo. But, after all, that's all that ships is good for, anyway; just to sail from land to land and take people and things from place to place. The sea's between like."

"You look at it the wrong way, mate. Certain of us men have sense enough to live on the sea, and keep away from land, except for water and provision. We go from sea to sea, and land's between."

"And what would you do for a country if we had no land? You're always talking about lovin' your country, bosun."

"Ay, that I do," said the old man. "I look upon a country, that is a land country, as a kind of necessary evil. My country's this ship, and yon flag, what it means and stands for. It means liberty, free waters, no interference with peaceful traders on the high seas, following their rightful pursuits, by British ships-of-war. Every man that has ever been aboard of one of those floating hells knows what liberty is not, well enough. No taxing of us by a Parliament on t' other side of the world, neither. No king but the captain. Freedom! So free that the lubberliest landsman on shore has a right to govern himself—if he can—subject to discipline and the commands of his superior officer, of course; and, besides, it's like a man's wife; if he's got to have one, he may beat her and abuse her, perhaps, but nobody else shall. No! Land's a pretty poor sort of a thing in general, but that aft there is the best there is going, and it's our own. We'll die for it, yes, for love of it, if it comes to that, even if we do hate it, on general principles mind, you understand."

There was evidently a trace of Irish blood in the old sailor, it would seem, and so saying, with a wave of his hand, which brushed aside further argument, he turned abruptly on his heel and walked aft. In spite of all his words, which only reflected the usual opinion of sailors, in those days at least, he yielded to no man in patriotism and devotion to the cause of liberty and the land that gave him birth. And no man in all Washington's army had done better service, marched more cheerfully, or fought harder than this veteran seaman. The men on the forecastle generally agreed with him in his propositions, but the obstinate old carpenter, with the characteristic tenacity of the ancient tar, maintained the discussion forward, until the sharp voice of the officer of the deck sent all hands to the braces. The ship was brought to the wind on the starboard tack, a manoeuvre which was followed in succession by the other vessels of the squadron, which had been previously directed to keep, though still within signal, at long distances from each other during the day, closing up at night, in order to spread a broad clew and give greater chance of meeting the enemy.

The young captain paced the quarter-deck alone—no man is ever so much alone among his fellows as the commander of a ship—a prey to his own sad thoughts. Those who had known him the gayest of gay young sailors in Philadelphia were at a loss to account for the change which had come over him. He had become the gravest of the grave, his cheery laugh was heard no more, and the baffled young belles of Charleston had voted him a confirmed woman-hater; though his melancholy, handsome face, graceful person, distinguished bearing, and high station might have enabled him to pick and choose where he would. But there was room in his heart for no more passions. Even his love of country and liberty had degenerated into a slow, cold hate for the British, and a desperate resolve to do his duty, and make his animosity tell when he struck. A dangerous man under whom to sail, gentleman of the Randolph, and a dangerous man to meet, as well. He could not forget Kate, and, except in the distraction of a combat, life was a mere mechanical routine for him. But because he had been well trained he went through it well—biding his time.

CHAPTER XXXI

SEYMOUR'S DESPERATE RESOLUTION

Six rather uneventful days passed by, during which prizes to the number of five fell to the lot of the squadron, one loaded with military stores, and another with provisions of great value. The lively little Fair American, being far to windward of the fleet, had also a smart action with a heavily armed British privateer, which struck her flag before the others could get within range, and was found to be loaded with valuable portable goods, the siftings of a long and successful cruise. Young Wilton had manoeuvred and fought his ship well, and had been publicly complimented in general orders by Seymour for skill and gallantry. The fleet had been exercised in signals and in various simple evolutions, the weather was most pleasant, the men in excellent spirits, and all that was necessary to complete their happiness was the appearance of the looked-for squadron of the enemy. The eager lookouts swept the seas unweariedly, but in vain, until early in the afternoon of the sixth day, the fleet being in Longitude 58 degrees 18 minutes West, Latitude 14 degrees 30 minutes North, about forty leagues east of Martinique, heading due west on the starboard tack, it was reported to Seymour, who was reading in the cabin, that the Fair American, again far in the lead and somewhat to windward, had signalled a large sail ahead. A short time should make her visible, if the vessels continued on the present course, and, after having called his fleet about him by signal, Seymour stood on for a nearer look at the stranger. An hour later she was visible from the deck of the Randolph, a very large ship, evidently a man-of-war under easy sail. The careful watchers could count three tiers of guns through the glass, which proclaimed her a ship of the line. From her motions, and the way she rose before them, she was evidently a very speedy ship, capable of outsailing every vessel of Seymour's little fleet without difficulty, except possibly the brig Fair American. It would be madness for the squadron of converted and lightly armed merchantmen to attack a heavy ship of that class,—all who got near enough to do so would probably be sunk or captured; yet the approaching vessel must be delayed or checked, or the result would be equally serious to the fleet. Seymour at once formed a desperate resolution. Signalling to the four State cruisers and the six prizes to tack to the northeast, escape if possible, and afterward make the best of their way back to Charleston, he himself stood on with the little Randolph to engage the mighty stranger. At first the older seamen could scarce believe their eyes. Was it possible that Captain Seymour, in a small thirty-two-gun frigate, was about to engage deliberately and wilfully in a combat with a ship of the line, a seventy-four!—the difference in the number of guns giving no indication of the difference in the offensive qualities of the two ships, which might better be shown by a ratio of four or five to one in favor of the ship of the line. It was like matching a bull terrier against a mastiff. The men half suspected some wily manoeuvre which they could not divine; but as the moments fled away and they saw the rest of the fleet and the prizes slipping rapidly away to the northeast, the Fair American lagging unaccountably behind the rest of the fleet, while they still held their even course, they began to comprehend that they were to fight to save the fleet, and Seymour meant to sacrifice them deliberately, if necessary, in the hope of so crippling the enemy that his other little cruisers, and the prizes, might escape. They were not daunted, however—your true Jack is a reckless fellow—by the daring and desperate nature of the plan; quite the contrary!

In a few moments the familiar tones of Bentley's powerful voice, seconded by the cheery calls of his mates, rang through the frigate,—

"All hands clear ship for action—Ahoy!"

The piercing whistling of the pipes which followed was soon drowned by the steady and stirring roll of the drums, accompanied by the shrill notes of the fifes, beating to quarters. The old call, which has been the prelude to every action on the sea, ushering in with the same dreadful note of preparation every naval conflict for twice two hundred years, went rolling along the decks. At the first tap of the drum the men sprang, with the eagerness of unleashed hounds before the quarry, to their several stations.

In an instant the orderly ship was a babel of apparently hopeless confusion; the men running hastily to and fro about their various duties, the sharp commands of the officers, the shrill piping of the whistles, and the deep voices of the gun captains and the boatswain's mates, made the usually quiet deck a pandemonium. Some of the seamen stowed the hammocks on the rail to serve as a guard against shot and splinters, others triced up stout netting fore and aft, as a protection against boarders. The light and agile sail-trimmers rove extra slings on the yards, and put stoppers on the more important rigging, and tightened and strengthened the boats' gripes. The cabin bulkheads were unceremoniously knocked down and stowed away, giving a clean sweep fore and aft the decks. The pumps were rigged and tried, and hose led along the deck. Arm chests were broken out and opened, and cutlasses and pistols distributed, and the racks filled with boarding-pikes. Division tubs filled with water were placed beside the guns, and the decks sanded lest they should grow slippery with blood. The magazine, surrounded by a wetted woollen screen to prevent fire, was opened, and grape and solid shot broken out and piled in the racks about the hatchways near the guns, the heavy sea lashings of which were cast loose by the different crews, after which they were loaded and run out and temporarily secured, the slow matches having been carefully examined and lighted. The oldest quartermasters took their places near the helm, and others, assisted by a small body of men, manned the relieving tackles below, to be used in case, as frequently happened, the wheel should be shot away. The officers, many of whom put on boarding caps of light steel with dropped cheek pieces, and covered with fur, fastened on their arms, looked to the priming of their pistols, and then hastened to their various stations.

Most of the watch officers, under the direction of the first lieutenant or executive officer, were to take charge of the different gun divisions in the batteries; though one of them remained aft near the captain, to look after the spars and rigging, command the sail-trimmers, and see that any order of the captain touching the moving of the ship was promptly carried out. The surgeon and his mates went below into the gloomy cockpit, spreading out the foreboding array of ghastly instruments and appliances, ready for the many demands certain to be made upon them. Some of the ubiquitous midshipmen commanded little groups of expert riflemen in the tops, which were well provided with hand grenades; others assisted the division lieutenants; and several were detailed as aids to the commanding officer. The little company of marines, under its own officers, was drawn up on the quarter-deck to keep down the fire of the enemy's small-arm men, and be ready to repel boarders, or head an attack, if the ships should come in contact. In that case grapnels, strong iron hooks securely fastened to the ends of stout ropes or slender iron chains, were provided at convenient intervals along the bulwarks, ready for catching and lashing the two ships together.

The men, their other duties performed, gradually settled down at the guns, or about the masts, or in the tops, in their several stations, many of them naked to the waist, and their deep voices could be heard answering to their names as they were mustered by the officers. In an incredibly short time the whole was done, and the impressive quiet was broken only by the excited voice of the first lieutenant, Nason—a young officer, and this his first serious battle—reporting to the gloomy captain that the ship was clear and ready for action.

Seymour had of course taken personal charge of the deck himself. Oh, he thought, after scanning closely the approaching ship with great care, if he had only a ship of the line under his command, instead of this little frigate, how gladly would he have entered the coming conflict! Or if his own small vessel had been, instead, one of those heavy frigates which afterward did so much to uphold the glory of American arms, and exhibit the skill and audacity of American seamen, in their subsequent conflict with Great Britain, he might have had a better chance; but none realized more entirely than he did himself the utter hopelessness of the undertaking which was before him. At the same time he was determined to carry it through, seeing, as few others could, the absolute necessity for the sacrifice, if he were to effect the escape of his fleet. Calling the men aft, he spoke briefly to them, pointing out the necessity for the conflict, and the nobility of this sacrifice. He entreated them, in a few brave, manly, thrilling words, to stand by him to the last, for the love of their country and the honor of their flag. As for him, he declared it to be his fixed purpose never to give up the ship, but to sink alongside rather, trusting before that happened, however, so to damage his mighty antagonist as to compel her to relinquish the pursuit. The men, filled with the desire for battle, and inspired by his heroic words, were nerved up to the point where they would cheerfully have attacked not one line-of-battle ship but a whole fleet! They answered him with frantic cheers, swearing and vowing that they would stand by him to the bitter end; and then, everything having been done that could be done, in perfect silence the taut frigate boldly approached her massive enemy.

Cyrus Townsend Brady

CHAPTER XXXII

THE PRISONERS ON THE YARMOUTH

It is usually not difficult for an individual to define the conditions of happiness. If I only had so and so, or if I only were so and so, and the thing is done. Each successive state, however, suggests one more happy, and each gratified wish leads to another desire more imperative. Miss Katharine Wilton, however, did not confine her conditions to units. There were in her case three requisites for happiness,— perfect happiness,—and could they have been satisfied, in all probability she would have come as near to the wished-for state as poor humanity on this earth ever does come to that beatific condition. She certainly thought so, and with characteristic boldness had not refrained from communicating her thoughts to her father.

The astonishing feature of the situation was that he was inclined to agree with her. There was nothing astonishing in itself in his agreement with her, for he usually did agree with her, but in that her conditions were really his own. For it is rare, blessedly so, that two people feel that they require the same thing to complete the joy of life, and when they parallel on three points 't is most remarkable. Even two lovers require each other—very different things, I am sure. Stop! I am not so sure about the third proviso with the colonel. I say the third, because Miss Wilton put it number three, though perhaps it was like a woman's postscript, which somehow suggests the paraphrase of a familiar bit of Scripture,—the last, not will be, but should be, first!

Here are the requisites. One: The flag floating gracefully from the peak of the spanker gaff above them, in the light air of the sunny afternoon, should be the stars and stripes, instead of the red cross of St. George! Two: The prow of the ship should be turned to the wooded shores of Virginia, and the Old Dominion should be her destination instead of the chalk cliffs of England! Three: that a certain handsome, fair, blue-eyed, gallant sailor, who answered to the name of John Seymour, should be by her side instead of another, even though that other were one who had once saved her life, and to whose care and kindness and forethought she was much indebted. Her present attendant was certainly a gentleman; and to an unprejudiced eye—which hers certainly was not— quite as handsome and distinguished and gallant as was his favored rival, and boasting one advantage over the other in that he bore a titled name—not such a desideratum among American girls at that time, however, as it was afterwards destined to become; and in a girl of the stamp of Miss Katharine Wilton, possibly no advantage at all.

But, could the heart of that fair damsel be known, all talk of advantage or disadvantage, or this or that compensating factor, was absolutely idle! She was not a girl who did things by halves; and the feeling which had prompted her to give herself to the young sailor, though of sudden origin, had grown and grown during the days of absence and confine- ment, till, in depth and intensity, it matched his own. She was not now so sure that, among the other objects of her adoration, he would have to take the second place; that, in case of division, her heart would lead her to think first of her country. Insensibly had his image supplanted every other, and with all the passionate devotion of her generous southern nature she loved him.

Lord Desborough had ample opportunity for ascertaining this fact. He had seen her risk her life for Seymour's own. He could never forget the glorious picture she made standing across the prostrate form of that young man, pistol in hand, keeping the mob at bay, never wavering, never faltering, clear-eyed, supreme. He would be almost willing to die to have her do the like for him. He could still hear the echo of that bitter cry,—"Seymour! Seymour!"—which rang through the house when they had dragged her away. These things were not pleasant reminiscences, but, like most other unpleasant memories, they would not down. In spite of all this, however, he had allowed himself—nay, his permission he vowed had not been asked—to fall violently in love with this little colonial maiden, and a country maiden at that! Not being psychologically inclined, he had never attempted to analyze her charm or to explain his sensations. Realizing the fact, and being young and therefore hopeful, he had not allowed himself to despair. Really, he had some claims upon her. Had he not interfered, she would have been murdered that night in the dining-room. He had earned the gratitude then and there of her father, and of herself as well; and he had earned more of it too when he had shot dead a certain brutal marauding blackguard by the name of Johnson, at the first convenient opportunity, having received incidentally, in return for his message of death, a bullet in his own breast to remind him that there are always two persons and two chances in a duel. A part of the debt of the Wiltons had been paid by the assiduous and solicitous care with which they— Katharine chiefly, of course—had nursed him through the long and dangerous illness consequent upon his wound. It was his interest which had prevented further ill treatment of them by the brutal and tyrannous Dunmore, and, had Katharine so elected, would have secured her freedom. She had, however, to Desborough's great delight, chosen to accompany her father to England, where he was to be sent as a prisoner of high political consequence.

After waiting many weary days at the camp of the fugitive and deposed governor at Gwynn's Island, they had been separated from Desborough, and unceremoniously hustled on board the frigate Radnor, which was under orders for England. They had stopped long enough at Norfolk to witness Dunmore's savage and vindictive action in bombarding and burning that helpless town; and from that point Katharine had been enabled to send her letter to Seymour, through a friendly American spy, just before taking departure for their long voyage across the seas. The orders of the Radnor had been changed at the last moment, however, and she had been directed to go in pursuit of Jones and the Ranger, which it was currently reported had got to sea from the Delaware Bay, bound for Canada and the Newfoundland coast. No vessel being ready for England at that time, the two prisoners had been transferred, fortunately for them, to a small ship bound to the naval station at Barbadoes; and thence, after another weary dreary wait, had been sent on board his Britannic majesty's ship Yarmouth, Captain John Vincent, bound home for England. The first lieutenant of this ship happened to be a certain Patrick Michael Philip O'Neal Drummond, Lord Desborough, son and heir to the Earl of Desmond! He congratulated himself most heartily upon his good fortune.

Providence had, then, thrown a lover again at Katharine's feet. Not that there was anything unusual in that. She might not regard it in a providential light, however; but he, at least did so, and he had intended to improve the shining hours of what would be a long cruise, in the close association permitted by the confined limits of the ship, to make a final desperate effort to win the heart which had hitherto so entirely eluded him that he could not flatter himself that he had made the least impression upon it. His success during the first three or four days of the cruise had not been brilliant. She had been unaffectedly glad to see him apparently, and gentle and kind in her reception,—too kind, he thought, with the circumspection of a lover,—but that was all. To add to his trials, he soon found himself not without rivals nearer at home than Seymour. Judging by present results, Washington, if he had a few regiments of Katharines, could carry consternation to the whole British army! For the captors had, apparently, taken the oath of allegiance to the captured, and the whole ship's company, from that gruff old sailor Captain Vincent down through all the other officers to the impudent and important little midshipman, were her devoted slaves. Even Jack forward, usually entirely unresponsive to the doings aft on the quarterdeck, put on an extra flourish or so, and damning his eyes, after the manner of the unsophisticated sailorman, gazed appreciatively upon her beauty, envying those fortunate mortals privileged to radiate about her person. Vincent might be the captain, but Katharine was certainly the queen of the ship. Colonel Wilton, too, shone, not altogether by reflected lustre either; and the considerate officers had done everything possible to make him forget that he was a prisoner.

Early one afternoon in the beginning of February, the Yarmouth, being under all plain sail with the wind two or three points abaft the beam, was bowling along under a fresh breeze about a day's sail east of Martinique. The weather was perfect, and because of the low latitude, in spite of the winter season, there was no touch of sharpness in the air, which was warm and delightful. All the necessary drills and exercises having been concluded earlier in the day, the whole ship's company was enjoying a period of unusual relaxation and idleness. The men at the wheel, the lookouts kept constantly at the mastheads, the marines doing sentry duty, with the midshipmen of the watch and the officer of the deck busily pacing to and fro, were the only people, out of the six hundred and odd men who made up the ship's complement, who presented any appearance of activity whatever. The men of the watch on and the watch off, dinner being over, were sitting or lounging about in all sorts of easy attitudes,—some of them busy with their needles; others overhauling their clothes-bags, to which they had been given access that afternoon; others grouped about some more brilliant story-teller than the rest, eagerly drinking in the multifarious details of some exciting personal experience, or romantic adventure, or never-ending story of shipwreck or battle, or mystery—technically, yarns! Colonel Wilton was standing aft with Captain Vincent in the shadow of the spanker. Miss Wilton, with Chloe, her black maid, behind her chair, was sitting near the break of the poop-deck, looking forward, surrounded by several lieutenants; Desborough being at her right hand, of course, feeling and looking unusually gloomy and morose. One or two of the oldest and boldest midship-men were also lingering on the outskirts of the group, as near to their divinity as they dared come in the presence of their superior officers. The conversation happening to turn, as it frequently did, upon the subject of the present war between England and the colonies engaged in rebellion against the paternal power, was unusually animated.

CHAPTER XXXIII

TWO PROPOSALS

"Oh, you know, Miss Wilton, if the colonies—" began one of the officers, vehemently.

"Pardon me, Mr. Hollins, that is hardly the correct term. The *late* colonies would be better," interrupted Katharine, with much spirit.

"Oh, well, you know, I am merely anticipating, of course; we'll have them back fast enough, after while. Now, if they—"

"Pardon me again, sir, but that is another contention I can hardly admit. You'll never have them back,—never, never!"

"Oh, come, Miss Wilton," said another, "you surely do not think the colonies—oh, well, the late colonies, if you will insist upon it—can maintain a fight with the power of Great Britain, for any length of time! Why, madam, the English spirit—"

"Well, sir, what else have we but the English spirit? What other blood runs in our veins, pray? Just as you love and prize your liberty, so too do we, and we will not be dominated and ruled over, even by our brothers. No, no, Mr.

Beauchamp, or you, either, Mr. Hollins; it is no use. We are just as determined as you are; and there is but one way to win back the colonies, as you call them, to their allegiance."

"And how is that, pray?"

"Why, by depopulating them, overwhelming them, killing the people, and wasting the land. Only a war of extermination will serve your purpose."

"Well," said Hollins, doggedly, "if they must have it, they must—let it be extermination! The authority of the king and the power of Parliament must be upheld at all hazards."

"Ah, that is easy enough to say," replied Katharine, "but three millions of English-speaking liberty-loving people are not to be blotted out by a wave of the hand; they are not so easily exterminated, as you will find. Besides, it is easy to speak in general terms; but thousands and thousands are young and helpless, or old and feeble,—grandsires or women or children,—how about them? As long as there is a woman left or a child, your task is yet unfulfilled. Make a personal application of it; I am one of them. Do you wish to exterminate me, sir?" she said, looking up at him brilliantly, with her glorious brown eyes.

"Oh, you—you are different, of course," said the lieutenant, hesitatingly, not liking to face this intensely personal application of his intemperate remark.

"Not I! I am just like the rest—"

"Treason! I won't hear it," said Desborough, softly. "There are no others like you on earth."

"Just like the rest," she continued emphatically, unheeding

the interruption, which the others had hardly caught, "and I will tell you that never again will that flag at the gaff there be the flag of America. You have lost us for good."

"Oh, don't say that. Make a personal exception of yourself at least, Miss Wilton, and give us room to hope a little."

"No, no," she laughed. "You have lost us all—me included."

There was a chorus of expostulation and argument immediately, but Miss Wilton was not to be overborne.

"Father!" she called quickly to the colonel, who, followed by the captain, at once joined the little group of officers. "These gentlemen seem to doubt me when I say their sometime colonies are gone for good. Won't you help me to state the point so they will understand it?"

"Gentlemen," said the old colonel, slowly and impressively, "the colonies were the most loyal and devoted portion of the king's dominion at one time. I have been up and down the length and breadth of them, I know the feeling. I was for years a soldier of the king myself,—with your fathers, young sirs,—and I can bear witness that no part of the kingdom responded with such alacrity to every legitimate demand upon it by the home government. Never did men so readily and willingly offer themselves and their goods for the service of the king. But it is all changed now. The change came slowly, but it came inevitably and surely, and you could no more change the present conditions than you could turn back the sun in its course. England has lost her colonies—"

"Her late colonies," corrected Katharine, softly.

"Yes, yes, of course, her late colonies, that is, beyond

possibility of recovery. We will not be taxed without representation."

"But suppose that we gave you the representation for which you asked, colonel. How then? Would not there be a general return to allegiance in that event?" queried the captain.

"Sir," replied the colonel, proudly, "the child who has once learned to walk alone does not afterward go back to creeping and crawling, or stumbling along by the aid of his mother's hand. We have tasted our independence, enjoyed it, and now we mean to keep it."

"Splendid, sir! splendid, father!" cried the delighted Katharine. "There speaks the spirit of Runnymede, and Naseby, too, gentlemen!"

"Hush, hush, my child!" chided the colonel, half amusedly; "it is only the spirit of a plain man who has learned to love liberty by studying the history of his ancestry and his people."

"Ah, but, colonel, how are you going to get that liberty without fighting for it?" asked Beauchamp, with rash temerity. "Howe and Cornwallis, for instance, have been pursuing Washington for six months, and could never get near enough to fire a shot at him, so they say."

"Fight, sir, fight!" exclaimed the colonel, in astonished wrath; "why, God bless me, sir, I am willing to stand out now and show you how they can fight!"

But Miss Katharine sprang to her feet: "And Bunker Hill, Mr. Beauchamp, and Long Island!" she cried impetuously.

Beauchamp backed away precipitately from before her in

great confusion, which invoked much mocking comment from the laughing officers round about him.

"Here is one time the English forces are routed by a rebel!" said Hollins.

"Yes," added Desborough, "but then Beauchamp is no worse off than the rest of us would be, if Miss Wilton were opposed to us."

"Well," continued another, coming to the rescue, "we won both of those engagements, you know, Miss Wilton, after all."

"Won! Who said anything about winning, sir? Anybody can win, if they have men enough or strength enough and money enough—we were talking about fighting, sir."

"But really, you know," went on Beauchamp, recovering, and returning to the charge, "Washington's army haven't fought since those days you speak of, and they must be wiped out of existence by now, I should suppose."

"Not if George Washington is still alive," interrupted the colonel, his anger at the inconsiderate officer having somewhat abated. "I know him well. I have known him from a boy,—met him first when I used to go shooting with Lord Fairfax out at Greenway Court. I knew his family; his brother Lawrence too, I was with him at Cartagena,—where I met your father, Lord Desborough, by the way,—and the world does not yet know the quality of that man. If he retreats, it is because he absolutely has to; and you will see, he will turn and strike Howe and Cornwallis some day such a blow as will make them reel. I should not wonder if he had done so already. 'T is six long weeks since we have heard any news from home. Trust me, gentlemen, the Americans will fight; and if there is a God of justice, they will win too."

"I would fight myself, had I but the opportunity," said Katharine, resolutely. "And there are hundreds of other women with the same feeling."

"Oh, Miss Wilton, you would find no enemies here to fight. We are all captives of your bow and spear now, and crave your mercy," said Desborough, meaningly.

"True, Mistress Katharine. I hardly know now who commands this ship, you or I!" said the captain, smiling at her.

"Alas, you do, Captain Vincent; were I the commander, we would be going that way," she replied, pointing off over the quarter, and gazing wistfully over the cool, sparkling water, the white-capped waves breaking beautifully away in every direction. "Oh, my poor, poor country, when shall I see you again?" she murmured; "when—"

"Sail ho!" floated down from the foremast head at this moment, and the idle ship awoke again.

"Where away?"

"Right ahead, sir."

Holmes and Beauchamp walked forward to get a look at the stranger, and the captain and the colonel stepped across to the weather side of the deck. Chloe was sent below to procure a wrap for her mistress, and Katharine was left alone for a few moments with Desborough. It was his first opportunity.

"Have you no curiosity as to the sail reported, Lieutenant Desborough?"

"No, Mistress Katharine, none whatever. I take no interest in anything but you. No, please don't go now," he went on in humble entreaty. "I wish to speak to you a moment. When you came aboard I hoped to see you often, to be with you alone—to win you—" His voice sank to a passionate whisper.

"My lord, my lord! it were best to go no further," she interrupted gravely. "'T is no use; you remember."

"Yes, yes, I remember everything,—everything about you, that is. I shut my eyes and feel the soft touch of your cool hand on my fevered head again, as when I had that bullet in my breast. Oh, it thrills me, maddens me! I'd be wounded so again, could I but feel those hands once more—Listen to me, you must listen! It cannot hurt you to hear me, and I am sure one of the others will be back in a moment; you are never alone," he said, detaining her almost forcibly. "I love you; you must know that I do. What is that land, or any land, beside my love? You are my country! I can give you lands, title, rank, luxury—Be pitiful to me, Mistress Katharine. What can I do or say or promise? You shall grace the court of the king, and be at the same time queen of my heart," he went on impetuously, his soul in his eager whisper. She turned and walked over to the lee rail, whither he followed her.

"I'd rather be in that land off yonder than be the king himself. I hate the king, and I could not love the enemy of my country! No, no," she replied, "it cannot be—it can never be!"

"Pshaw! Your country,—that's not the reason; you love him

still," he went on jealously, "that sailor."

"Yes, 't is true; I love a sailor—you are not he."

"But he is dead! You left him lying there on the floor in the hall, you remember, and since then have heard nothing. He is surely dead."

"It is cruel of you to say it," she went on relentlessly, "but I shall love his memory then. No, 't is useless—I respect you, admire you, am grateful to you, but my heart is there!" and she pointed away again.

"Won't you let me try to win you?" he persisted. "Don't say me nay altogether, give me some hope. If he be dead, let me have a chance. Oh, Katharine Wilton, I would give up anything for—"

A midshipman touched him on the arm. "Captain wants to see first lieutenant, sir!" he said with a wooden, impassive face, saluting the while.

With a smothered expression of rage, Desborough sprang across the deck,—for such a summons is not to be disregarded for an instant; even love gives way to the captain, on shipboard at least. The little midshipman was a great favorite with Katharine, and, grateful for the interruption, she accordingly laid her hand lightly and affectionately on the shoulder of the Honorable Giles Montagu, aged thirteen, one of the youngest and smallest middies in the ship; but he stood very straight and rigid, the personification of dignity, and endeavored to look very manly indeed.

"Thank you, Mr. Montagu," she said, somewhat to his surprise.

"Don't mention it, nothing at all, madam—orders! Got to obey orders, you know."

Katharine laughed. "You dear sweet child!" she said, and suddenly stooped and kissed him. The Honorable Giles turned pale, then flushed violently and burst into unmanly tears.

"Why, what is it? Don't you like to have me kiss you?" she said, amazed.

"It isn't that, Miss Wilton. I'd rather kiss you than—than anything; but you call me a boy, and treat me like a child, and—and I can't stand it. I—I've challenged all the men in the steerage about you already," alluding to the other little fellows of like rank; "they call me a baby there, too, because I 'm so little and so young. But I'll grow. And—I love you," he went on abruptly and determinedly, choking down his sobs and swallowing his tears, while fingering the handle of his dirk, and furtively rubbing his eyes with his other hand. "Oh, madam, if you would only wait until I got a frigate! Won't you? But no! You don't treat me like a man," he exclaimed bitterly, stamping his foot and turning away.

"Well, I never!" cried the astonished and abashed Katharine, completely overawed for the moment by this novel declaration. "What next?"

Truly, they made men out of boys early in those days. The next moment the hoarse cries of the boatswain and his mates, and the beating drums, called all hands to clear the ship for action and startled everybody into activity at once. The Honorable Giles, the manly if lachrymose midshipman, sprang forward to his station as rapidly as his small but sturdy legs could carry him.

CHAPTER XXXIV

CAPTAIN VINCENT MYSTIFIED

While the big ship was rapidly and methodically being stripped for the possible emergency, the captain was engaged in busy conversation with the colonel. They had steadily drawn near the reported sail until the lookouts could plainly make out a small fleet of small ships. Never dreaming that they could be American ships, Captain Vincent had his ship prepared for action, more through the habitual wariness of an experienced sailor than from any premonition of an impending battle. But as the two forces drew near, the actions of the opposing fleet became suddenly suspicious; all but one of them tacked ship, and stood off to the northeast, in a compact group in close order, under all possible sail, though one, the smallest and a brig, it was noticed, lagged behind the rest of the group in a way which bespoke either very slow sailing qualities or deliberate purpose of delay. The remaining ship, the largest of them all, stood boldly on its original course. This latter, it was plain to see, was a small frigate, possibly a twenty-eight or a thirty-two. Taking into account the respective rates of speed, the frigate, whose course made a slight angle with that of the ship of the line, would probably cross the bows of the latter within range of her battery. None of the opposing vessels showed any flags as yet, and their movements completely mystified

Captain Vincent.

"Certainly a most extraordinary performance going on there!" he said, after a long look through his glass, which he then handed to the colonel. "They show no flags, but I cannot conceive of their being anything but a squadron or a convoy of ours. What do you make them out, Colonel Wilton?"

Now, the colonel was morally certain that they were Americans, or, at least, that the first and nearest one was an American ship. He had been one of the naval committee which had taken charge of the building of the men-of-war ordered by Congress in '75; he had seen the Randolph frequently on the ways and after she was launched, and was entirely familiar with her lines. Perhaps the wish also was father to the thought, for the old soldier was not sufficiently versed in nautical affairs to detect at that distance the great disparity in force between the two ships, to which for the moment he gave no thought, or he would not have entertained hopes for a release from confinement by recapture,—a patent impossibility to a seaman. So he answered the captain evasively, returning the glass and pleading his ignorance of nautical matters to excuse his indefinite opinion.

"It must be the Carrysford, with Hythe's squadron; she is a thirty-two. But why they should act this way, I cannot see. He must know what we are now, as there are no ships of our size in these waters, except our own, and why should he send the rest of them off there? They are leaving us pretty fast, except that brig. Now, if it were a colonial convoy, I should say that this frigate was going to engage us in the hope of so crippling us as to effect the escape of the rest; but I hardly think that your men are up to that yet."

"Think not?" said the colonel indifferently, violently repressing an inclination to strike him. "It may be as you say,

Captain Vincent; still, I think we are up to almost anything that you are."

"Oh, colonel," laughed the captain, good-naturedly, "you are not going to compare the little colonial forces with his majesty's navy, are you! Now, I am morally certain that is a king's ship. See the beautiful set of her sails, the enormous spread of the yards; notice how trim and taut her rigging and running gear stand out, and then, too, see how smartly she is handled. Only English ships are thus. Hythe is a sailor, every inch of him," he went on in genuine admiration for the approaching vessel. "See! He has the weather gauge of us now, or will have. Not that it matters anything. We could afford to let him have it even if he were an enemy; but what he means by this sort of performance, I don't understand. However, we shall know in half an hour at least."

"Well, sir?" he said, turning toward Lieutenant Desborough, who at that moment stepped on the poop in fighting uniform, sword in hand.

"Ship's ready for action, sir!"

"Very good. Keep the people at their quarters, and stand on as we are. Ah, Mr. Montagu, will you step below and fetch me my sword out of my cabin. What do you think of her, Desborough?"

"We think she is an American, sir," said Desborough.

"Oh, you do, do you? Well, I think she is one of ours. No American would dare to lead down on us in that way! We can blow him out of the water with a broadside or two, you know, but we'll give him a hint all the same. Fire a gun there, to leeward, and hoist our colors."

As the smoke rolled away along the water, the stops were broken, and there flew out from each masthead the splendid English flag. It was answered soon afterward by a small English flag at the gaff of the approaching ship, which apparently mystified the captain more than ever, though it confirmed him in his previous opinion.

"Oh, father," whispered Katharine, clinging to the colonel, "what do you think it is? See that English flag!"

"Kate, I 'm morally sure that it is an American ship; it is just the plan and size of those ordered by Congress in '75. One of those ships should be in commission by now. If I am right, this should be the Randolph. I saw her a dozen times in Philadelphia; and if that's not she, I shall never pretend to know a ship again."

"But did you hear what Captain Vincent said?" continued Katharine; "how many guns would the Randolph carry?"

"About forty, and most of them small ones at best," answered the colonel, with a sigh.

The two ships were much nearer now, and their disparity in force was apparent even to the most unskilful eye.

"The little ship can't fight this great one, father, can it?"

"No, my dear; that is, not with any chance of success. But I fear—or hope, rather—that they mean to engage us, and sacrifice themselves in order not to allow us to capture the little fleet, probably prizes, off yonder. The man who commands her is a hero, certainly."

"Just what Mr. Seymour would do. Oh, if it were he!" she exclaimed, clasping her hands, her eyes filling with tears at the possibility.

"Well, it may be, of course. He was certain to be posted captain soon, and 'tis like him truly. But, Kate, the ships are drawing nearer every moment. You must go below in case of action, my dear."

"Yes, Miss Wilton," said Desborough, who had at that moment approached them, looking very handsome, having heard the last words of the colonel; "we have arranged a safe place for you and your maid, in the cable tiers, way below the water-line, and out of the way of shot, though I hardly expect much of it from that fellow. Will you allow me to conduct you there? Perhaps you too, colonel, would be safer if you would—"

"Pardon me, sir, unless force is used, I shall remain on deck. The idea of me, sir—skulking in the hold during an action! Why, sir,—"

"And the idea of me, either, doing the same thing!" said Katharine defiantly, in a ringing voice in which there was a clear echo of her father's determination.

Both men looked at her smiling.

"Oh, you are different, Miss Wilton," said Desborough.

"No use, Katharine: you must go," added her father.

"Oh, please!"

"My daughter—"

"Oh, father, let me stay just a little longer—there is no danger yet. Take Chloe down, if you will, Mr. Desborough, and have a place ready for me. I'll go down when the battle begins—indeed I will, father!" she continued entreatingly.

"Well," said the colonel, uncertainly, "let her stay a little longer, my lord."

"Very well, sir," replied Desborough, bowing and turning forward.

"Here, you Jack, take this girl below and stow her away in the cable tiers by the main hatch," he said, pointing to Chloe, who was led unresistingly away, her teeth chattering with undefined but none the less overwhelming terror. The colonel stepped forward beside Captain Vincent, and Desborough descended to the main-deck to superintend the fighting of the batteries, while Katharine, grateful for the respite, and determined not to go below at all, stepped aft in the shelter of the rail, her heart already beating madly, as the two ships approached each other in silence.

CHAPTER XXXV

BENTLEY SAYS GOOD-BY

The men on the Randolph were in excellent spirits, and as they drew nearer and nearer became more and more anxious for the fray.

"She's a big one, ain't she?" said one young seaman, glancing over a gun through a port-hole forward; "but we ain't afraid of her, mates. We'll just dance up and slap her in the face with this, and then turn around and slap her with t' other side," laying his hand at the time on one of the long eighteens which constituted the main battery of the frigate.

"Yes, and then what will she do to us? Blow us into splinters with a broadside, youngster! Not as I particularly care, so we have a chance to get a few good licks at her with these old barkers," said an older man, pointing, like the first, to a gun.

"That's the talk, men," said Seymour, who was making a tour of inspection through the ship in person, and who had stopped before the gun and heard the conversation. "Before she sinks us we will give it to her hard. I can depend upon you, I know."

"Yes, yes, your honor."

"Ay, ay, sir—"

"We's all right, sir—"

"We's with you, your honor—" came in a quick, strong chorus from the rough-and-ready men, and then some one called for three cheers for Captain Seymour, and they were given with such a will that the oak decks echoed and re-echoed again and again.

"Pass the word to serve out a tot of grog to each man; let them splice the main-brace once more before they die," said Seymour, grimly, amid a chorus of approving murmurs from the sailors, as he walked slowly along the lines, greeting men here and there with plain, bluff words of cheer, which brought smiles of pleasure to their stern, weather-beaten faces.

"Now, ain't he a beauty?" whispered the captain of number two gun to his second. "Blow me if 't ain't a pleasure to serve under sich a officer, and to die for him, too! Here is to a speedy fight and lots of damage to the Britisher," he cried loudly, lifting his pannikin of rum and water to his lips, amid a further chorus of approval.

Old Bentley was standing on the forecastle forward, looking earnestly at the approaching ship, when Seymour came up to him. The rest of the men, mindful of the peculiar relationship between the two, instinctively drew back a little, leaving them alone.

"Well, Bentley, our work is cut out for us there."

"Ay, Captain Seymour. I 'm thinking that this cruise will end right here for this ship—unless you strike, sir."

"Strike! Do you advise me to do so, then?"

"God forbid! Except it be with shot and these," said the old man, lifting an enormous cutlass, ground to a razor edge, which he had specially made for his own personal use in battle. "No, no; we've got to fight him till he's so damaged that he can't get at the rest. Do you see, sir, how the brig lags behind them?" he went on, pointing out toward the slowly escaping squadron. "The boy's got her luffed up so she makes no headway at all!"

"I know it. I have signalled to him twice to close with the rest—he can sail two feet to their one; but it is no use,—he pays no attention. He shouldn't have been given so responsible a command until he learned to obey orders," said Seymour, frowning.

"Let the boy alone, Master John; he'll do all right," said Bentley; "he's the makings of a good sailorman and a fine officer in him. I've watched him."

"Ha! there goes a shot from the liner," cried Seymour, as a puff of smoke broke out from the lee side followed by the dull boom of a cannon over the water, and then the flags rippled bravely out from the mastheads. "Well, we did not need that sort of an introduction. Aft there!" cried the captain, with his powerful voice.

"Sir."

"Show a British flag at the gaff. That will puzzle him for a while longer. Well, old friend, I must go aft. It's likely we won't both of us come out of this little affair alive, so good-by, and God bless you. You've been a good friend to me, Bentley, ever since I was a child, and I doubt I've requited you ill enough," he said, reaching forth his hand. The old sailor shifted his cutlass into his left hand, took off his hat, and grasped Seymour's hand with his own mighty palm.

"Ay, ever since you were a boy; and a properer sailor and a better officer don't walk the deck, if I do say it myself, as I've had a hand in the making of you. But what you say is true, sir: we'll probably most all of us go to Davy Jones' locker this trip; but we couldn't go in a better way, and we won't go alone. God Almighty bless you, sir! I—" said the old seaman, breaking off suddenly and looking wistfully at the young man he loved, who, understanding it all, returned his gaze, wrung his hand, and then turned and sprang aft without another word.

The ships were rapidly closing, when Seymour's keen eye detected a dash of color and a bit of fluttering drapery on the poop of the line-of-battle ship. Wondering, he examined it through his glass.

"Why! 't is a woman," he exclaimed. Something familiar in the appearance made his heart give a sudden throb, but he put away the idea which came to him as preposterous; and then stepping forward to the break of the poop, he called out,—

"My lads, there is a woman on yon ship, on the poop, way aft. We don't fight with women; have a care, therefore, that none of you take deliberate aim at her, and spare that part of the deck where she stands in the fight, if you can. Pass the word along."

"Well, I 'm blessed," said one old gun captain, *sotto voce*, "be they come out against us with wimmen!"

The Randolph had the weather-gage of the Yarmouth by this time; and Seymour shifted his helm slightly, rounded in his braces a little, and ran down with the wind a little free and on a line parallel to the course of his enemy, but going in a different direction. He lifted the glass again to his eye, and looked long and earnestly at the woman's figure half hidden by the rail on the ship. Was it—could it be—indeed she? Was fate bringing them into opposition again? It was not possible. Trembling violently, he lifted the glass for a further investigation, when an officer, trumpet in hand, sprang upon the rail of the Yarmouth forward and hailed.

CHAPTER XXXVI

THE LAST OF THE RANDOLPH

"Pass the word quietly," said Seymour, rapidly, to one of his young aids, "that when I say, 'Stand by to back the maintopsail,' the guns are to be fired. Bid the gun captains to train on the port-holes of the second tier of guns. Mind, no order to fire will be given except the words, 'Stand by to back the maintopsail.' The men are to fire at the word 'topsail.' Do you understand? Tell the division officers to hold up their hands, as a sign that they understand, as you pass along, so that I can see them. Lively now! Quartermaster, standby to haul down that flag and show our colors at the first shot."

The frigate was now rapidly drawing near the ship of the line, until, at the moment the officer hailed, the two ships were nearly alongside of each other. The awful disparity between their sizes was now painfully apparent.

"Ship ahoy! Ahoy the frigate!" came down a second time in long hollow tones through the trumpet from the officer balancing himself on the Yarmouth's rail by holding on to a back-stay. "Why don't you answer?"

"Ahoy the ship!" replied Seymour at last through his own

trumpet. "What ship is that?"

"His Britannic majesty's ship of the line, Yarmouth, Captain Vincent. Who are you? Answer, or I will fire!"

The flying boom of the Randolph was just pointing past the Yarmouth's quarter, and the two ships were abreast each other; now, if ever, was the time for action.

"This is the American Continental ship, Randolph, Captain Seymour," cried the latter, through the trumpet, in a voice heard in every part of the ship of the line.

At least two hearts in the Yarmouth were powerfully affected by that announcement. Katharine's leaped within her bosom at the sound of her lover's voice, and beat madly while she revelled in thought in his proximity; and then as she noticed again the fearful odds with which he was apparently about to contend, her heart sank into the depths once more. In one second she thrilled with pride, quivered with love, trembled with despair. He was there—he was hers—he would be killed! She gripped the rail hard and clenched her teeth to keep from screaming aloud his name, while her gaze strained out upon his handsome figure. Pride, love, death,—an epitome of human life in that fleeting moment,—all were hers!

On the main-deck of the frigate the name carried consternation to Lieutenant Lord Desborough. So Seymour was alive again! Was that the end of my lord's chance? No. Joy! The rebel was under the guns of the battle-ship! Never, vowed the lieutenant, should guns be better served than those under his command. Unless the man surrendered, he was doomed. So, he spoke eagerly to his men, bidding them take good aim and waste no shot, never doubting the inevitable issue. These thoughts took but a moment, however.

Beauchamp, who had done the talking, now stepped aft to Captain Vincent's side, and replied to Seymour's hail by calling out,—

"Do you strike, sir?"

"Yes, yes, of course; that's what we came down here for. We'll strike fast enough," was the answer.

A broad smile lighted up Captain Vincent's face; he turned to the colonel, laughing, and said with a scarcely veiled sneer,—

"I told you they were not up to it. The cad! he might have fired one shot at least for the honor of his flag, don't you see?"

The colonel with a sinking heart could not see at all. Cowardice in Seymour, in any officer, was a thing he could not understand. The world turned black before Katharine. What! strike without a blow! Was this her hero? Rather death than a coward! In spite of her faith in her lover, as she heard what appeared to be a pusillanimous offer of surrender, Desborough's chances took a sudden bound upward, while that gentleman cursed the cowardice of his enemy and rival, which would deprive him of a pleasing opportunity of blowing him out of the water. Most of the men at the different guns relaxed their eager watchfulness, while sneers and jeers at the "Yankee" went up on all sides.

"Heave to, then," continued Beauchamp, peremptorily and with much disgust, "and send a boat aboard!"

"Ay, ay, sir!"

Oh, it was true, then; he was going to surrender tamely without—

"Stand by!" there was a note of preparation in the words in spite of Seymour's effort to give them the ordinary intonation of a commonplace order,—a note which had so much meaning to Katharine's sensitive ear that her heart stopped its beating for a moment as she waited for the next word. It came with a roar of defiance. "Back the maintopsail!" But the braces were kept fast and the unexpected happened. In an instant sheets of flame shot out from the muzzles of the black guns of the Randolph, which were immediately wreathed and shrouded in clouds of smoke. At the moment of command Seymour had quickly ordered the helm shifted suddenly, and the Randolph had swung round so that she lay at a broad angle off the quarter of the Yarmouth. The thunderous roar of the heavy guns at short range was immediately followed by the crashing of timber, as the heavy shot took deadly effect, amid the cheers and yells and curses and groans and shrieks of the wounded and startled men on the liner, while three hearty cheers rang out from the Randolph.

The advantage of the first blow in the grim game, the unequal combat, was with the little one.

"How now, captain!" shouted the colonel, in high exultation. "Won't fight, eh! What do you call this?"

"Fire! fire! Let him have it, men, and be damned to you! The man's a hero; 't was cleverly done," roared the captain, excitedly. "I retract. Give it to him, boys! Give it to the impudent rebel!" he roared.

Katharine, forgot by every one in the breathless excitement of the past few moments, bowed her head on her hands on the rail, and breathed a prayer of thankfulness, oblivious of everything but that her lover had proved himself worthy the devotion her heart so ungrudgingly extended him. There was great confusion on board the Yarmouth from this sudden and unexpected discharge, which, delivered at short range, had done no little execution on the crowded ship; but the officers rallied their men speedily with cool words of encouragement.

"Steady, men, steady."

"Give it back to them."

"Look sharp now."

"Aim! Fire!"

And the forty-odd heavy guns roared out in answer to the determined attack. The effect of such a broadside at close range would have been frightful, had not the Randolph drawn so far ahead, and her course been so changed, that a large part of it passed harmlessly astern of her. One gun, however, found its target, and that was one aimed and fired by the hand of Lord Desborough himself: a heavy shot, a thirty-two, from one of the massive lower-deck guns of the Yarmouth, which the pleasant weather permitted them to use effectively, came through one of the after gun-ports of the Randolph, and swept away the line of men on the port side of the gun. Some of the other shot did slight damage also among the spars and gear, and several of the crew were killed or wounded in different parts of the ship; but the Randolph was practically unharmed, and standing boldly down to cross the stern of the Yarmouth to rake her. But the English captain was a seaman, every inch of him, and his ship could not have been better handled; divining his bold little antagonist's purpose, the Yarmouth's helm was put up at once, and in the smoke she fell off and came before the wind almost as rapidly as did the Randolph, her promptness frustrating the endeavor, as Seymour was only able to make an ineffectual effort to rake her, as she flew round on her heels. The starboard battery of the Yarmouth had been manned as she fell off, and the port battery of the Randolph was rapidly reloaded again. The manoeuvre had given the Englishmen the weather-gage once more, the two ships now having the wind on the port quarter. The two batteries were discharged simultaneously, and now began a running fight of near an hour's duration.

Seymour was everywhere. Up and down the deck he walked, helping and sustaining his men, building up new gun's crews out of the shattered remains of decimated groups of men, lending a hand himself on a tackle on occasion; cool, calm, unwearied, unremitting, determined, he desperately fought his ship as few vessels were ever fought before or since, imbuing, by his presence and example and word, his men with his own unquailing spirit, until they died as uncomplainingly and as nobly as did those prototypes of heroes,—another three hundred in the pass at Thermopylae!

The guns were served on the Randolph with the desperate rapidity of men who, awfully pressed for time, had abandoned hope and only fought to cripple and delay before they were silenced; those on the Yarmouth, on the contrary, were fired with much more deliberation, and did dreadful execution. The different guns were disabled on the Randolph by heavy shot; adjacent ports were knocked into one, the sides shattered, boats smashed, rails knocked to pieces, all of the weather-shrouds cut, the mizzenmast carried away under the top, and the wreck fell into the sea,—fortunately, on the lee side, the little body of men in the top going to a sudden death with the rest. The decks were slippery with blood and ploughed with plunging shot, which the superior height of the Yarmouth permitted to be fired with depressed guns from an elevation. Solid shot from the heavy main-deck batteries swept through and through the devoted frigate; half the Randolph's guns were useless because of the lack of men to serve them; the cockpit overflowed with the wounded; the surgeon and his mates, covered with blood, worked like butchers, in the steerage and finally in the ward room; dead and dying men lay where they fell; there were no hands to spare to take them below, no place in which they could lie with safety, no immunity from the searching hail which drove through every part of the doomed ship. Still the men, cheered and encouraged by their officers, stood to their guns and fought on. Presently the foretopmast went by the board also, as the long moments dragged along, Seymour was now lying on the quarter-deck, a bullet having broken his leg, another having made a flesh-wound in his arm; he had refused to go below to have his wounds dressed, and one of the midshipmen was kneeling by his side, applying such unskilful bandages as he might to the two bleeding wounds. Nason had been sent for, and was in charge, under Seymour's direction. That young man, all his nervousness gone, was most ably seconding his dauntless captain.

The two ships were covered with smoke. It was impossible to tell on one what was happening on the other; but the steady persistence with which the Randolph clung to her big enemy had its effect on the Yarmouth also, and the well-delivered fire did not allow that vessel any immunity. In fact, while nothing like that on the frigate, the damage was so great, and so many men had fallen, that Captain Vincent determined to end the conflict at once by boarding the frigate. The necessary orders were given, and a strong party of boarders was called away and mustered on the forecastle, headed by Beauchamp and Hollins; among the number were little Montagu, with other midshipmen. Taking advantage of the smoke and of the weather-gage, the Yarmouth was suddenly headed for the Randolph. As the enormous bows of the line-of-battle ship came slowly shoving out of the smoke, towering above them, covered with men, cutlass or boarding pike in hand, Seymour discerned at once the purpose of the manoeuvre. Raising himself upon his elbow to better direct the movement,—

"All hands repel boarders!" he shouted, his voice echoing through the ship as powerfully as ever.

This was an unusual command, as it completely deprived the guns of their crews; but he rightly judged that it would take all the men they could muster to repel the coming attack, and none but the main-deck guns of the Yarmouth would or could be fired, for fear of hitting their own men in the melee on the deck. The Randolph was a wreck below, at best; but while anything held together above her plank shears, she would be fought. The men had reached that desperate condition when they ceased to think of odds, and like maddened beasts fought and raved and swore in the frenzy of the combat. The thrice-decimated crew sprang aft, rallying in the gangway to meet the shock, Nason at their head, followed close by old Bentley, still unwounded. As the bow of the Yarmouth struck the Randolph with a crash, one or two wounded men, unable to take part in repelling the boarders but still able to move, who had remained beside the guns, exerted the remaining strength they possessed to discharge such of the pieces as bore, in long raking shots, through the bow of the liner; it was the last sound from their hot muzzles.

The Yarmouth struck the Randolph just forward of the mainmast; the men, swarming in dense masses on the rail and hanging over the bowsprit ready to leap, dropped on her deck at once with loud cheers. A sharp volley from the few marines left on the frigate checked them for a moment,— nobody noticing at the time that the Honorable Giles had fallen in a limp heap back from the rail upon his own deck,

Cyrus Townsend Brady

the blood staining his curly head; but they gathered themselves together at once, and, gallantly led, sprang aft, handling their pistols and pikes and waving their cutlasses. Nason was shot in a moment by Hollins' pistol, Beauchamp was cut in two by a tremendous sweep of the arm of the mighty Bentley, and the combat became at once general. Slowly but surely the Americans were pressed back; the gangways were cleared; the quarter-deck was gained; one by one the brave defenders had fallen. The battle was about over when Seymour noticed a man running out in the foreyard of the Yarmouth with a hand-grenade. He raised his pistol and fired; the man fell; but another resolutely started to follow him.

Bentley and a few other men, and one or two officers and a midshipman, were all who were able to bear arms now.

"Good-by, Mr. Seymour," cried Bentley, waving his hand and setting his back against the rail nearest to the Yarmouth, which had slowly swung parallel to the Randolph and had been lashed there. The old man was covered with blood from two or three wounds, but still undaunted. Two or three men made a rush at him; but he held them at bay, no man caring to come within sweep of that mighty arm which had already done so much, when a bullet from above struck him, and he fell over backward on the rail mortally wounded.

Seymour raised his remaining pistol and fired it at the second man, who had nearly reached the foreyard arm; less successful this time, he missed the man, who threw his grenade down the hatchway. Seymour fainted from loss of blood.

"Back, men! back to the ship, all you Yarmouths!" cried Captain Vincent, as he saw the lighted grenade, which exploded and ignited a little heap of cartridges left by a dead powder-boy before the magazine. Alas! there was no one there to check or stop the flames. The English sailors sprang back and up the sides and through the ports of their ship with frantic haste; the lashings were being rapidly cut by them, and the braces handled.

"Come aboard, men, while you can," cried Captain Vincent to the Americans. "Your ship's afire; you can do no more; you'll blow up in a moment!"

The little handful of Americans were left alone on their ship. The only officer still standing lifted his sword and shook it impotently at the Yarmouth in reply; the rest did not stir. The smoke of battle had now settled away, and the whole ghastly scene was revealed. A woman's cry rang out fraught with agony,—"Seymour, Seymour!" and again was her cry unheeded; her lover could not hear. She cried again; and then, with a frightful roar and crash, the Randolph blew up.

Cyrus Townsend Brady

CHAPTER XXXVII

FOR LOVE OF COUNTRY

The force of the explosion occurring so near to the line-of-battle ship drove her over with irresistible power upon her beam-ends until she buried her port main-deck guns under water; her time was not yet come, however, for, after a trembling movement of sickening uncertainty, she righted herself, slowly at first, but finally with a mighty roll and rush as if on a tidal wave. For a few seconds the air was filled with pieces of wreck, arms, spars, bodies, many of which fell on the Yarmouth. The horrified spectators saw the two broken halves of the ill-fated frigate gradually disappearing beneath the heaving sea, sucking down in their inexorable vortex most of the bodies of those, alive or dead, who floated near. The fire had come in broad sheets through the portholes of the main-deck guns of the ship from the explosion, driving the men from their stations, and, by heating the iron masses or igniting the priming, caused sudden and wild discharges to add their quota of confusion to the awful scene. Pieces of burning wreck had also fallen in the tops, or upon the sails, or lodged in the standing rigging, full of tar as usual, and dry and inflammable to the last degree. The Yarmouth, therefore, was in serious danger,—more so than in any other period of the action,—her little antagonist having inflicted the most damaging blow with the last gasp, as it were; for little columns of flame and smoke began to rise ominously in a dozen places. Then was manifested the splendid discipline for which British ships were famous the world over. Rapidly and with unerring skill and coolness the proper orders were given, and the tired men were set to work desperately fighting once more to check and put out the fire. Long and hard was the struggle, the issue much in doubt; but in the end the efforts of her crew were crowned with merited success, and their ship was eventually saved from the dangerous conflagration which had menaced her with ruin, not less complete and disastrous than had befallen the frigate.

While all this was being done, a little scene took place upon the quarter-deck which was worthy of notice. Something heavy and solid, thrown upward by the tremendous force of the discharge, struck the rail with a mighty crash at the moment of the explosion, just at the point where Katharine, wide-eyed, petrified with horror, after that one vivid glance in which she apparently saw her lover dead on his own quarter-deck beneath her, stood clinging rigidly to the bulwarks as if paralyzed. It was the body of a man; instinctively she threw out her strong young arm and saved it from falling again into the sea on the return roll of the ship. One or two of the seamen standing by came to her assistance, and the body was dragged on board and laid on the deck at her feet. Something familiar in the figure moved Katharine to a further examination. She knelt down and wiped the blood and smoke and dust from the face of the prostrate man, and recognized him at once. It was old Bentley, desperately wounded, his clothes soaked with blood from several severe wounds, and apparently dying fast, but still breathing. A small tightly rolled up ball of bunting was lying near her on the deck; it was a flag from the Randolph, which had been blown there by the force of the explosion. She quickly picked it up and pillowed the head of the unconscious man upon it. Then she ran below to her cabin, coming back in a moment with water and a cordial, with which she bathed the head and wiped the lips of the dying man. The fires were all forward, and, the wind being aft, the danger was in the fore part of the ship; no one therefore paid the least attention to her. There was, in fact, save the captain and one or two midshipmen, no one else on the poop-deck except her father, who like herself had been overwhelmed by the sudden and awful ending of the battle. Being without anything to do, the colonel, who had been watching the men fight with the fire, happened to look aft for a moment and saw his daughter by the side of the prostrate man. He stepped over to her at once.

"Katharine, Katharine," he said to her in a tone of stern reproof and surprise, not as he usually spoke to her, "you here! 'T is no place for women. When did you come from below?"

"I've not been below at all, father," she replied, looking up at him with a white, stricken face which troubled his loving heart.

"Do you mean to tell me that you have been on deck during the action?"

"Yes, father, right here. Do you not understand that it was Mr. Seymour's ship—I could not go away!"

"By heavens! Think of it! And I forgot you completely—The fault was mine, how could I have allowed it?" he continued in great agitation.

"Never mind, father; I could not have gone below in any case. Do you think he—Mr. Seymour—can be yet alive?" she asked, still cherishing a faint hope.

The colonel shook his head gloomily, and then stooping down and looking at the prostrate form of the man on the deck, he asked,—

"But who is this you have here?"

The man opened his eyes at this moment and looked up vacantly.

"William Bentley, sir," he said in a hoarse whisper, as if in answer to the question; and then making a vain effort to raise his hand to his head, he went on half-mechanically, "bosun of the Randolph, sir. Come aboard!"

"Merciful Powers, it is old Bentley!" cried the colonel. "Can anything be done for you, my man? How is it with you?"

Katharine poured a little more of the cordial down his throat, which gave him a fictitious strength for a moment, and he answered in a little stronger voice, with a glance of recognition and wonder,—

"The colonel and the young miss! we thought you dead in the wreck of the Radnor. He will be glad;" and then after a pause recollection came to him. "Oh, God!" he murmured, "Mr. Seymour!"

"What of him? Speak!" cried Katharine, in agony.

"Gone with the rest," he replied with an effort "'T was a good fight, though. The other ships,—where are they?"

"Escaped," answered the colonel; "we are too much cut up to pursue."

"Why did you do it?" moaned Katharine, thinking of

Seymour's attack on the ship of the line.

The old man did not heed the question; his eyes closed. He was still a moment, and then he opened his eyes again slowly. Straight above him waved the standard of his enemy.

"I never thought—to die—under the English flag," he said slowly and with great effort. Supplying its place with her own young soft arm, Katharine drew forth the little American ensign which had served him for a pillow— stained with his own blood—and held it up before him. A light came into his dying eyes,—a light of heaven, perhaps, no pain in his heart now. One trembling hand would still do his bidding; by a superhuman effort of his resolute will he caught the bit of bunting and carried it to his lips in a long kiss of farewell. His lips moved. He was saying something. Katharine bent to listen. What was it? Ah! she heard; they were the words he said on the deck of the transport when they saw the ship wrecked in the pass in the beating seas,— the words he had repeated in the old farmhouse on that winter night to the great general, when he told the story of that cruise; the words he had made to stand for the great idea of his own life; the words with which he had cheered and soothed and sustained and encouraged many weaker men who had looked to his iron soul for help and guidance. They were the words to which many a patriot like him, now lying mute and cold upon the hills about Boston, under the trees at Long Island, by the flowing waters and frowning cliffs of the Hudson, on the verdant glacis at Quebec, 'neath the smooth surface of Lake Champlain, in the dim northern woods, on the historic field of Princeton, or within the still depths of this mighty sea now tossing them upon its bosom, had given most eloquent expression and final attestation. What were they?

"For—for—love—of—country." The once mighty voice

died away in a feeble whisper; a child might still the faintly beating heart. The mighty chest—rose—fell; the old man lay still. Love of country,—that was his passion, you understand.

Love of country! That was the great refrain. The wind roared the song through the pines, on the snow-clad mountains in the far north, sobbed it softly through the rustling palmetto branches in the south-land, or breathed it in whispers over the leaves of the oak and elm and laurel, between. The waves crashed it in tremendous chorus on rock-bound shores, or rolled it with tender caress over shining sands. Under its inspiration, mighty men left all and marched forth to battle; wooed by its subtle music, hero women bore the long hours of absence and suspense; and in its tender harmonies the little children were rocked to sleep. Ay, love of country! All the voices of man and nature in a continent caught it up and breathed it forth, hurled it in mighty diapason far up into God's heaven. Love of country! It was indeed a mighty truth. They preached it, loved it, lived for it, died for it, till at last it made them free!

CHAPTER XXXVIII

PHILIP DISOBEYS ORDERS

"Who is this, pray?" said Captain Vincent, at this moment stepping back to the silent little group.

"The boatswain of the Randolph," replied the colonel. "He has just died."

"Poor fellow! but there are many other brave men gone this day. What think you was the complement of the frigate, colonel?"

"Over three hundred men certainly," replied the colonel (the actual number was three hundred and fifteen). "Most of them not already done for were lost in the explosion, I presume?"

"Yes, assuredly; and now I owe you an apology, my dear sir. I never saw a more gallant action in my life. The man's gone, of course, but he shall have full credit for it in my report; 'twas bravely done, and successfully, too. We are frightfully cut up, and in no condition to pursue. In fact, I will not conceal from you that some of our spars are so severely wounded, and the starboard rigging so damaged and scorched and cut up, that I know not how we could stand a heavy blow. Twenty-five are killed, and upward of sixty wounded too, and about thirty missing, killed, or wounded men of the boarding party, who were undoubtedly blown up with the frigate. Beauchamp is gone; and that little fellow there," pointing to a couple of seamen bringing a small limp body aft, "is Montagu. Poor little youngster!"

"This has indeed been a frightful action, captain," replied the colonel. "I knew young Seymour well. He was a man of the most consummate gallantry. This sacrifice is like him," he continued softly, looking at Katharine and then turning away. Perhaps the captain understood. At any rate he stepped to her side and said gently,—

"Mistress Katharine, this is no place for you; you must go below. Indeed, I must insist. I shall have to order you. Come—" and then laying his hand on her arm, he started back in surprise. "Why, you are wounded!"

"'Tis nothing, sir," said Katharine, faintly. "I welcome it; 'twas an American bullet. Would it had found my heart!"

"Only a flesh-wound, colonel; no cause for alarm," said the captain, looking at it with the eye of experience. "It will be all right in a day or two. But now she must go below. I can't understand how you were allowed to stay here, or be here. What were they thinking of? But you saw one of the hottest and most desperate battles ever fought between two ships since you were here. They can fight; you were right, colonel," he went on in ungrudging admiration.

"Here, Desborough," he added, addressing the lieutenant, who just then put his foot on the deck, "take Miss Wilton below, and ask the surgeon to attend her at his convenience; she's gone and got herself wounded by her friends."

Lieutenant Desborough, black and grimy, streaked with

smoke and powder, turned pale at the captain's words, and sprang forward anxiously and led the object of his love down the steps to her cabin. "Wounded!" he murmured. "Oh, my love, why did no one take you to a place of safety?"

"'T is nothing," she replied, going on as if in a dream.

Desborough had his wish: his rival was gone; he had the field to himself; but he was too manly to feel any exultation now that it was over, and too sorry for the vacant despair he saw on her face. He tenderly whispered to her as he led her on,—

"Believe me, dear Katharine, it is not thus I would have triumphed over Mr. Seymour. He was in truth a knightly gentleman."

Overwhelming pity for her filled his heart, and he went on magnanimously,—

"I am sorry—"

She made no answer; she did not hear. In the cabin the body of little Montagu was lying on a table. He would never get his frigate now. How small and frail and boyish looked the Honorable Giles to-day! Why did they send children like that to war? Had he no mother?—poor lad! Moved by a sudden impulse, she stooped and kissed him, as she had done an hour before. No throb of the proud little heart answered responsive to her caress now. Alas! she might kiss him when and as she pleased; he would not feel it, and he would not heed. Entering her own berth at last, she closed the door and sank down upon her knees,—alone with God!

"A sail coming down fast,—the little brig, sir," reported the officer of the deck to Captain Vincent. "Shall we come about and give him a broadside?"

"No, no; we dare not handle the braces yet,—not until the gear and spars have been well overhauled."

"Shall we use the stern-chaser then, sir?"

The Yarmouth had left the scene of the explosion some distance away by this time, but she was still within easy gun-shot. Captain Vincent earnestly examined the brig; as he looked, she came up to the wind, hove to, and dropped a boat in the water. There was a bit of spar still floating there. The captain saw that three or four men were clinging to it.

"No; she's on an errand of mercy. There are men in the water on that topmast there. Let her go free," he said generously. "We've done enough to-day to satisfy any reasonable man."

The colonel grasped his hand warmly and thanked him. The little brig picked up her boat, swung her mainyard, and filled away again on the port tack, in the wake of the rest of the little squadron now far ahead; then, understanding the forbearance of the big ship, she fired a gun to leeward and dipped her ensign in salute.

The force of the explosion had thrown Seymour, from his advantageous position aft, far out into the water and away from the sinking ship. The contact with cold water recalled him to his senses at once; and with the natural instinct of man for life, he struck out as well as he might, considering his broken leg and wounded arm and weakened state. There was a piece of a mast with the top still on it floating near by. He struggled gallantly to make it,—'twas no use, he could do no more; closing his eyes, he sank down in the dark water. But help was near: a hand grasped him by his long hair and drew him up; one of his men, unwounded fortunately, had saved him. The two men presently reached the bit of wreck; the sailor scrambled up on it, and by a great effort drew his captain by his side; two more men swam over desperately, and finally joined the little group. They clung there helpless, hopeless, despairing, fascinated, watching the remains of the Randolph disappear, marking a few feeble swimmers here and there struggling, till all was still. Then they turned their eyes upon their late antagonist, running away before the wind in flames; they saw her fight them down successfully; appalled, none spoke. Presently one of the seamen glanced the other way, and saw the little brig swiftly bearing down upon them.

"God be praised! Here's the brig, the Fair American," he cried. "We shall be saved—saved!"

The brig was handled smartly; she came to the wind, backed the maintopsail, and lay gently tossing to and fro on the long swells. The young captain stood on the rail, clinging to the back-stays, anxiously watching. The boat was dropped into the water, and with long strokes shot over to them. The men sprang aboard; rude hands gently and tenderly lifted the wounded captain in. They pulled rapidly back to the brig; the falls were manned, and the boat was run up, the yard swung, and she filled away. Seymour was lifted down; Philip received him in his arms.

"I ought to arrest you for disobedience of orders," said the captain, sternly. "Why did you pay no attention to my signals? You have jeoparded the brig. Yon ship can blow you out of the water; you are quite within range."

But they soon saw that no motion was made by the ship; and in accordance with Seymour's orders the gun was fired and the colors dipped,—a salute which the ship promptly returned.

"I ought to put you under arrest, Philip," again said Seymour, faintly, while he was lying in the tiny cabin, having his wounds dressed; "but I will not. 'T was gallantly done; but obey orders first hereafter,—'t is the first principle of action on the sea." That was rather cool comfort for the young officer, considering that his somewhat reckless action had just saved Seymour's life. He made brief reply, however, and then resumed his station on the deck of his little vessel, which was rapidly overhauling the rest of the fleet. As soon as the night fell, the wind permitting, they were by Seymour's direction headed for the harbor of Charleston once more. Now that his mind was free again, Seymour's thoughts turned to that woman's form of which he had one brief glimpse ere the line-of-battle ship disappeared in the smoke. Could it indeed have been Katharine Wilton? Could fate play him such a trick as to awaken once more his sleeping hope? Through the long night he tossed in fevered unrest in his narrow berth. Again he went over the awful scenes of that one hour of horror. The roar of the guns, the crash of splintered timbers, the groans of the wounded men, rang in his fretted ear. They seemed to rise before him, those gallant officers and men, the hardy, bold sailors, veterans of the sea, audacious youngsters with life long before them, Bentley, his old, his faithful friend,—lost—all lost. Was there reproach in their gaze? Was it worth while, after all? Ay, but duty; he had always done his duty—duty always— duty—Ah, they faded away, and Katharine looked down upon—it was she—love—duty—love—duty! Was that the roar of battle again, or only his beating heart? They found him in the morning, delirious, shouting orders, murmuring words of love, calling Kate,—babbling like a child.

CHAPTER XXXIX

THREE PICTURES OF THE SEA

A short time before sunset that same evening the Yarmouth was hove to, and the hoarse cry of the boatswain and his mates was once more heard through the ship, calling,—

"All hands! Bury the dead."

Skilled hands had been working earnestly all the afternoon to repair the damage to the vessel; much had been accomplished, but much more still remained to be done. However, night was drawing on, and it was advisable to dispose of the dead bodies of those who had been killed in the action, or who had died since of their wounds, without further delay. Some of the sailmaker's mates had been busy during the afternoon, sewing up the dead in new, clean hammocks, and weighting each one with heavy shot at the feet to draw it down. The bodies were laid in orderly rows amidships, forward of the mainmast, and all was ready when the word was passed. The crew assembled in the gangways facing aft, the boatswain, gunner, carpenter, sailmaker, and other warrant officers at their head. The captain, attended by Colonel Wilton and the first lieutenant in full uniform, and surrounded by the officers down to the smallest midshipman, stood facing the crew on the quarter-deck; back of the officers, on the opposite side of the deck, the marine guard was drawn up. At the break of the poop stood the slender, graceful figure of a woman, alone, clearly outlined against the low light of the setting sun, looking mournfully down upon the picture, her heart, though filled with sadness and sorrow particularly her own, still great enough to feel sympathy for others.

The chaplain, clothed in the white vestments of his sacred office, presently came from out the cabin beneath the poop-deck, and stopped opposite the gangway between the line of men and officers. Two of the boatswain's mates, at a signal from the first lieutenant, stepped to the row of bodies and carefully lifted up the first one and laid it on a grating, covering it at the same time with a flag. They next lifted the grating and placed one end of it on the rail overlooking the sea, and held the other in their hands and waited. The captain uncovered, all the other officers and the men following his example.

The chaplain began to read from the book in his hand. The first body on the grating was a very small one,—only a boy, looking smaller in contrast to those of the men by which it had lain. The little figure of the Honorable Giles looked pathetic indeed. Some of the little fellow's messmates had hard work to stifle their tears; here and there in the ranks of the silent men the back of a hand would go furtively up to a wet eye, as the minister read on and on.

How run the words?

"Forasmuch as it hath pleased Almighty God, in His wise Providence, to take out of this world the soul of our deceased brother—" Was it indeed Thy pleasure, O God, that this little "brother" should die? Was Thy Providence summed up in this little silent figure? Alas, who can answer?

And then as the even voice of the priest went on with the solemn and beautiful words which never grow familiar,— "we therefore commit his body to the deep,"—the first lieutenant nodded to the watching sailors. They lifted the inboard end of the grating high in the air; a fellow midshipman standing by pulled aside the covering flag; the little body started, moved slowly,—more rapidly; there was a flash of light in the air, a splash in the water alongside.

The chaplain motioned for another; it was a man this time,— all the rest were men; four of the seamen lifted him up. Again the few short sentences, and the sailor was launched upon another voyage of life. Tears were streaming from eyes unused to weeping, tracing unwonted courses down the strangely weather-beaten, wrinkled cheeks; men mourning the loss of shipmate and messmate, friend and fellow. The last one in the row was a gigantic man; over his bosom was laid a little blood-stained flag of different blazoning: there was the blue field as in the heavens, white stars, and red and white stripes that enfolded him like a caress. The sailors lifted him up and waited a moment, until the tall, stately, distinguished figure of the colonel, in his plain civilian dress, stepped out from the group of officers and stood beside the grating; he put his hand upon the flag of his country, glad to do this service for a faithful if humble friend. It was soon over; with a little heavier splash old Bentley fell into the sea he had so loved, joining that innumerable multitude of those who, having done their duty, wait for that long-deferred day when the sea shall give up her dead! The woman hid her face within her hands, the great bell of the ship tolled solemnly forward, the sun had set, the men were dismissed, the watch called, and the night fell softly, while the ship glided on in the darkness.

Another week had elapsed. The Yarmouth had been driven steadily northward, and by contrary winds prevented from making her course. She was in a precarious condition too; a further examination had disclosed that some of her spars, especially the mainmast, had been so severely and seriously wounded, even more so than at first reported, as scarcely to permit any sail at all to be set on them, and not fit in anyway to endure stress of weather. The damages had been made good, however, as far as possible, the rigging knotted and spliced, the spars fished and strengthened as well. The ship had been leaking slightly all the time, from injuries received in the fight, in all probability; but a few hours at the pumps daily had hitherto kept her free, and though the carpenter had been most assiduous in a search for the leaks, and had stopped as many as he had been able to come at, some of them could not be found. The weather had steadily changed for the worse as they had reached higher latitudes, and it was now cold, rainy, and very threatening. The captain and his officers were filled with anxiety and foreboding. Katharine kept sedulously in her cabin, devoured by grief and despair; and the once cheery colonel, full of deep sympathy for his unfortunate daughter, went about softly and sadly during the long days.

The day broke gloomily on one certain unfortunate morning; they had not seen the sun for five days, nor did they see it then. No gladsome light flooded the heavens and awoke the sea; the sky was deeply overcast with cold, dull, leaden clouds that hung low and heavy over the mighty ship; a horror of darkness enshrouded the ocean. Away off on the horizon to the northeast the sky was black with great masses of frightful-looking clouds; through the glass the watchful officers saw that rain was falling in torrents from them, while the vivid lightning played incessantly through them. Where the ship was, it had fallen suddenly calm, and she lay gently rolling and rocking in the moderate swell; but they could see the hurricane driving down upon them, coming at lightning speed, standing like a solid wall, and flattening the waves by sheer weight. All hands had been called on deck at once, at the first glimpse of the coming hurricane. Desborough had the trumpet; the alert and eager topmen were sent aloft to strip the ship of the little canvas which the heavy weather and weakened spars had permitted them to show. It was a race between them and the coming storm. The men worked desperately, madly; some of them had not yet reached the deck when the rain and the wind were upon them. By the captain's direction, the colonel had brought Katharine from below, and she was standing on the quarter-deck sheltered by the overhang of the poop above, listlessly watching. Desborough had made no progress in his love-affairs; he had too much tact and delicacy to press his suit under the present untoward circumstances, and indeed had been too incessantly occupied with the pressing exigencies of the shattered ship, and the duties of his responsible position thereon, to have any time to spare for more than the common courtesies. The awful storm was at last upon them: a sudden change in its direction caused the first fierce blow to fall fairly upon the starboard side of the ship; it pressed her down on her beam-ends; over and over she went, down, down. Would she ever right again? Ah, the spliced shrouds and stays on the weather-side, which had been that attacked by the Randolph, finally gave way, the mainmast went by the board about halfway below the top, the foremast at the cap, and the mizzentopmast, too; relieved of this enormous mass of heavy top hamper, the ship slowly righted herself. The immense mass of wreckage beat and thundered against the port side; it was a fearful situation, but all was not yet lost. Gallantly led by Desborough himself, who saw in one sweeping glance that Katharine was still safe, the men, with axes and knives, hacked through the rigging which held the wreck of the giant spars to the ship, and after a few moments of sickening suspense she drifted clear; a bit of storm canvas was spread forward on the wreck of the foremast, and the ship got before the wind and drove on, laboring and pitching in the heavy sea. The decks were cleared; and indeed there was little left to clear, the waves having broken over her several times when she lay in the trough of the sea, sweeping everything out with them, and the vessel was a total wreck,—the spars gone, rails and bulwarks battered in and smashed, boats lost, the battle having destroyed these on the starboard side, and the wreck and the sea the others. Stop! there was one boat left amidships, a launch capable of holding about forty persons in a pinch, and still seaworthy; it was, by the captain's order, promptly made as serviceable as possible in view of the probable emergency.

About four o'clock in the afternoon the carpenter came aft with the sounding-rod of the well in his hand. The strain had been too much for her; some of the weakened timbers had given way, or some of the seams had opened, or perhaps a butt had started, for the ship was leaking badly. Still those dauntless men did not despair. The crew were told off in gangs to work, and all night the clank, clank, of the pumps was heard. Katharine dutifully laid down as she was bidden; but there was no sleep for her nor any one else on the ship that long night. The day broke again finally, but brought them no cheer: their labor had been unavailing; the leak had gained on them so rapidly that the ship lay low in the water, listless and inert, rolling in a sick, sluggish, helpless way in the trough of the sea. The wind had abated somewhat, and a boat well handled might live in the water now. By Captain Vincent's direction the men were sent to their stations on the spar, or upper deck. The boat's crew was chosen by selecting every fifteenth man in the long lines, the division officers doing the counting. The boat was launched without tackles, by main strength, sliding on rollers over the side through the broken bulwarks. Katharine, listless and indifferent, still attended by Chloe, was put aboard. Captain Vincent looked about among his officers; whom should he put in charge? They all looked deprecatingly and entreatingly at him. None desired to go; no one wished to be singled out to abandon the ship and his brother officers. His glance fell on Desborough.

"The duty is yours; you are the first officer of the ship."

"Oh, Captain Vincent, do not send me, I beg you. My place surely is on the ship with you. Cannot some one else—"

"No, you must go. My last command to you, my lord," he said, smiling faintly and extending his hand. Desborough, seeing the futility of further appeal, grasped it warmly in both his own, bowed to the other officers, and with a wave of his hand stepped on the rail and sprang into the tossing boat alongside.

"Are there any others to go?" he said.

The captain's eye fell upon the figure of the colonel standing among the officers.

"You are to go, sir. Nay, I will hear of no objections. You are my prisoner, and I am bound to see you delivered safely. Go, colonel. I mean it; I will have you put aboard by a file of marines if you do not go at once."

Katharine awoke from her apathy and stretched out her hands with a piteous cry,—

"Father, father, oh, I cannot lose you too."

"Prisoner or no prisoner, sir," said the colonel, "let me say that I am proud of my connection with you and your officers and your men. If I live to reach the shore, the world shall hear of this noble ending. Good-by, captain; good-by, gentlemen. I would fain stay with you."

"No, no!" was the cry from this band of heroes; and then Hollins sprang forward and shouted,—

"Lads! Three cheers for the colonel and for our shipmates in the launch! Let them tell at home that we were glad to stay by the old ship."

The hearty cheers came with a roar from five hundred throats.

"Good-by, good-by; God bless you!" cried the colonel, choking and utterly overcome, as he got into the boat, and sank down in the stern sheets beside his daughter.

"Colonel, we haven't a moment of time," whispered Desborough, who saw that the ship was sinking.

"Shove off, men; pull hard!"

A few moments of hard rowing in the heavy sea put them some little distance away, and the boat waited under just enough way to give them command of her. The men of the ship kept their stations; calm and peaceful, they also waited. The ship settled lower and lower; a man stepped hurriedly aft; and a moment later the bold and brilliant ensign of Old England, which never waved over braver men, fluttered out in the heavy breeze from the wrecked mast-head, the vivid red of the proud flag making a lurid dash of color against the gray sky-line. The ship was lower now. Now she plunged forward; the water rose; the captain raised his hand; three hearty cheers rang out; the drums beat; the marines presented arms. She was gone! The flag streamed out bravely on the surface of the water, and then it was drawn down; a confused mass of heads and waving arms was seen in the water, and they too in a moment were slowly drawn down into the vortex caused by the sinking ship. The woman again hid her face in her hands; the colonel laid his arm across the shoulder of his daughter; Desborough and the men in the boat stared horribly at the spot left vacant; a deep groan broke from them; they rose on the crest of a wave, sank down again, rose once more and looked again,—the little boat was alone on that mighty sea!

Oh, the agony of those long and frightful days in that little boat! Never a sail did they sight, as day after day they rowed or sailed to the westward, eagerly scanning the horizon for a landfall. The waves washed over them, saturating their clothing; the chill winds of winter froze them. First their provisions gave out, though served with the most rigid economy by Desborough himself; then the water, husbanded as no precious jewel was ever hoarded, was exhausted to the last drop, and that drop, by common consent, Desborough forced between Katharine's reluctant lips, though she would fain have refused it, claiming no indulgence beyond the others. The rare qualities of that young officer showed themselves brilliantly in this frightful peril. It was due to his skill and careful management that they were not swamped a dozen times; tireless, unselfish, cheerful, unsparing of himself, without him they would have died. The men bore their sufferings, when all food and water failed them, with the sturdy resolution of British sailors; Desborough his, with the courage of the hero that he was, his fiercest pang being for the white-faced girl who suffered in uncomplaining silence. The colonel exhibited the stoical indifference of a seasoned old soldier, as to his own personal condition, all his thoughts being centred upon his daughter, who passed through the dreadful experience with the calm resignation of a woman who had nothing left to live for, and, strange to say, seemed to feel it less acutely than the rest; even black Chloe, who had impartially shared with her mistress in all the favors accorded to her, being in a state of utter exhaustion, amounting to collapse.

When the pangs of hunger and thirst got hold of them, they refused—and were indeed entirely unable—to work longer with the oars, so that, unless the wind was fair and the sail was set, they simply drifted on.

One by one the sailors died. Waking from a troubled sleep of short duration, Katharine one day found Chloe's dead hand around her feet, her cold lips pressed upon them. Some of the men grew mad before they died, and raved and babbled of green fields and running brooks until the end came, and still the little boat drifted on. Few and short were the prayers the living said as, day by day they cast the dead into the sea. Desborough, the resolute, with undying strength kept steadily at the helm. Once only did he speak to Katharine in words of love. As their situation grew more and more hopeless, and even his resolute optimism began to fail him, he bent down and whispered in her ear,—

"I would not trouble you now, Katharine, but before we die I must tell you once again that I love you. Will you believe it?"

"I will believe it," she answered dully, giving him her hand. Oh, he thought in agony, as he bent over it and kissed it, how thin and white and feeble it was I One morning, after hope was dead, he was listlessly scanning the line of the horizon as the rising sun threw it into relief, more from habit than expectancy, when his heart almost stopped its feeble beating, for land was there before him if his strained eyes did not deceive him. Doubting the evidence of his weakened senses, and fearing the delusions of a disordered imagination, he refrained from communicating his impressions to any of the others until the light of day determined the accuracy of his vision. Then he whispered the news to Katharine, the apathetic woman told it to the sinking colonel, and then Desborough cried it to his dying crew. The wind sprang up at the moment too, and in a few hours they beached the boat upon a low sandy shore, with the waves breaking gently over it in long easy rollers. It was a desolate coast, sparsely wooded with small trees, and having little evidence of human habitation about it; but no glimpse of heaven could have more rejoiced a dying soul than this bleak haven to which they had been brought. They staggered, half fell, out of the boat, and lay exhausted, with ghastly haggard faces, on the shining sands, giving thanks to God for His mercy.

Desborough, as the strongest of the party, started inland, finding by and by a little stream of fresh water, and farther on, on higher ground, seeing a house, the smoke curling from its chimneys showing that it was inhabited. To the bubbling spring he half led, half dragged his shipwrecked party. They drank sparingly by his direction, and were refreshed, for with the cool water life and hope came back to them once more. Then he left them again and went on to the house. They had landed on the shore of Virginia, and the people of the house welcomed and cared for the poor castaways, sharing with them their humble store with the kindly hospitality for which the land was famous. Their long voyage was at an end, their troubles were over. The colonel and Katharine would be free again; they might go home once more, and Desborough would be a prisoner.

BOOK V

THE DEAD ALIVE AGAIN

CHAPTER XL

A FINAL APPEAL

It was springtime again in Virginia. The sky, its blue depths accentuated by the shifting clouds, was never more clear, wherever it appeared in the intervals of sunshine, nor the air more fresh and pure, even in that land famed for its bright skies and its mild climate, than it was this April day; which, with its sunshine and showers in unregulated alternation, seemed symbolical of life,—that life of which every tender blade of grass, every venturesome flower thrusting its head above the sod, seemed to speak. There was health and strength in the gentle breeze which wantonly played with the budding leaves of the great trees, already putting forth little evangels of that splendid foliage with which they decked themselves in the full glory of summer. That merry wind which swept through the open boat-house at the end of the wharf laid a bold hand upon the curls which fell about the neck of the young girl sitting there by the door near the water on one of the benches, gazing out over the broad reaches of the quiet, ever beautiful Potomac, rippled gently by the wind under the late afternoon sun. The gallant little breeze, fragrant with balm and perfume of the trees and flowers, kissed a faint color into her pale cheek, and seemed to whisper to her despondent heart in murmuring sounds that framed themselves into the immortal words "hope, hope."

The young girl had but yesterday entered upon her twentieth spring. Four months ago there had not been a merrier, lighter-hearted, gayer, more coquettish young maiden in tidewater Virginia; and to-day, she thought, as she looked down at her thin hand outlined so clearly upon the vivid cardinal cloak she wore, which had dropped unheeded on the seat by her side, to-day she was like that man in the play of whom her father read,—a grave man. No, not a man at all. Once, in her enthusiasm, she had fondly imagined that she had possessed all those daring qualities of energy and action, those manly virtues, which might have been hers by inheritance could the accident of sex have been reversed. But now she knew she was but a woman, after all,—so weak, so feeble, so listless. What had she left to live for? Once it was her father, then it was her country, then it was her lover; now? Nothing! Her father at the request of Congress would soon resume his interrupted duties in France, now become more important than ever. He was a man of the world and a soldier, a diplomat. The hard experiences of the past few months were for him episodes, exciting truly, but only part of a lifetime spent in large adventure, soon forgotten in some other strenuous part demanded by some other strenuous exigency. But she,—no, she was not a man at all, but a woman,—unused to such scenes and happenings as fate had lately made her a participant in. Her father might have his country,—he had not lost his love, his heart was not buried out in the depths of the cruel sea. What had become of that Roman patriotism upon which she prided herself in times past? Her country! What had changed her so? There were many answers.

There was Blodgett's grave at the foot of the hill. She had played in childhood with that faithful old soldier. Many a tale had he told her of her gallant father when, as a young man, he gayly rode away to the wars, leaving her lady mother in tears behind. She could sympathize with waiting women now, and understand. Those were such deeds of daring that the rude recital of the old man once stirred her very heart with joy and terror; now she was sick at the thought of them. And Blodgett was gone; he had died defending them, where he had been stationed. That was an answer.

There, too, far away in another State, lay the lover of her girlhood's happy day,—the bright-eyed, eager, gallant, joyous lad. What good comrades they had been! How they had laughed, and played, and ridden, and rowed, and hunted, and danced, and flirted, through the morning of life,—how pleasant had been that life indeed! He was quiet now; she could no longer join in his ringing laugh, the sound of his voice was stilled, they might never play together again,— was there any play at all in life? That was another answer.

There was the white-haired mother, the stately little royalist, Madam Talbot, who slept in peace on the hill at Fairview Hall, her ambitions, her hopes, and her loyalty buried with her, leaving the place untenanted save by wistful memories; she too had gone.

Answers?—they crowded thick upon her! There were the officers of the Yarmouth, Captain Vincent, Beauchamp, Hollins, and the little boy, the Honorable Giles, and all the other officers and men with whom she had come in contact on that frightful cruise. There were the heroic men who had stayed by their ship, who had seen the favored few go away in the only boat that was left seaworthy, without a murmur at being left behind, who had faced death unheeding, unrepining, sinking down in the dark water with a cheer upon their lips. There was the old sailor, too, with his unquenchable patriotism, her friend because the friend of her lover; and Philip, her brother; and there was Seymour himself. Ah, what were all the rest to him! Gone, and how she loved him!

She leaned her head upon her hand and thought of him. Here in this boat-house he had first spoken to her of his love. Here she had first felt his lips touch her cheek. There, rocked gently by the light breeze, upon the water at her feet was the familiar little pleasure-boat; she had not allowed any one to row her about in it since her return, in spite of much entreaty. It was this very cloak she wore that day, nearly the very hour. The place was redolent with sweet memories of happy days, though to think on them now broke her heart. It all came back to her as it had come again and again. She briefly reviewed that acquaintance, short though it was, which had changed the whole course of her life. She saw him again, as he struck prompt to defend her honor in the hall, resenting a ruffian's soiling hand stretched out to her; she saw him lying wounded and senseless there at her feet. She saw him stretched prone on that shattered deck, on that ruined ship, pale, blood-stained, senseless again, again unheeding her bitter cry. She would have called once more upon him, save that she knew humanity has no voice which reaches out into the darkness by which it may call back those who are once gone to live beyond. She did not weep,—that were a small thing, a trifle; she sat and brooded. What had she lost in the service of her country? What sacrifices had been exacted from her by that insatiable country! Alas, alas, she thought, men may have a country, a woman has only a heart.

Four short months had changed it all. How young she had been! Would she ever be young again? How full of the joy of life! Its currents swept by her unheeded now. Why had not God been merciful to her, that she could have died there upon the sea, she thought. Ah, poor humanity never learns His mercy; perhaps it is because we have no measure by which to fathom its mighty depths. She saw herself old and lonely, forgotten but not forgetting. But even then lacked she not opportunity; woman-like, in spite of her constancy, she took a melancholy pleasure in the thought that there was one still who hungered for the shattered remnants of her broken heart, who lived for the sound of her voice and the glance other eyes and the light of her face. One there was, handsome, brave, distinguished, gentle, of ancient name, assured station, ample fortune, who longed to lay all he was or had at her feet.

But what were these things? Nothing to her, nothing. There was but one, as she had said on the ship to Desborough: "I love a sailor; you are not he." And yet her soul was filled with pity for the gallant gentleman, and she thought of him tenderly with deep affection.

Presently she heard quick footsteps on the floor of the boat-house, and turning her head she saw him. He held a letter, an official packet, with the seal broken, open in his hand.

"Oh, Miss Wilton, you here?" he said. "I have looked everywhere for you. Do you not think the evening air grows chill? Is it not too cold for you out here in the boat-house? Allow me;" and then, with that gentle solicitude which women prize, he lifted the neglected cloak and tenderly wrapped it about her shoulders.

"Thank you," she said gratefully, faintly smiling up at him, "but I hardly need it. I do not feel at all cold. The air is so pleasant and the sun is not yet set, you see. Did you wish to see me about anything special, Lord Desborough?"

"No—yes—that is—Oh, Mistress Katharine, the one special want of my life is to see you always and everywhere. You know that,—nay, never lift your hand,—I remember. I will try not to trespass upon your orders again. I came to tell you that—I am going away."

"Going away," she repeated sadly. "Has your exchange

been made?"

"Yes; a courier came to the Hall a short time since, and here it is. My orders, you see; I must leave at once."

"I am sorry, indeed sorry that you must go."

He started suddenly as if to speak, a little flash of hope flickering in his despondent face; but she continued quickly,—

"It has been very pleasant for us to have you here, except that you have been a prisoner; but now you will be free, and for that, of course, I rejoice. But I have so few friends left," she went on mournfully, "I am loath to see one depart, even though he be an enemy."

"Oh, do not call me an enemy, I entreat you, Katharine. Oh, let me speak just once again," he interrupted with his usual impetuosity; "and talk not to me of freedom! While the earth holds you I am not free: ay, even should Heaven claim you, I still am bound. All the days of my captivity here I have been a most willing and happy prisoner,—your prisoner. I have looked forward with dread and anguish to the day when I might be exchanged and have to go away. Here would I have been content to pass my life, by your side. Oh, once again let me plead! My duty, my honor, call me now to the service of my king. I no longer have excuse for delay, but you have almost made me forget there was a king. Now that I must go, why should I go alone?" he went on eagerly. "I know, I know you love the—the other,—but he is gone. You do not hate me, you even like me; you regret my going; perhaps as days go by, you will regret it more. We are at least friends; let me take care of you in future. Oh, it kills me to see you so white, and indifferent to life and all that it has or should have for you. You are only a girl yet,—I cannot bear to see all the

Cyrus Townsend Brady

color gone out of your sweet face, the light out of your eyes; the sight of that thin hand breaks my heart. Won't you live for me to love,—live, and let me love you? Your father goes to-morrow, so he says, and you will be left alone here; why should it be? Go with me. Give me a right to do what my heart aches to do for you,—to coax the roses back into your cheek, to woo the laugh to your lips, to win happiness back to your heart; to devote my life to you, darling. Have pity on me, have pity on my love,—have pity!"

His voice dropped into a passionate whisper; as he pleaded with her, he sank down upon one knee by her side, beseeching by word and gesture and look that she should show him that pity he could see in her eyes, that he knew was in her heart, and to which he made his last appeal; and then, lifting the hem of her dress to his lips with an unconscious movement of passionate reverence, he waited.

She looked at him in silence a moment. So young, so handsome, so appealing, her heart filled with sorrow and sympathy for him. There was hope in his eyes which she had not seen for many days; how could she drive it away and crush his heart! It might be cruel, but she had no answer, no other answer, no new word, to tell him. Her eyes filled with tears; she could not trust herself to speak, she only shook her head.

"Ah," he said, rising to his feet and throwing up his hands with a gesture of despair, "I knew it. Well, the dream is over at last. This is the end. I sought life, and found death; that, at least, if it shall come I shall welcome. Would God I had gone down with the ship! You have no pity; you let a dead image—an idea—stand between you and a living love. Will you never forget?"

"Never," she said softly. "Love knows no death. He is

alive—here. But do not grieve so for me; I am not worth it. You will go away and forget, and—"

"No; you have said it, 'Love knows no death.' I, too, cannot forget. As long as I live I shall love—and remember. How if I waited and waited? Katharine, I would wait forever for you," he said, suddenly catching at the trifle.

"No, it would be no use. My friend, we both must suffer; it cannot be otherwise. I esteem you, respect you, admire you. You have protected me, honored me; my gratitude—" She went on brokenly, "You might ask anything of me but my heart, and that is given away."

"Let me take you without it, then. I want but you."

"No, Lord Desborough, it cannot be. Do not ask me again. No, I cannot say I wish it otherwise."

His flickering hope died away in silence. "Katharine, will you promise me, if there ever comes a time—"

"I promise," she said; "but the time will never come."

He looked at her as dying men look to the light, there was a long silence, and then he said,—

"I must go now, Katharine. I suppose I must bid you good-by now?"

"Yes, I think it would be best."

"I shall pass this way again on my journey to Alexandria in half an hour; may I not speak once more to you then?"

"No," she said finally, after a long pause. "I think it best that we should end it now. It can do no good at all. Good-by, and may God bless you."

He bent and kissed her hand, and then stopped a moment and looked at her, saying never a word.

"Good-by, again," she said.

On the instant he turned and left her.

CHAPTER XLI

INTO THE HAVEN, AT LAST

Two weary horsemen on tired horses were slowly riding up the river road just where it entered the Wilton plantation. One was young, a mere boy in years; but a certain habit of command, with the responsibility accompanying, had given him a more manly appearance than his age warranted. The other, to a casual glance, seemed much older than his companion, though closer inspection would show that he was still a young man, and that those marks upon his face which the careless passer-by would consider the attributes of age had been traced by the fingers of grief and trouble. The bronzed and weather-beaten faces of both riders bespoke an open-air life, and suggested those who go down upon the great deep in ships, a suggestion further borne out by the faded, worn naval uniforms they wore. In spite of the joy of springtime which was all about them, both were silent and both were sad; but the sadness of the boy, as was natural, was less deep, less intense, than that of the man. He was too young to realize the greatness of the loss he had sustained in the death of his father and sister; and were it not for the constant reminder afforded him by the presence of his gloomy companion, he would probably, with the careless elasticity of youth, have been more successful in throwing off his own sorrow. The man had not lost a father or a sister, but some one dearer still. He looked thin and ill, and under the permanent bronze of his countenance the ravages wrought by fever, wounds, and long illness were plainly perceptible; there were gray hairs in his thick neatly tied locks, too, that had no rightful place there in one of his age. The younger and stronger assisted and watched over his older companion with the tenderest care and attention.

They rode slowly up the pleasant road under the great trees, from time to time engaging in a desultory conversation. Philip endeavored to cheer his companion by talking lightly of boyhood days, as each turn of the road brought familiar places in the old estate in view. Here he and Katharine and Hilary had been wont to play; there was a favorite spot, a pleasant haunt here, this had been the scene of some amusing adventure. These well-meant reminiscences nearly drove Seymour mad, but he would not stop them. Finally, they came to the place where the road divided, one branch pursuing its course along the river-bank past the boat-house toward the Talbot place, the other turning inland from the river and winding about till it surmounted the high bluff and reached the door of the Hall. There Philip drew rein.

"This is the way to the Hall, you know, Captain Seymour," he said, pointing to the right. Seymour hesitated a moment, and said finally,—

"Yes, I know; the boat-house lies over there, does it not, beyond the turn? I think I will let you go up to the house alone, Philip, and I will go down to the boat-house myself. I will ride back presently."

"Well, then, I will go with you," said Philip. "I really think you are too weak, you know, especially after our long ride to-day, to go alone."

"No, Philip," said Seymour, gently, "I wish to be alone for a few moments."

The boy hesitated.

"Oh, very well," he said, beginning to understand, "I will sit down here on this tree by the road and wait for you. I'll tie my horse, and you can leave yours here also, if you wish. There is nothing at the Hall, God knows, to make me hurry up there now, since father and Katharine are gone," he continued with a sigh. "Go on, sir, I'll wait. You won't mind my waiting?"

"No, certainly not, if you wish it I shall be back in a few minutes anyway. I just want to see the—the—ah—boat-house, you know."

"Yes, certainly, I understand, of course," replied Philip, bluntly, but carefully looking away, and then dismounting from his tired horse and assisting Seymour to do the same from his.

"Poor old fellow!" he murmured, as he saw the man walk haltingly and painfully up the road and disappear around the little bend.

Left to himself Seymour stumbled alone along the familiar road over which a few short months before he had often travelled light-heartedly by the side of Katharine. As he pressed on, he noticed a man leave the boat-house and climb slowly up the hill. Desirous of escaping the notice of the stranger, who, he supposed, might be the factor or agent of the plantation, he waited in the shadow of the trees until the man disappeared over the brow of the hill, and then he staggered on. A short time after, he stood on the landward end of the little pier, and then his heart stood still for a second, and then leaped madly in his breast, as he seemed to hear a subtle voice, like an echo of the past, which whispered his name, "Seymour! Seymour!" Stepping toward the middle of the pier so that he could see the interior of the boat-house through the inner door, his eyes fell upon the figure of a woman standing in the other doorway looking out over the water, stretching out her hands. The sun had set by this time, and the gray dusk of the evening was stealing over the river. He could not see distinctly, but there was light enough to show him a familiar scarlet cloak at her feet, and although her back was turned to him, he recognized the graceful outlines of her slender figure. It was Katharine, or a dream! But could the dead return again? Had the sea given up her dead indeed?

He could not believe the evidence of his bewildered senses. It might be an hallucination, the baseless fabric of a vision, some image conjured from the deep recesses of his loving heart by his enfeebled disordered imagination, and yet he surely had heard a living voice, "Seymour—John—Oh, my love!" Stifling the beating of his heart, holding his breath even, stepping softly, lest he should affright the airy vision, he staggered to the door and stood gazing; then he whispered one word,—

"Katharine!"

It was only a whisper she heard, but it reached the very centre of her being.

"Katharine," he said softly again, with so much passionate entreaty in his wistful voice, that under its compelling influence she slowly turned and looked toward the other door from whence the sound had come. Then as she saw him, lifting one hand to her head while the other unconsciously sought her heart, she shrank back against the wall, and stared at him in voiceless terror. He dropped unsteadily to his knee, as if to worship at a shrine.

"Oh, do not go away," he whispered. "I know it is only a dream of mine—so many times have I seen you, ever since the night the frigate struck and I sent you to your death on that rocky pass, in that beating sea. Ay, in the long hours of the fever—but you did not shrink away from me then, you listened to me say I love you, and you answered." He stretched out his hand toward her in tender appeal. She bent forward toward him. He rose to his feet, half in terror.

"Kate," he said uncertainly, "is it indeed you? Are you alive again?"

She was nearer now. One glad cry broke from her lips; he was in her arms again, and she was clasped to his heart!—a real woman and no dream, no vision. What the wind could only faintly shadow forth upon her cheek, sprang into life under the touch of his fevered lips, and color flooded them like a wave. Laughing, crying, sobbing, she clung to him, kissed him with little incoherent murmurs, gazed at him, wept over him, kissed him again. All the troubles of the intervening days of sadness and privation faded away from her like a disused chrysalis, and she sparkled with life and love like a butterfly new born.

He that was dead was alive again, he had come back, and he was here! As for him, in fearful surprise, he held her to his breast once more, still unbelieving. She noticed then an empty sleeve, and raised it tenderly to her lips.

"I lost it after an action with the British ship Yarmouth,—it was only a flesh wound at first,—we were long in reaching Charleston; the arm had to be amputated. It was a fearful action."

Cyrus Townsend Brady

"I know it," she interrupted; "I was there."

"You, Katharine! Ah, that woman on the ship! I was not deceived then, and yet I could not believe it."

"Yes, 'twas I. I gloried in your bravery, until I saw you lying, as I thought, dead on the deck. Oh, John, the horror of that moment! Then I called you, and you did not answer. Then I wanted to die, too, but now I am alive again, and so happy— but for this;" she lifted the empty sleeve to her lips. "How you must have suffered, my poor darling," she went on, her eyes filling with tears, her heart yearning over him. "And how ill you look, and I keep you standing here,—how thoughtless! Come to the bench here and sit down. Lean on me."

"Nay, but, Kate, you too have suffered. See!" He lifted her arm, the loose sleeve fell back. "Oh, how thin it is, and how smooth and round and plump it was when I kissed it last," he said, as he raised it tenderly again to his lips.

"It is nothing, John. I shall be all right now that you are here. You poor shattered lover, how you must have suffered!" she went on, with a sob in her voice.

"Oh, Katharine, this," looking down at his empty sleeve, "was nothing to what I suffered before, when I thought I had killed you!"

"When you thought you had killed me!" she said in surprise. They were sitting close together now, and she had his hand in both her own. "How—when, was that?"

And then he told her rapidly about the loss of the Radnor, and the idea which her note had given that she was on board of it.

"And you led that ship down to destruction, believing I was on her! How could you do it, John?" she said reproachfully.

"It was my duty, darling Kate," he said desperately.

"And did you love your duty more than me?"

"Love it? I hated it! But I had to do it, dearest," he went on pleadingly. "Honor—you told me so yourself, here, in this very spot; I remember your words; do you not recall them?—'If I stood in the pathway of liberty for a single instant I should despise the man who would not sweep me aside without a moment's hesitation.' Don't you know you said that, Katharine?"

"Did I say it? Ah, but that was before I loved you so, and you swept me aside,—well, I love you still, and, John, I honor you for it too; but I could not do it. You see, I am only a woman."

"Kate, don't say 'only a woman' that way; what else would I have you, pray? But tell me of yourself."

Briefly she recited the events that had occurred to her, dwelling much upon Desborough's courage and devotion to her in the first days of her captivity, the death of Johnson, the burning of Norfolk, the death of Bentley. He interrupted her there, and would fain hear every detail of the sad scene over again, thanking her and blessing her for what she had done.

"It was nothing," she said simply; "I loved to do it; he was your friend. It seemed to bring me closer to you." Then she told him of the foundering of the ship, of the frightful voyage in the boat, and rang the changes upon Desborough's name, his cheerfulness, his unfailing zeal and energy, until Seymour's heart filled with jealous pain.

"Kate," he said at last, "as I came up the road I saw a man leave the boat-house and climb the hill; who was it?"

"It was Lord Desborough, John."

Seymour was human, and filled with human feeling. He drew away from her.

"What was he doing here?" he said coldly. She smiled at him merrily.

"Bidding me good-by. He was made prisoner, of course, by the first soldier we came across after we landed, and has been spending the days of his captivity with us. He was exchanged to-day, and leaves to-night."

"Katharine, he was in love with you!" he said, with what seemed to him marvellous perspicacity.

"Yes, John," she answered, still smiling.

"Was he making love to you here?"

"Yes."

"And you? You praise this man, you like him, you—"

"I think him the bravest man, the truest gentleman in the world—except this one," she said, laying her hand upon his shoulder and her head upon his breast. "No, no; he pleaded in vain. I only pitied him; I loved you. Do not be jealous, foolish boy. No one should have me. I am yours alone."

"But if I had not come back, Kate,—how then?"

"It would have made no difference. I told him so."

Neither of them in their mutual absorption had noticed that a horse had stopped in the road opposite the boat-house, and a horseman had walked to the door and had halted at the sight which met his eyes. Desborough recognized Seymour at once, and he had unwittingly heard the end of the conversation. He was the second. The man was back again. It was true. The gallant gentleman stood still a moment, making no sound, then turned back and mounted his horse, and rode madly away with despair in his heart.

"Oh, Katharine," Seymour said at last, "do you know that I am a poor man now? Lame! See, I can no longer walk straight." He stood up. "Poor surgery after the battle did that."

"The more reason that in the future you should not go alone," she said softly, standing by his side.

"And with but one arm," he continued.

"No, three," she said again, "for here are two."

"Besides, my trading ships have been captured by the enemy, my private fortune has been spent for the cause. I am a poor man in every sense."

"Nay, John, you are a rich man," she said gayly.

"Oh, yes, rich in your love, Katharine."

"Yes, that of course, if that be riches, and richer in honor too; but that's not all."

"What else pray, dearest?"

"Did you know that Madam Talbot had died?" she answered,

with apparent irrelevance.

"No, but I am not surprised at it. After her son's death I expected it, poor lady. He loved you too, Kate. We fought about you once," he said; and then he told her briefly of Talbot's end, his burial, the interview he had with Talbot's mother, and the letter.

"I have seen that letter since I returned," she said. "It is at Fairview Hall now awaiting you, awaiting its master like the other things there,—and here. Shall we live there, think you, John?"

"Awaiting me! Its master! Live there! What mean you, Kate?" he cried in surprise.

"Yes, yes, it is all yours," she replied, laughing at his astonishment. "A codicil to her will, written and signed the day before she died, the day after you saw her, left it all to you. It was to have been her son's and then mine; and when she believed us dead, as she had no relatives in this land she left it to you, 'As,' I quote her own words, 'a true and noble gentleman who honors any cause, however mistaken, to which he may give his allegiance.' I quote them, but they are my own words as well. You are a rich man, John, and the two estates will come together as father and Madam Talbot had hoped, after all."

"I am glad, Kate, for your sake."

"It is nothing. I should have taken you, if you had nothing at all."

A young man ran down the little pier and into the house at this moment. "Kate," he cried, "where are you? It is so dark here I can hardly see—Ah, there you are!" he ran forward and kissed her boisterously. "You'll have to forgive me, I could not wait any longer, Captain Seymour. Father rode down the hill after Lord Desborough galloped by me, and met me there, waiting. Oh, I was so glad to know you were alive again! We felt like a pair of murderers, didn't we, Captain Seymour? Father told me you were here, Kate, and then we waited until now, to give you a little time, and then I couldn't stand it any longer, I had to see you. Father's coming too, but I ran ahead."

"Why, Philip," cried Kate, as soon as he gave her an opportunity, kissing him again and laughing light-heartedly as she has not done for days, "how you have grown! You are quite a man now."

"It is entirely due to Philip, Katharine, that I am here," said Seymour. "He commanded the little brig which ran down to the Yarmouth at the risk of destruction, and picked me up. Disobeyed orders too, the young rogue. He brought me into Charleston, nursed me like a woman, and then brought me here. I should have died without him."

"Oh, Philip," said the delighted girl, kissing the proud and happy youngster with more warmth than he had ever known before, "promise me always to disobey your orders. How can I thank you!"

"Very bad advice that. Promise nothing of the kind, Philip; but what are you thanking him for, Kate?" said the cheery voice of the colonel as he came in the door.

"Thanking him for Seymour, father."

"Ah, my boy," said the colonel, grasping his hand, "you don't know how glad I am to see you. It is like one returning from the dead. But it is late and cold and quite dark. Supper is ready, let us go up to the Hall. I shall see the Naval Commissioners in a few days, Seymour, and get you another and a better ship. The country is full of your action; they've struck a medal for you and voted you prize money and thanks, and all that. I make no doubt I can get you the best ship there is on the ways, or planned. 'T was a most heroic action—"

"Not now, father," said Katharine, jealously, throwing her arm about her lover. "He shall not, cannot, go now; he must have rest for a long time, and he must have me! We are to be married as soon as he is well, and the country must wait. Is it not so, John?"

"What's that?" said the colonel, pretending great surprise.

"Sir," answered Seymour, nervously, "I have something to say to you,—something I must say. Will you give me the privilege of a few moments' conversation with you?"

"Seymour," said the colonel, smiling, "you asked me that once before, did you not?"

"Yes, sir, I believe so."

"And I answered you—how?"

"Why, you said, if my memory serves me, that you—"

"Exactly, that I would see you after supper, and so I will. Come, children, let us go in; this time I warrant you there will be no interruptions."

The father and son turned considerately and walked away, leaving the two lovers to follow.

"You won't leave me, John, will you, now that you have just

come back?"

"No, Kate, not now; I am good for nothing until I get strong."

"Good for me, though; but when you do get strong?"

"Then, if my country needs me, dearest, I shall have to go. But I fear there will be no more ships of ours to get to sea, the blockade is getting more strict every day. I can be a soldier, though. No, Kate, do not beg me. My duty to my country constrains me."

"Don't talk about it now, then, John. At least I shall have you for a long time; it will be long before you are well again."

"Yes, I fear so," he said with a sigh.

"Why do you sigh, dearest?"

"Because I want to stay with you, and I ought to welcome any opportunity to enter active service. Think what old Bentley would say."

"Old Bentley did not love you," she replied quickly, with a jealous pang.

"Ah, did he not!" said Seymour, softly.

There was a long pause.

"Well," said Katharine at last, "I suppose nothing will move you if your duty calls you, but I warn you if you get killed again, I shall die. I could not stand it another time," she cried piteously.

"Well, dearest, I shall try to live for you. Now we must go to the Hall."

But, to anticipate, fate would be kinder toward Katharine in the future than she had been in the past and it was many a day before her lover, her husband rather, was able to get to sea; and, as if they had suffered enough, he went through the rest of the war on land and sea scatheless, and was one of those who stood beside the great commander before the trenches of Yorktown, when the British soldiers laid down their arms. But this was all of the future, and now they turned quietly and somewhat sadly to follow the others.

This time it was Katharine who helped Seymour up the hill. Slowly, hand in hand, they walked across the lawn, up the steps of the porch, and toward the door of the Hall. The night had fallen, and the house was filled with a soft light from the wax candles. They paused a moment on the threshhold; Katharine resolutely mastered her fears and resolved to be happy in the present, then, heedless of all who might see, she kissed him.

"Home at last, John," she said, beaming upon him. And there, with the dark behind, and the light before, we may say good-by to them.

ABOUT THE AUTHOR

Cyrus Townsend Brady (1861-1920) was a journalist, historian and adventure writer. His most well-known work is "Indian Fights and Fighters". He was born in Allegheny, Pennsylvania on December 20, 1861 and graduated from the U.S. Naval Academy in 1883. He was also a deacon in the Episcopal church. His first wife was Clarissa Guthrie, who died in 1890. His second wife was Mary Barrett.

Choose from Thousands of 1stWorldLibrary Classics By

A. M. Barnard
Ada Leverson
Adolphus William Ward
Aesop
Agatha Christie
Alexander Aaronsohn
Alexander Kielland
Alexandre Dumas
Alfred Gatty
Alfred Ollivant
Alice Duer Miller
Alice Turner Curtis
Alice Dunbar
Allen Chapman
Alleyne Ireland
Ambrose Bierce
Amelia E. Barr
Amory H. Bradford
Andrew Lang
Andrew McFarland Davis
Andy Adams
Angela Brazil
Anna Alice Chapin
Anna Sewell
Annie Besant
Annie Hamilton Donnell
Annie Payson Call
Annie Roe Carr
Annonaymous
Anton Chekhov
Archibald Lee Fletcher
Arnold Bennett
Arthur C. Benson
Arthur Conan Doyle
Arthur M. Winfield
Arthur Ransome
Arthur Schnitzler
Arthur Train
Atticus
B.H. Baden-Powell
B. M. Bower
B. C. Chatterjee
Baroness Emmuska Orczy
Baroness Orczy
Basil King
Bayard Taylor
Ben Macomber
Bertha Muzzy Bower
Bjornstjerne Bjornson

Booth Tarkington
Boyd Cable
Bram Stoker
C. Collodi
C. E. Orr
C. M. Ingleby
Carolyn Wells
Catherine Parr Traill
Charles A. Eastman
Charles Amory Beach
Charles Dickens
Charles Dudley Warner
Charles Farrar Browne
Charles Ives
Charles Kingsley
Charles Klein
Charles Hanson Towne
Charles Lathrop Pack
Charles Romyn Dake
Charles Whibley
Charles Willing Beale
Charlotte M. Braeme
Charlotte M. Yonge
Charlotte Perkins Stetson
Clair W. Hayes
Clarence Day Jr.
Clarence E. Mulford
Clemence Housman
Confucius
Coningsby Dawson
Cornelis DeWitt Wilcox
Cyril Burleigh
D. H. Lawrence
Daniel Defoe
David Garnett
Dinah Craik
Don Carlos Janes
Donald Keyhoe
Dorothy Kilner
Dougan Clark
Douglas Fairbanks
E. Nesbit
E. P. Roe
E. Phillips Oppenheim
E. S. Brooks
Earl Barnes
Edgar Rice Burroughs
Edith Van Dyne
Edith Wharton

Edward Everett Hale
Edward J. O'Biren
Edward S. Ellis
Edwin L. Arnold
Eleanor Atkins
Eleanor Hallowell Abbott
Eliot Gregory
Elizabeth Gaskell
Elizabeth McCracken
Elizabeth Von Arnim
Ellem Key
Emerson Hough
Emilie F. Carlen
Emily Bronte
Emily Dickinson
Enid Bagnold
Enilor Macartney Lane
Erasmus W. Jones
Ernie Howard Pie
Ethel May Dell
Ethel Turner
Ethel Watts Mumford
Eugene Sue
Eugenie Foa
Eugene Wood
Eustace Hale Ball
Evelyn Everett-green
Everard Cotes
F. H. Cheley
F. J. Cross
F. Marion Crawford
Fannie E. Newberry
Federick Austin Ogg
Ferdinand Ossendowski
Fergus Hume
Florence A. Kilpatrick
Fremont B. Deering
Francis Bacon
Francis Darwin
Frances Hodgson Burnett
Frances Parkinson Keyes
Frank Gee Patchin
Frank Harris
Frank Jewett Mather
Frank L. Packard
Frank V. Webster
Frederic Stewart Isham
Frederick Trevor Hill
Frederick Winslow Taylor

Friedrich Kerst	Hayden Carruth	James Branch Cabell
Friedrich Nietzsche	Helent Hunt Jackson	James DeMille
Fyodor Dostoyevsky	Helen Nicolay	James Joyce
G.A. Henty	Hendrik Conscience	James Lane Allen
G.K. Chesterton	Hendy David Thoreau	James Lane Allen
Gabrielle E. Jackson	Henri Barbusse	James Oliver Curwood
Garrett P. Serviss	Henrik Ibsen	James Oppenheim
Gaston Leroux	Henry Adams	James Otis
George A. Warren	Henry Ford	James R. Driscoll
George Ade	Henry Frost	Jane Abbott
Geroge Bernard Shaw	Henry James	Jane Austen
George Cary Eggleston	Henry Jones Ford	Jane L. Stewart
George Durston	Henry Seton Merriman	Janet Aldridge
George Ebers	Henry W Longfellow	Jens Peter Jacobsen
George Eliot	Herbert A. Giles	Jerome K. Jerome
George Gissing	Herbert Carter	Jessie Graham Flower
George MacDonald	Herbert N. Casson	John Buchan
George Meredith	Herman Hesse	John Burroughs
George Orwell	Hildegard G. Frey	John Cournos
George Sylvester Viereck	Homer	John F. Kennedy
George Tucker	Honore De Balzac	John Gay
George W. Cable	Horace B. Day	John Glasworthy
George Wharton James	Horace Walpole	John Habberton
Gertrude Atherton	Horatio Alger Jr.	John Joy Bell
Gordon Casserly	Howard Pyle	John Kendrick Bangs
Grace E. King	Howard R. Garis	John Milton
Grace Gallatin	Hugh Lofting	John Philip Sousa
Grace Greenwood	Hugh Walpole	John Taintor Foote
Grant Allen	Humphry Ward	Jonas Lauritz Idemil Lie
Guillermo A. Sherwell	Ian Maclaren	Jonathan Swift
Gulielma Zollinger	Inez Haynes Gillmore	Joseph A. Altsheler
Gustav Flaubert	Irving Bacheller	Joseph Carey
H. A. Cody	Isabel Cecilia Williams	Joseph Conrad
H. B. Irving	Isabel Hornibrook	Joseph E. Badger Jr
H.C. Bailey	Israel Abrahams	Joseph Hergesheimer
H. G. Wells	Ivan Turgenev	Joseph Jacobs
H. H. Munro	J.G.Austin	Jules Vernes
H. Irving Hancock	J. Henri Fabre	Julian Hawthrone
H. R. Naylor	J. M. Barrie	Julie A Lippmann
H. Rider Haggard	J. M. Walsh	Justin Huntly McCarthy
H. W. C. Davis	J. Macdonald Oxley	Kakuzo Okakura
Haldeman Julius	J. R. Miller	Karle Wilson Baker
Hall Caine	J. S. Fletcher	Kate Chopin
Hamilton Wright Mabie	J. S. Knowles	Kenneth Grahame
Hans Christian Andersen	J. Storer Clouston	Kenneth McGaffey
Harold Avery	J. W. Duffield	Kate Langley Bosher
Harold McGrath	Jack London	Kate Langley Bosher
Harriet Beecher Stowe	Jacob Abbott	Katherine Cecil Thurston
Harry Castlemon	James Allen	Katherine Stokes
Harry Coghill	James Andrews	L. A. Abbot
Harry Houidini	James Baldwin	L. T. Meade

L. Frank Baum
Latta Griswold
Laura Dent Crane
Laura Lee Hope
Laurence Housman
Lawrence Beasley
Leo Tolstoy
Leonid Andreyev
Lewis Carroll
Lewis Sperry Chafer
Lilian Bell
Lloyd Osbourne
Louis Hughes
Louis Joseph Vance
Louis Tracy
Louisa May Alcott
Lucy Fitch Perkins
Lucy Maud Montgomery
Luther Benson
Lydia Miller Middleton
Lyndon Orr
M. Corvus
M. H. Adams
Margaret E. Sangster
Margret Howth
Margaret Vandercook
Margaret W. Hungerford
Margret Penrose
Maria Edgeworth
Maria Thompson Daviess
Mariano Azuela
Marion Polk Angellotti
Mark Overton
Mark Twain
Mary Austin
Mary Catherine Crowley
Mary Cole
Mary Hastings Bradley
Mary Roberts Rinehart
Mary Rowlandson
M. Wollstonecraft Shelley
Maud Lindsay
Max Beerbohm
Myra Kelly
Nathaniel Hawthrone
Nicolo Machiavelli
O. F. Walton
Oscar Wilde

Owen Johnson
P.G. Wodehouse
Paul and Mabel Thorne
Paul G. Tomlinson
Paul Severing
Percy Brebner
Percy Keese Fitzhugh
Peter B. Kyne
Plato
Quincy Allen
R. Derby Holmes
R. L. Stevenson
R. S. Ball
Rabindranath Tagore
Rahul Alvares
Ralph Bonehill
Ralph Henry Barbour
Ralph Victor
Ralph Waldo Emmerson
Rene Descartes
Ray Cummings
Rex Beach
Rex E. Beach
Richard Harding Davis
Richard Jefferies
Richard Le Gallienne
Robert Barr
Robert Frost
Robert Gordon Anderson
Robert L. Drake
Robert Lansing
Robert Lynd
Robert Michael Ballantyne
Robert W. Chambers
Rosa Nouchette Carey
Rudyard Kipling
Saint Augustine
Samuel B. Allison
Samuel Hopkins Adams
Sarah Bernhardt
Sarah C. Hallowell
Selma Lagerlof
Sherwood Anderson
Sigmund Freud
Standish O'Grady
Stanley Weyman
Stella Benson
Stella M. Francis

Stephen Crane
Stewart Edward White
Stijn Streuvels
Swami Abhedananda
Swami Parmananda
T. S. Ackland
T. S. Arthur
The Princess Der Ling
Thomas A. Janvier
Thomas A Kempis
Thomas Anderton
Thomas Bailey Aldrich
Thomas Bulfinch
Thomas De Quincey
Thomas Dixon
Thomas H. Huxley
Thomas Hardy
Thomas More
Thornton W. Burgess
U. S. Grant
Upton Sinclair
Valentine Williams
Various Authors
Vaughan Kester
Victor Appleton
Victor G. Durham
Victoria Cross
Virginia Woolf
Wadsworth Camp
Walter Camp
Walter Scott
Washington Irving
Wilbur Lawton
Wilkie Collins
Willa Cather
Willard F. Baker
William Dean Howells
William le Queux
W. Makepeace Thackeray
William W. Walter
William Shakespeare
Winston Churchill
Yei Theodora Ozaki
Yogi Ramacharaka
Young E. Allison
Zane Grey